A DEADLY LEGACY

A HOPGOOD HALL MYSTERY

E.V. HUNTER

Boldwood

First published in Great Britain in 2024 by Boldwood Books Ltd.

Copyright © E.V. Hunter, 2024

Cover Design by Rachel Lawston

Cover Images: Rachel Lawston

Every effort has been made to obtain the necessary permissions with reference to copyright material, both illustrative and quoted. We apologise for any omissions in this respect and will be pleased to make the appropriate acknowledgements in any future edition.

A CIP catalogue record for this book is available from the British Library.

Paperback ISBN 978-1-83561-340-5

Large Print ISBN 978-1-83561-339-9

Hardback ISBN 978-1-83561-338-2

Ebook ISBN 978-1-83561-341-2

Kindle ISBN 978-1-83561-342-9

Audio CD ISBN 978-1-83561-333-7

MP3 CD ISBN 978-1-83561-334-4

Digital audio download ISBN 978-1-83561-336-8

This book is printed on certified sustainable paper. Boldwood Books is dedicated to putting sustainability at the heart of our business. For more information please visit https://www.boldwoodbooks.com/about-us/sustainability/

Boldwood Books Ltd, 23 Bowerdean Street, London, SW6 3TN

www.boldwoodbooks.com

For my friend, Andy Berks.
Ever the gentleman. (Well, usually!) x

1

'Why now? Just when things have been running smoothly, with no dramas.'

Alexi glanced at her friend, Cheryl Hopgood, through the partially open kitchen door of the boutique hotel in Lambourn that Cheryl and her husband owned and in which Alexi was a minority shareholder. Cheryl had been putting a brave face on things but now, unaware that she was being observed, her devastation was obvious.

'It's so unfair,' Alexi complained. 'Why did this have to happen now, of all times? I want so much to help her and Drew through this trauma but have absolutely no idea what to do.' She glanced up at her partner, Jack Maddox, through tear-stained eyes. 'You're good with people. Tell me how to go about it.'

'It's a tough one.' Jack ran a reassuring hand across Alexi's shoulders. 'I know it's a cliché but time's a great healer. Just be there for Cheryl and I'll do the same for Drew. The funeral's out the way, the grieving widow has taken her leave and we'll get our friends through it between us.'

Alexi shot Jack a dubious look. 'I guess.'

Alexi turned away from the kitchen door before Cheryl saw them lurking in the corridor. She would be embarrassed to be caught crying and probably claim that her emotions were all over the place due to the fact that she was six months pregnant. They very likely were, but that wasn't the cause of her grief, Alexi knew.

'It's not as though Drew and his brother were close any more,' Alexi added, leaning against the wall immediately outside the private kitchen in Hopgood Hall. 'But still, Frank was only in his forties. His death is a needless tragedy.'

'Accidents happen, darling.'

'I know, but...'

Alexi dashed at an errant tear. She'd only met Frank a couple of times and hadn't really known him well. Now that he was dead, it seemed wrong to admit, if only to herself, that she hadn't much liked him. He was different to Drew in every possible way. A restless spirit in perpetual search of that elusive something. He hadn't wanted to know about restoring Hopgood Hall when his and Drew's parents had died and had forced Drew into taking out a loan that he couldn't afford in order to buy out his half-share of their joint inheritance.

'Go and sit with Cheryl. She's been bottling it all up ever since the funeral last week. Something's obviously bothering her. See if you can get her to talk about it. Talking always helps, especially when the listener is sympathetic.'

'Yeah, I guess.'

'I'll go and track Drew down and do the same thing.'

Alexi swallowed, nodded once and plastered a smile on her face. Followed by her feral cat, Cosmo and his faithful sidekick, Silgo, a dog of questionable pedigree that Alexi had acquired recently, she took a deep breath and walked into the kitchen. Cheryl had taken Alexi under her wing when she'd been fired from her post on the *Sunday Sentinel* and allowed her to lick her wounds here in Lambourn until she got her act together. It was more than time to return the favour.

'Hey,' she said, ensuring she made enough noise to alert Cheryl of her arrival. Not that she'd needed to. The moment Toby, Cheryl's little terrier, caught sight of Cosmo and Silgo, he went into a frenzy of excited yapping and danced round the cat and much larger dog like a performing seal. 'You'd think they'd been separated for months,' Alexi added, her voice artificially bright.

'Toby suffers from separation issues,' Cheryl replied with a watery smile.

Alexi gave her friend a big hug, the gesture impeded by her baby bump. 'Feeling low?' she asked.

'It's the hormones, I suppose. They're all over the place,' she replied, plonking herself down at the table and sighing.

Alexi went to the fridge, poured orange juice for Cheryl and coffee for herself from the pot kept permanently on the go on the side. She sat across from her friend and waited her out in silence, sensing that she wanted to talk, but perfectly happy to remain quiet if that's what Cheryl preferred.

'Life's shit sometimes,' Cheryl eventually said, flapping a hand across her damp cheeks. 'Not sure why I'm getting so upset. Frank is gone, before his time, it's true, but like I say, there are no guarantees. Besides, we hadn't seen him or had much to do with him for three years now. Not since Drew bought out his share of this house.'

'I remember Frank from our time at uni. He was a real party animal. He and Drew were tight in those days. I often wondered what happened. Having no siblings myself, I have no idea what changes occur when we're obliged to grow up and become responsible.'

'Frank didn't ever grow up.' Cheryl rolled her eyes. 'That was half the problem.'

'Drew needed him to invest in the house, not clear you out so he could take his half share and scarper.'

Cheryl's head shot up. 'I never told you that.'

'You didn't need to. I can read between the lines. It's what I do.'

'Well, you're right.' Cheryl spread her hands. 'Frank never could knuckle down to anything for long. And yeah, we could have done without raising such a big loan to give him his share of the inheritance. But he was a man in a hurry with all sorts of business opportunities he couldn't wait to explore. In the end, Drew said it would be better just to bite the bullet and pay him out, then we'd be free to develop this hotel the way we thought best, without Frank contributing wild and untenable ideas.'

'I seem to remember you telling me that Frank was averse to turning it into a hotel in the first place.'

'Right. He wanted it to remain a family home but chose to ignore the fact that it was crumbling around our ears.' Cheryl rested her elbow on the table and the side of her face against her cupped hand. 'Frank was a dreamer. A charming guy without a practical bone in his body. He drove Drew crazy with his unrealistic plans. Anyway, he swanned off to Australia once we paid him off, vowing to return a millionaire. Of course, that never happened. We were never sure what he got up to Down Under but then...'

'Then he came back married to Stella The Stunner. But then, we shouldn't be surprised. He always was a bit of a babe magnet.'

'Yeah, Stella's half his age and a real ball-breaker. Into PR and ambitious as you like. I never thought to see the day when any woman would run rings around Frank, but she had him by the short and curlies, no question.' Cheryl flashed a wan smile. 'I am not, in case you hadn't already guessed it, her greatest fan.'

'Yeah, I saw her at the funeral, turning it into the Stella show,' Alexi replied, wrinkling her nose. 'All that pseudo-grief. It was sickening. Well, I say pseudo. Perhaps it was genuine and I'm just being a bitch, but somehow, I don't think that's the case. I overheard her on her mobile, discussing a business opportunity with someone, which really turned me against her. I mean, who does that at her husband's funeral?' Alexi let out a prolonged sigh, having neglected to say that she'd been madly flirting with whoever she'd been speaking to. Cheryl didn't need to know that. 'Anyway, why did they come back to the UK?'

'We never could get to the bottom of that one, mainly because she kept Frank away from Drew. Anyway, they came back a few months ago. Drew said he didn't recognise his vibrant brother any more. It was as though the life had been sucked out of him. He'd turned into Stella's lapdog and Drew reckoned that he couldn't use the bathroom without his wife's permission.'

'Okay, but that still doesn't explain why they came back.'

Cheryl lifted one shoulder. 'Not sure but, like I say, Stella seemed to make all the decisions, so I guess it was her call. What Stella wanted, Stella got, and I imagine there are more opportunities for a go-getter like her here in the UK. Being married to Frank meant she could come. And stay.'

'Okay. And where is she living now?'

'Absolutely no idea. We'd only had one brief visit from

them together since their return, and that was more than enough. I took against Stella and the way she eyed this property up, as though assessing its potential. She kept banging on about it being Frank's childhood home and how much he missed it.' Cheryl shuddered. 'It gave me the creeps.'

'You don't need to have anything more to do with her now,' Alexi replied, reaching across to touch Cheryl's hand. 'She'll probably sink her claws into her next victim before the ink on Frank's death certificate is dry. Sorry,' she added hastily, holding up a hand to reinforce the apology. 'That was insensitive.'

'But true, I'm sure.' Cheryl sighed. 'I don't care what she does, just so long as I don't have to see her. No, what's bothering me is the manner of Frank's death. I just can't believe that he had a climbing accident, of all things. Climbing was his life and he took safety very seriously. He wouldn't climb on his own either. He knew better than that.'

'There was an investigation into his death?'

'Sure, but perfunctory. According to Stella, he got up early one morning to climb with an old friend at Harrison's Rocks in East Sussex.'

'Never heard of them.'

'Nor had I until after the accident. They are sandstone outcrops, apparently, and lure climbers from all over because they have more than 380 routes, suitable for all abilities. Placing gear is prohibited, I've subsequently found out, due to the fragile rock surface.'

'So free climbing, I suppose.' Alexi pursed her lips. 'If Frank had become as downtrodden as you imply then I'm guessing that climbing was his escape, and that the fragrant Stella didn't join him.'

'Very likely, but as I already said, he would never climb alone.'

'The Frank you once knew wouldn't have, but it sounds as though he'd changed in more ways than one.'

'Well anyway, you know the rest.' Cheryl took a swig of her juice. 'He was found in a mangled heap at the bottom of the rocks early in the morning by other climbers when they turned up. Frank was alone and none of his climbing buddies had been due to join him. He'd gone rogue was the assumption made, perhaps for the reasons you suggest.'

'I guess we'll never know.'

'I wish I could get it out of my head that it was nothing more than an accident.' Cheryl tapped an irritated tattoo on the table's surface with the fingers of one hand. 'That way, I'd be able to move on, but I know that despite their differences Drew is traumatised by the loss of his big brother. He tries to keep it from me, which is infuriating. I'm pregnant, not mentally deficient, and we should talk about his suspicions.'

'Who would want to deliberately harm Frank?' Alexi asked, fairly sure that she already knew the answer to her own question. 'I can understand if you suspect Stella, but Frank wasn't mega-rich so if the marriage had run its course, the divorce courts would have been a better option.'

'I know and I agree with you.' Cheryl frowned as she struggled to articulate her thoughts. 'It's Drew's bottled-up emotions and obvious doubts that get to me. Like I say, Frank was too experienced to climb alone but for whatever reason, he did, and so we just have to let it go.' Cheryl placed a protective hand over her protruding stomach. 'We have to put our family's interests first. Frank's gone and Stella will never be family because she made it abundantly clear that she didn't want to be. Like I say, we only saw her the once before Frank's death. I tried to be friendly but she really didn't want to know, so that's that. It'll just be the four of us now.'

Silgo, even more intuitive to human angst than Cosmo, walked up to Cheryl and pushed his wet nose beneath her hand. Cheryl smiled and tugged gently at his shaggy ears, seeming to find comfort in the gesture.

'We have the big society wedding to occupy us,' Alexi said, her tone upbeat, as she referred to the marriage of a local trainer to one of his grooms. 'They're pushing the boat out *and* not fretting over the arrangements, which is a welcome change from all the other weddings that we've put on here so far.'

'Absolutely.' Alexi smiled and leaned forward to squeeze Cheryl's hand.

'It's still a few weeks away. Hopefully, the autumnal leaves will do their bit and make the perfect backdrop for the photos. It'll be the first indoor wedding we've staged.' Cheryl spoke in a lacklustre tone; her habitual enthusiasm and perfectionism, her burning desire to promote the interests of Hopgood Hall and get every little detail right, were nowhere in sight. Alexi was really starting to worry about her state of mind. 'All the others have been summer affairs.'

'True, but at least being inside, we don't have to worry about the weather messing with our plans.'

Drew and Jack joined them at that point and the conversation turned to weddings. Drew joked about Alexi and Jack taking their turn to exchange vows, but Alexi could tell that his heart wasn't really in it. Not sure what more she could say to reassure Cheryl, Alexi stood.

'We'll get out of your hair,' she said. 'Jack ought to be working on his latest case,' she added, referring to his career as a private investigator, 'and I'm on a deadline. Need to get my second round of proofreads done by the end of the week.'

'Is Polly happy with your efforts?' Cheryl asked, showing a little animation.

She was referring to the book that Alexi, who was an investigative journalist, had written about a murder recently committed in Lambourn. One of four recent murders, she reminded herself with a shudder. Polly, a B&B proprietor, had been one of Alexi's main detractors in the small community, until she'd found herself accused of murdering her lover. Then she'd run to Alexi and Jack, cap in hand, desperate for their help. Against all the odds, she and Jack had been able to uncover the identity of the real culprit and now Polly and her friend Maggie were Alexi's greatest fans.

'She seems to be. I think that exposing the duplicitous character of a man that Polly and Maggie both had feelings for is helping them to get over their traumatic loss. I hope so anyway.'

'So do I,' Cheryl said with feeling, probably thinking about Frank's untimely demise and her husband's inability to cope.

The conversation flowed around Alexi and she allowed her mind to wander, thinking about Frank's accident. She suspected that Cheryl and Drew would know no peace of mind until the matter was more thoroughly investigated since the funeral had, if anything, only intensified their concerns. Alexi had hoped it would give them some closure, but that was clearly not the case. Even so, what was there to investigate so long after the event? There were no obvious suspicious circumstances, if one overlooked an experienced climber breaking all the safety rules by going it alone, no witnesses, nada. Be that as it may, Cheryl's doubts were rubbing off on

Alexi and, she suspected, Drew had probably made Jack equally curious. As an ex-police detective, Jack was programmed to see shadows on a cloudy day. Drew only needed to say the word.

They might as well ask just a few preliminary questions. Alexi would make the suggestion when she and Jack were alone. They could perhaps delve a little deeper into the state of Frank's marriage, as well as into Stella's past. Alexi wouldn't even consider it but for the fact that Stella was definitely a woman on a mission. She had gotten what she wanted insofar as her marriage to Frank had secured her the right to British citizenship – if that had been her intention – but Alexi sensed a far greater ambition lurking beneath that attractive surface.

Alexi and Jack said their goodbyes, collected up cat and dog, and were about to leave the kitchen when a low growl rumbled at the back of Silgo's throat. He was ordinarily such an easy-going dog that everyone looked at him askance. Alexi could see that his body had gone rigid. Once a down-trodden, unloved guard dog, he had found his courage since being taken into Alexi's household but seldom felt the need to growl at anyone.

'What is it, boy?' Jack asked, rubbing his ears.

Jack's question was answered when the door opened and Stella's athletic form filled the aperture.

'Hey,' she said. 'Sorry to drop by unannounced but I was in the area. Besides, we're related now and have never gotten to know one another properly. It's beyond time that we rectified that situation, don't you think?'

* * *

Jack shared a glance with Alexi and could see that Stella's sudden appearance had made her highly suspicious, as it had him. Drew had just told him that Stella's entrance into his brother's life had sounded the death knell for their relationship. Not that there had been much of a relationship once Frank took off for Australia. Stella, it transpired, wasn't willing to share Frank with anyone – not even his family.

Drew had welcomed the fact that his playboy brother had finally settled down and was anxious to meet the lady who had brought that situation about, but Stella had apparently made it clear that Frank was now off limits. Drew hadn't understood why, and still didn't, but now that the woman had shown her face, perhaps matters would become clearer. Jack was unable to decide if that would be a good thing. Judging from Drew's wary expression, he felt the same way, but would likely give her an opportunity to explain.

'Stella,' Drew said. 'This is unexpected.'

'It's all been so awful,' Stella replied, flouncing into the nearest chair and giving a little shriek when Cosmo growled at her and Silgo's arched back displayed raised hackles. 'Do we really have to...'

She glanced at the aggrieved animals and her words trailed off. Stella flicked her long hair over one shoulder and smiled at Drew, clearly thinking that a smile was all it would take to have him evict Cosmo and Silgo from his kitchen. Drew simply shrugged, his expression set in stone. Jack sensed a vulnerability beneath the confident and attractive exterior the woman showed to the world, but it was so deeply hidden that it would only be visible to a person who looked carefully enough. Stella would probably hate knowing that she appeared to be anything other than confident, worldly and capable. Jack wondered if she had really loved Frank and was grieving for her loss. He would give her the benefit of the doubt for now, even though Cosmo had taken against her and his judgement was usually spot on.

'You have something against domestic pets?' he asked in a neutral tone.

'Well no... it's just that I was hoping to catch you both alone. We have stuff to talk about and...' She glanced at Alexi and Jack and nodded. 'Would you excuse us please.'

Up until that point, Stella had spoken only to Drew. She'd spared Jack a probing once over but had yet to make eye contact with either Cheryl or Alexi. Jack watched the ladies as they exchanged a glance and was proud of Alexi when she managed not to roll her eyes. This woman didn't appear to like her own sex very much, and seemed to think that Drew would dance to her tune. Jack observed Drew's darkening expression and prepared himself to enjoy the show.

'This is Jack Maddox and Alexi Ellis,' Drew said, 'but you already met them at the funeral.' He reached out an arm and slung it around Cheryl's shoulders. 'Alexi is a major investor in this hotel, as well as a respected journalist.'

'Of course.' Stella lowered her gaze, finally, reached into the pocket of her impossibly tight jeans and produced a tissue that she used to dab at her eyes. 'Sorry if I'm coming across as a bit of a dork, Cheryl. My world's been turned on its head.' She gave a little sob. 'You look so much like Frank, Drew, that it's uncanny.'

'Given that we were brothers, not so uncanny,' Drew replied, clearly unmoved by Stella's performance and making no offer of refreshment. 'So, what can we do for you?'

Stella jerked upright at his clipped tone and anger briefly fuelled her expression. 'What makes you suppose that I want anything?'

'How long do you plan to stay in the area?' Cheryl asked. 'Where are you staying, come to that?'

'Well, that's the thing. I wondered if I could stay here, just for the time being.'

'Here?' Drew and Cheryl said together.

'In the hotel,' Drew added alone, scratching his chin. 'What on earth do you plan to do in Lambourn?'

'It's more a case of assessing my options,' Stella said. 'Frank and I had big plans but he died before we could put them into play.'

'What sort of plans?' Drew asked. 'My brother was always big on ideas but shoddy when it came to following through.'

Jack felt like he and Alexi were intruding on a private family moment. Judging by the frequent glances that Stella sent their way, she agreed with that assessment but Alexi's *shall-we-leave-you-to-it* glance at Cheryl was met with a firm shake of the head. Jack was glad. This woman wanted something from Drew and although Drew was perfectly capable of fighting his own battles, there was no harm in offering him a little moral support.

'Well, that's the thing, you see.' Stella paused to moisten impossibly shiny lips. 'Frank was thinking of resuming his role in this place.'

2

Alexi watched Drew as his jaw literally fell open. It took a degree of willpower to prevent her own from doing the same thing. Whatever game this woman thought she was playing, it hadn't once crossed Alexi's mind that she would attempt to muscle in on Hopgood Hall's success. She glanced at Cheryl, whose expression showed a combination of shock and outrage.

'Frank sold out his share in this place,' Drew said, his tone tightened by barely suppressed anger. 'But then, you must already be aware of that.'

'You look surprised,' Stella responded. 'Nice try, but you can't be, not really. Frank said he'd been negotiating with you.'

Drew sent her a speculative look. 'News to me.'

'Don't make this more difficult than it has to be.' Stella turned on the charm for Drew, completely ignoring everyone else in the room. Silgo sensed the tension and growled. Cosmo stalked up to her, hissing. Alexi didn't call the animals off, but Stella acted as though they weren't there. That was either brave or exceedingly foolhardy. Silgo was untried in situations such as this but Cosmo, left to his own devices, had been known to draw blood if he took a dislike to a person. 'Despite your differences, you and Frank were brothers, he cared about you and knew that together, you'd be able to take the hotel to an even higher level. Absolute exclusivity, in other words. He had plans to make it world famous. That's the thing about hotels nowadays. Cities are too expensive and high-end country establishments with top-notch chefs are in vogue. Coupled with my ability to create publicity, it couldn't have failed. But then, he told you all this and you encouraged him to come home and explore the possibilities.'

When no one reacted to her ridiculous claims, she finally appeared to realise that she was preaching to a hostile audience and her words dried up. Only Cosmo's posturing and Silgo's rumbling growls broke the crystalline silence.

'I haven't seen or spoken to Frank without you being there, not since he left England,' Drew eventually said in a mordant tone. 'But if I had and if he'd made the ludicrous suggestion you just voiced then I would have told him in no uncertain terms to take a hike.'

'He has no claim on this hotel, Stella,' Cheryl added, 'and he wouldn't have tried to pretend otherwise. I find it contemptable that you'd even attempt to put this on the dead guy, just to feather your own nest.'

'Ah, I see how it's going to be.' Stella lowered her head into her splayed hands and sighed. 'Frank said he didn't think you'd treat him fairly.'

Drew's face turned puce. He swallowed, blew air through his lips and clenched his fists at his sides. He was the easiest-going man Alexi had ever met. Nothing seemed to faze him. He always saw the best in everyone, but this woman with her outrageous claims had clearly got him rattled and he was on the verge of losing it. Hardly surprising. Alexi knew that Drew had treated Frank more generously than he'd deserved or had any right to expect. Far more generously than Drew could afford, simply because he was that type of guy. And now, this money-grabbing schemer had come along, using Frank's death to turn up the emotional blackmail and extract money from Drew, presumably because she'd run through Frank's inheritance and was on the make.

It defied belief.

'Frank received half the value of the property at the time of our mother's death,' Drew said. 'He had plans for that cash. I assume he squandered it all with your help which is perhaps why you returned to England, but I can assure you that he didn't come to me cap in hand.'

'Show us proof of these negotiations you insist were insti-gated,' Jack said into the ensuing silence.

'Excuse me, but this is none of your business,' Stella said archly, her Australian twang pronounced. 'It's a family affair.'

Cheryl glowered at the woman. 'And you are not family, nor will you ever be.'

'Even so...' Stella waved a hand vaguely in the direction of Alexi and Jack.

'Alexi has a shareholding in this hotel,' Drew reminded her, 'and she has a right to hear your ridiculous fiction before I throw you out. You're upsetting my wife and if Cheryl's upset then so am I. And believe me, you really don't want to upset me.'

'Sorry.' But the apology sounded trite, insincere. 'Look, Frank told me you'd spoken, that you were considering his request and that he was coming to talk to you about it after... well, on the day of that fatal climb.'

'You didn't climb with him?' Jack asked.

'God, no!' She shuddered. 'I'm afraid of heights. The sea is more my thing. I love surfing.'

I'll just bet you do! Alexi had no trouble imagining the woman posing in a tight-fitting wetsuit. Annoyingly, she'd be able to carry it off but that was not the issue.

'I'd be interested to know why Frank thought he still had any interest in this place,' Alexi said.

Stella's gaze briefly rested on the top of Alexi's head and was as quickly averted. Instead, it landed on Jack but if she thought her performance of fragility and injured pride would find an ally in that quarter then she must have quickly realised her mistake. 'The value was decided upon the probate figure.'

'And?' Drew and Jack said together.

'It was too low.' She spread her hands. 'Look, you probably don't know this, but Frank had a bit of a breakdown when your mother died, Drew. They were close, apparently, and her death hit him hard.'

Drew nodded, his expression set in stone. 'It was devastating for us both but not unexpected.'

'He fell apart once she was gone and needed to get away, which is why he sold out so cheaply.'

'There was nothing cheap about the split!' Cheryl cried, outraged. 'Frank wanted out, couldn't wait to get away and, for the record, he seemed to be of perfectly sound mind. He was full of plans for the future. He said he needed to spread his wings. Lambourn was holding him back and with his mother gone, there was nothing to keep him here.'

'Presumably, Frank sought medical help for the mental condition you suggest he suffered from,' Jack suggested.

'Well, no.' Stella looked suitably distraught. 'You know

how sensitive men can be about that sort of stuff. It's not macho to admit to frailties of any type, especially mental.'

'So we only have your word for the fact that there was anything wrong with him,' Alexi said. 'Or that he'd come home to extract money from Drew and Cheryl.'

'You think that I...' Stella pointed to her own chest for emphasis, her expression one of righteous indignation. 'That I would try and con my husband's relations.'

The outrage was almost convincing.

Almost.

'I think I speak for us all when I say that the thought crossed our collective minds,' Drew replied.

Anger invaded Stella's expression. 'Look, your parents' will clearly left the property to the two of you jointly.'

'Tell me something I don't know,' Drew said, tapping his fingers restlessly against the work surface he was leaning against.

'But the deeds were transferred into your sole name, Drew.'

'After Frank almost bankrupted me by taking half the probate value.'

'And the agreement that Frank signed ceding his half of the property to you in exchange for monetary reward is lodged where?' she asked sweetly.

The air left Drew's lungs in an extravagant whoosh. 'Frank signed over his half of the property to me and our solicitor lodged the deeds in my sole name. We were brothers. There was no need for a formal contract.' Drew shot a look of total disdain Stella's way. 'Or so we thought.'

'Well, I'm sorry it's come to this,' Stella said, standing. 'I thought we'd be able to resolve this matter in a civilized fashion, but it seems I was wrong about that. Frank was a fool to let his inheritance go so cheaply. He realised that after he'd come to his senses and wanted to redress the balance. As his widow, I have no choice but to carry out his wishes, albeit posthumously.'

'Just so you're aware,' Alexi said, standing close to the woman and invading her space, 'Drew and Cheryl were on their knees financially when I came along and that was because they'd borrowed so heavily to buy Frank out. They couldn't get a further business loan because the hotel hadn't taken off at that point.'

Alexi's mind briefly drifted in the direction of her own large investment that had enabled Drew and Cheryl to turn their failing business around. If this woman did have a legitimate claim, then where would that leave Alexi? She pushed the thought aside. It wouldn't come to that. She and Jack would find a way to expose Stella for the fraud that she was and protect the interests of Hopgood Hall.

'What Alexi isn't saying is that her investment turned us around and without her, we'd have gone under and sold up long since,' Cheryl added, standing at Alexi's shoulder and echoing her thoughts as she continued to glower at Stella. 'Do whatever you feel you have to do to cash in on your husband's death, but you won't be stealing our livelihood *and* living beneath our roof. Now get out and if you need to speak with us again, do so through your solicitor.'

Alexi had never seen Cheryl so riled before and wanted to applaud her. Drew stood behind her, an arm resting protectively on her shoulders, and pointed towards the door.

'Don't let it hit your backside on the way out,' he said.

Stella glanced at four hostile faces and two intimidating animals, picked up her handbag and left the room without saying another word.

The moment she was gone, the friends looked at one another, none of them appearing to know quite what to say.

'Sit down, darling,' Drew said, breaking the silence, 'before you fall down.' He pulled out a chair and helped Cheryl into it. 'I have never wanted to kill anyone in my entire life, but I swear to God, I was on the verge of throttling the damned woman.'

'You'd have had to join the queue,' Alexi replied, sitting beside Cheryl and squeezing her hand.

'Don't get mad, get even,' Jack advised, glancing at Drew. 'Stella's trying her luck, but we won't let her get away with it. That was an act of desperation, which showed her hand. We'll play on that desperation.' *Somehow*, he added *sotto voce*.

'Perhaps now I understand why I was so edgy around Stella and couldn't properly put Frank's death behind me,' Drew said. 'I took an instant dislike to Stella, which isn't normal for me. I tend to like everyone unless they give me a reason not to, but there was just something about her that put my back up. I sensed there was something brewing but never in my wildest dreams...'

'Wildest dreams about sums it up, I'd say,' Alexi replied. 'The woman saw an opportunity and thought she'd exploit it. She knows now that she'll get some strong opposition so hopefully, that's the last you'll hear from her.'

'I wouldn't count on it,' Jack said. 'Sorry to rain on your parade but in my line of work, I've come across women like her more times than enough. She's accustomed to getting what she wants and desperate enough to try her luck. Unfortunately for her, she's met her match this time.'

'Did you really not have Frank sign anything in return for giving up his half share?' Alexi asked gently.

Drew shook his head. 'Our solicitor advised it, but it

seemed so... well, businesslike. We were family, grieving the loss of our mother. We'd agreed on the way forward between us and that seemed like enough.'

'Was Frank as close to your mother as Stella implied?' Jack asked.

'She went into care towards the end but still had all her marbles. She was frail though and needed round-the-clock care, so it seemed like the right solution. She was happy enough in the home and Frank did visit her regularly.'

'Because unlike Drew, he wasn't attempting to work full time and keep this house from falling down around our ears,' Cheryl added hotly.

'Yeah, well...'

'And what Drew isn't saying is that some of her jewellery went missing.' Cheryl was clearly not done venting and Alexi thought it would do her good to articulate her feelings. 'Not that she had much but what she did have was old and quite valuable. We're pretty sure that Frank helped himself but couldn't prove it so rather than cause friction, Drew let it go.'

Drew threw up his hands and looked to be on the point of reaching for the cooking brandy. He changed his mind at the eleventh hour, which was probably just as well. Right now, he needed to keep a clear head. Alexi knew that Stella wouldn't just give up and go away. She must have known that she would meet with considerable opposition and, on the surface at least, had nothing to support her outrageous claims. *What the hell could her motive possibly be?* Alexi wondered for the hundredth time.

'I'm no lawyer but I'm pretty sure she has no claim,' Alexi said. 'But I'm also sure that won't stop her attempting to cause trouble. Why she'd want to is less certain.'

'What can she do?' Cheryl asked. 'There was no written

agreement about the sum Frank took but he *did* sign over his share of the house to Drew and there is documentation to prove it.'

A squeal echoing through the baby monitor alerted them all to the fact that Verity, Cheryl's and Drew's young daughter, had woken from her afternoon nap.

'I'll go,' Drew said, waving Cheryl back into her chair. They had help during the daytime with the little girl, but it was Susie's day off.

'Damn!' Cheryl buried her face in her hands and sighed. 'What the hell do we do to get rid of her?' Cheryl abruptly lifted her face again. 'Is that what she wants, do you suppose? A payoff to get her out of our hair?'

'It's one possibility,' Jack said, exchanging a glance with Alexi. 'Have you ever wondered if there was anything suspicious about Frank's death?'

'Well, we talked about it, obviously, and did think it was odd, but stranger accidents have happened.' Cheryl's eyes widened. 'Surely you don't think that...'

'They do,' Drew said, returning to the kitchen with a sleepy Verity in his arms. 'And now, so do I.'

'I actively dislike the woman, but surely she wouldn't go that far,' Cheryl said, sounding less than convinced by her own argument.

Alexi held out her arms and Drew passed Verity to her. She sat the little girl on her lap and jiggled her knees, making Verity giggle. 'Why would a woman who looks like Stella and thinks so much of herself marry a man twice her age?' she asked, focusing her attention on Verity as she voiced her suspicions. 'What was her motivation?'

Drew and Cheryl exchanged a prolonged look.

'Frank would have been flush with the cash he took from

this place when he arrived in Australia, full of impractical plans to increase it,' Drew said. 'And his money would have attracted Stella's attention. Besides, he wasn't a bad-looking bloke and could be the life and soul. Women were drawn to him because he didn't take himself too seriously.'

'He would have talked his circumstances up, too,' Cheryl added, 'just to impress her. It was clear to us from the emails he sent that he'd finally met a woman who could hold his interest for more than five minutes.' She sighed. 'Only to think, we were pleased for him.'

'It didn't occur to us to worry when the emails dwindled to a trickle,' Drew added. 'Presumably, she set about estranging him from us even before they tied the knot.'

'So,' Alexi said. 'You think he implied to Stella that he still had a share in this place, enticing her in by that means?'

'No, a simple search of the land registry would have shown Drew as the sole owner,' Jack pointed out.

'He probably spun her a story about an agreement between brothers that I'd reneged upon,' Drew said, rolling his eyes. 'It's the sort of thing he'd have said to impress her, never expecting her to latch onto it.'

'Owning a half share in a large house in a prestigious village, you mean?' Alexi asked.

'Right.'

Cheryl's expression remained grim, and unshed tears were in danger of blurring her vision. Alexi was furious on her friend's behalf, which strengthened her determination to get them out of this situation.

Somehow.

'What do we know about Stella?' Jack asked, clearly in business mode.

'Very little,' Drew replied. 'We received an email from

Frank saying he'd met "the one" and that they were getting married. We thought it was all a bit quick but were happy for him. We assumed that a wife would be a steadying influence and that he'd finally settle down and stick to something. Ha! Little did we know.'

'We saw a few pictures of the wedding on a beach but there didn't seem to be any guests. Well, none that made the pictures,' Cheryl said. 'Frank said she was into PR and had a number of high-flying clients. But she wanted to be over here, where there's more action. Frank was all for setting her up in her own company. She wanted to branch out into high-end wedding planning apparently, and Frank encouraged her to go for it. God only knows where the money was coming from.'

'You're assuming he ran through the funds he took from this place,' Alexi said.

'I'd put money on it, no pun intended,' Drew replied, his expression sombre. 'That was remarkably quick, even by his standards but having met Stella, I'm starting to realise how that situation arose.'

'You think she tried to persuade him that he'd been short-changed and should come after you for more?' Jack suggested.

Cheryl and Drew nodded in unison.

'I have absolutely no doubt about it,' Drew said with authority. 'Frank was one of life's chancers, but he had a conscience and would never have shafted me. That's why I thought it was unnecessary to go to the expense of having him formally sign away his half share in return for the agreed sum.' He sighed and rubbed his chin. 'I guess that being too trusting is gonna come back to haunt me now.'

'Not if we have any say in the matter,' Alexi replied resolutely.

'We're going to do a bit of digging, both into Stella's background and into Frank's. Point us in the right direction, Drew. What friends did Frank have in this country who he would have linked up with once he got back?'

'Well, there's Brian Hardy. The two of them were joined at the hip as kids and I know they stayed in touch when he was away. Brian's a trainer's assistant down the road here and comes in the bar occasionally. He'd always tell me if he'd heard from Frank and was as shocked as me when he heard that Frank was about to settle down to a life of domesticity.'

'I know that name.' Alexi closed her eyes, attempting to recall where she'd heard it recently. 'The wedding,' she said, opening her eyes again and snapping her fingers. 'The one here in a few weeks' time. His name is included in the wedding party. He's an usher, I think.'

'Yes, he is,' Cheryl confirmed.

'Okay,' Jack said, 'we'll track him down and have a word with him. Anyone else?'

Drew and Cheryl shared a look and simultaneously shook their heads.

'We don't know where Frank and Stella were living, or who they've been in touch with since they got back to the UK a few months ago. We asked, obviously, but Frank said their plans were fluid.'

'I got the impression that Stella wanted to be in London, "close to the action," as she put it, but obviously, that would have been expensive and I'm guessing there weren't enough funds to stretch to that,' Cheryl added.

Drew nodded. 'And Stella would probably have kept Frank well away from anyone who couldn't be of use to her – any of his old mates, that is – much as she kept him away from us.'

'Why though?' Alexi asked, frowning. 'Why was she so possessive? So determined to keep Frank to herself? She doesn't strike me as the type of woman who's suffered from a day's lack of confidence in her entire life so she can't possibly imagine that anyone else would pose a threat to her hold over Frank. You said yourself, Cheryl, that he appeared obsessed, and blind to her faults.'

'In order to answer that question, we need to find out more about the woman herself. Was she born in Australia, do we know?'

Drew shook his head. 'I gather she hailed from around these parts somewhere, but none of her relations came to Frank's funeral.'

'Oh, I just assumed she was Australian,' Alexi said, chiding herself for jumping to conclusions. As a journalist, she knew always to check her facts. 'She speaks with a bit of an Australian accent, but not all the time, now that I think about it.'

'She can tell one end of a horse from the other, that much I do know,' Drew said. 'But when I pressed Frank on the subject, he became reticent. Said she'd left for Australia after a bitter separation from her ex and it was a part of her life she didn't want to revisit.'

'But she latched onto Frank when she discovered his connection to Lambourn and encouraged him to return.' Alexi cupped her chin between the thumb and index finger of her left hand and took a moment to reflect. 'The lady definitely had an agenda and Frank, her lapdog, played a starring role, albeit unwittingly.'

'You think his death wasn't an accident, don't you?' Drew asked quietly.

'The thought crossed my mind,' Jack replied, 'and Alexi's too, I'm willing to bet.'

'Too right!' Alexi agreed with alacrity. 'It's as suspicious as hell. Sorry if that upsets you, Drew, but I just don't buy that Frank went climbing alone.'

'On the contrary, I'm glad you're considering the possibility.'

'We all know that Frank didn't approach you about taking a cut from this place, Drew,' Alexi said. 'Perhaps Frank developed a backbone. No, scrub that. We already know that he had standards, which she clearly doesn't, but she assumed she could pull his strings. When that failed, she had no further use for him.'

'Funnily enough, I got the impression that the blinkers had already come off from Frank's perspective,' Drew said in a musing tone. 'I did manage one brief conversation with him alone and he made obtuse comments about being disillusioned but before I could get him to expand, she joined us. I'd suggested a boys' night out, but we never got to do it before... before he died.'

'Stella wouldn't have allowed it,' Cheryl said, reaching across to touch Drew's hand. 'Not if she had her own agenda.'

Jack smiled and stood up, beckoning to Alexi who did the same thing. 'We'll get out of your hair, go home and decide how to tackle this. But don't worry, we're on the case. Stella won't get her grubby hands on any part of your property while I have breath in my body.'

'Thank you, Jack.' Cheryl stood to peck his cheek and then hug Alexi. 'It's a great relief to know you're fighting our corner.'

'Hey, my corner too,' Alexi protested. 'I'm not giving that conniving little madam one penny of our hard-earned profits.'

3

'Whoever reckoned that life is dull in the country has obviously never visited Lambourn,' Alexi said, as Jack drove her, with Cosmo and Silgo installed on the back seat, away from Hopgood Hall.

'Well, at least we know what it is that Stella's after and can fight back.'

Alexi frowned at the passing scenery. 'She's brazen, no question about that, but she can't possibly believe that Drew and Cheryl will simply roll over and give her what she wants if she asks nicely enough. She must have some alternative agenda.'

'Yeah.' Jack tapped his fingers on the steering wheel. 'That's what worries me. What we just saw was an opening salvo, that much I do know, and she's unlikely to go away, quietly or otherwise, unless we can persuade her that it would be in her best interests.'

'Well, if she wants a fight then she's come to the right place.'

Jack pulled his car into the driveway of their shared

cottage. Cat and dog vanished into the garden, tails swishing, the moment the doors were opened. Alexi reached for her keys and unlocked the front door, allowing a waft of warmth to mingle with the cool, autumnal air. She glanced up at darkening clouds that threatened rain.

'We can say goodbye to summer, I think,' she remarked absently.

'Okay,' Jack said, slipping his arms out of his leather jacket and throwing it over the newel post before heading for the kitchen and firing up his laptop. 'Let's see what we can discover about the not-so-lovely Stella North.'

'At least she kept her own name, which makes our life a little easier,' Alexi replied, reaching for the kettle and filling it. She made tea for them both, placed a mug at Jack's elbow and took the chair beside his.

'You're checking births, I take it,' she said.

'Yep.' He sat back and picked up his tea. 'Here we go.'

'This must be her,' Alexi said, peering at the screen as Jack scrolled down a list. 'The dates are about right. They'd make her twenty-four now. She was born in Reading.'

Jack took a screenshot of the entry and then reapplied his fingers to the keyboard. 'There's no sign of her marrying. At least not in this country. Doesn't mean she didn't have a long-term relationship though.'

'She told Frank that she went to Australia to get away from a possessive ex,' Alexi reminded him.

'Yeah, she did say that, didn't she, but after today's performance, I don't believe a word that spills from her lips.'

'The names of her parents are on that birth certificate,' Alexi remarked. 'It would be interesting to know if they're still alive.'

Jack did another search.

'Looks as though her mother died five years ago. Heart attack.'

'She must have been quite young,' Alexi said. 'That's tragic.'

'Her father, Ben North, appears to be still alive. I'll have Cassie see if she can work her magic and track him down,' he said, referring to his partner in their private investigation business. Cassie was a whizz with computers, and no one could hide from her for long.

'I wonder how Stella got involved with horses, given that she was born in the city,' Alexi said. 'We know she liked them. That's one thing Frank did reveal about her and something that Stella herself never sought to hide.'

'More to the point, was her involvement centred around Lambourn? That could be a reason why she got her claws into Frank. She clearly wanted to come back to the area for reasons we have yet to fathom.'

'Why couldn't she have done that without a big, strong man to guide her path?'

'Absolutely no idea,' Jack replied cheerfully. 'Yet.'

'A better avenue to explore would be her insistence upon being entitled to a share of Hopgood Hall's profits, even though she must know that she isn't. It would give her a legitimate reason to hang about, to say nothing of an income, while she pursues her real agenda.'

'You're probably right,' Jack said, frowning, 'but we can't just leave Drew and Cheryl hanging and hoping the threat will go away.'

'There's more to it than that, of course.'

Jack leaned back in his chair. 'I haven't forgotten about Frank's death.'

'Is there any way that we can prove he was murdered a month after the event, especially given that his body has been cremated?'

'We can certainly ask a few questions. Don't get your hopes up though. If there was anything suspicious, it would have come to light at the time. Anyway, his friend Brian Hardy would be as good a place as any to start, along with the people involved in the place where he climbed.'

'Not sure about the latter. Even if anyone was around, and they all said at the inquest that no one was there at first light, they'll probably close ranks in an effort to protect their business.'

Jack chuckled. 'And we've never been stonewalled in any of our investigations before now?'

Alexi smiled too. 'True.' She paused. 'We don't have much to go on this time though, do we?'

'Oh, I don't know. Stella's father, if we can find him, Brian Hardy and the climbing school are enough to be going on with.'

'I wonder if Brian and Stella knew one another before Stella left these shores?'

Jack looked surprised by the question. 'Any reason why they should have?'

'No, not really. It's just... I don't know.' Alexi threw her head back, wondering why she felt there could be any sort of connection. Desperate to help her friends, was she clutching at straws? 'Stella wanting to go into wedding planning and Brian being involved in the wedding we're hosting here...' She flapped a hand when Jack opened his mouth to prevent him from interrupting her flow. 'Tenuous, I know. But then there's Brian being involved with horses, and Stella appearing to be something of an expert in that field, too. Brian would also have known that Frank had come into money.' She blinked. 'Well, presumably he knew, given they were close friends. Stella and Frank then just happened to link up in Australia?' She cocked her head to one side and sent Jack a challenging look. 'What are the chances?'

'When you put it like that, it does seem like a stretch,' Jack conceded.

'Anyway, Brian's the only common denominator that we've found so far.'

Jack nodded. 'Yeah, we really need to make Brian our first port of call tomorrow.'

The cat flap rattled, and Cosmo stalked regally into the room. Jack and Alexi shared a smile, waiting for Silgo to indicate that he too was finished in the garden. He barked seconds later and still smiling, Jack got up to let him in.

'We'd get a dog flap, darling,' Alexi said, tugging at Silgo's ears, 'but it would have to be so big that it would be an open invitation to burglars.'

Silgo rubbed his head against Alexi's thigh, and she could have sworn that he smiled as he lapped up the attention that had been missing from his life for so long. Jack watched them for a moment, an indulgent smile playing about his lips, then reached for his phone.

'I'll get Cassie onto looking for Ben North,' he said.

A short conversation later, he cut the connection.

'Shall I order something in for supper, save us cooking?' he asked.

'A curry would hit the spot.'

'Consider it done.'

By the time their meal had been delivered and consumed,

Cassie had called back with an address for Ben North in Reading.

'That's close to the posh school we went to on the Natalie Parker case, isn't it?' Alexi asked, checking the address on her phone.

'Same direction. It's certainly not central Reading. It's much more rural, which could be how a young Stella came into contact with horses. Well, she'd have been hard pressed to miss them in that neck of the woods. Cassie also discovered that Stella has three older siblings.'

'Really?' Alexi raised a brow. 'As far as I'm aware, she never said anything about them to Cheryl and Drew. But then again, she revealed precious little about herself.'

'The more people we can find with a connection to Stella, the more we're likely to discover about her ambitions, and her reason for swanning off to Australia. We'll see her father tomorrow, after Brian, then run the siblings to ground.'

Alexi, with Cosmo on her lap and Silgo stretched across her feet, leaned back into the corner of the settee and yawned. 'Sounds like a plan,' she said.

'Come on you.' Jack stood and offered Alexi his hand. 'You look beat. Let's turn in and come at this fresh tomorrow.'

Cosmo leapt from Alexi's lap without having to be tipped from it and, tail aloft, led the procession up the stairs. The bedroom was too small for Silgo to join them in it and anyway, on the one occasion he'd tried it, Cosmo had made it very clear that he wasn't welcome. *One step too far*, as Jack had remarked at the time. He'd also pointed out that if Silgo joined them on the bed then there would be no room left for him and Alexi. A fair point and Silgo, being easy going, seemed perfectly content to sleep on the landing rug. It was, Alexi knew, a different world for him from the cold, outdoor kennel that he'd been chained to when he'd belonged to a local, now disgraced trainer.

* * *

'I reckon we should try our luck with Brian now,' Jack said, glancing at his watch over breakfast the following morning.

Alexi nodded. They'd been in Lambourn for long enough to know that trainers took several strings of horses out on the gallops early in the morning and watched them perform. Only after that did they stop for breakfast.

'Let's do it then,' she replied, standing to stash the plates in the dishwasher.

The animals had finished their breakfast and, predictably, it was Cosmo who led the way to the door, tail swishing.

'He's still pulling rank,' Jack said, laughing. 'He doesn't seem to realise that Silgo is perfectly happy to play second fiddle.'

'Silgo knows his place and is just grateful to be part of our family.'

'Well, there is that.'

Jack followed the instructions issued by his sat nav and drove them to one of the many training yards scattered around the rolling chalk downs surrounding Lambourn. Rain still threatened but had yet to materialise.

'This looks a bit more professional than Baxter's yard,' Alexi said, referring to the rundown establishment where Silgo had suffered for so long.

'Anything would.'

Jack pulled his car into the visitors' parking area, stopped next to a muddy four by four and cut the engine. Leaving Silgo and Cosmo in the car, he and Alexi walked towards the yard and asked a groom if Brian Hardy happened to be about.

'He's just finished breakfast,' the girl replied. 'He's over there, watching the vet walking that grey up.'

Jack and Alexi stood back while Brian conducted a conversation with the vet. Alexi took the opportunity to observe Brian before he realised they were there. He was a stocky individual whom she knew to be in his late forties. He looked older. His weathered face spoke of a man who worked outdoors, a trademark flat cap fixed firmly on his head.

He turned towards them once the vet left, his expression open and friendly. Affable enough, Alexi's first impression was favourable.

'Can I help you?' he asked.

'I hope so. I'm Jack Maddox.' he extended his hand. 'And this is Alexi Ellis.'

Brian shook each of their hands. 'I know who you are. I've seen you around Hopgood Hall. And at Frank's funeral too, but we never got a chance to talk.' He shook his head. 'Such a tragedy.'

'Do you have a moment?' Jack asked. 'Is there somewhere private we can go to talk? We have a few questions for you.'

'Sounds sinister,' Brian replied with a theatrical shudder. 'I read the local rag and know you two always get your man, so to speak. Should I be worried?'

'Not in the least,' Alexi replied, following Brian into a warm tack room, where the smell of leather prevailed. 'We're actually here to pick your brains.'

'About Frank, I assume.' Brian leaned his backside against a window ledge and crossed his arms over his torso. 'Not sure what I can tell you. Anyway, what do you want to know, and more to the point, why?'

'I gather the two of you were good friends,' Alexi said, avoiding giving a direct answer to Brian's question.

'From our school days.' A brief smile touched Brian's lips. 'We were always getting into scrapes. Drove our teachers bonkers, so we did. Frank was a great one for practical jokes, even as a kid, and I tagged along for the ride.' The smile turned into a wicked little grin. 'Not that I'm claiming to have been a saint. It's just that there always has to be a leader and that was always going to be Frank.'

Which isn't the way it turned out in his marriage, Alexi thought but did not say.

'What happened when you left school?' Jack asked. 'You both stayed in the district initially and presumably your friendship endured?'

'I did. I was always going to go into this business. I've taken over my dad's position here at this yard. He never quite made it to trainer status: always the understudy, a bit like me with Frank. And I prefer it that way. Don't want the stress and responsibility that goes with being the overall boss.' He let out a long breath. 'But you didn't come here to talk about my career aspirations, or lack thereof, so what is it that you do want to know?' He cocked his head to one side. 'And more to the point, why do you want to know it? Don't imagine I didn't notice your failure to answer that question earlier. I don't mean to be rude, but Frank's death was a tragic accident. There was an enquiry. And now he's been laid to rest, so...' He spread his hands and allowed his words to trail off.

'I'm Drew and Cheryl's partner in the hotel, as you probably know,' Alexi explained. 'Drew's having a hard time coming to terms with what happened and I'm just trying to help him find closure. He and Frank were close at one time, but I gather they drifted apart.'

'Well, Drew was always the steady one, but Frank... well, he bored easily and was always chasing the next big opportunity to make easy money, convinced that this time, he'd hit the jackpot. He was also convinced that fortune favoured the brave, to coin a phrase.' Brian signalled to the groom holding the grey to put it back in its stable. 'Of course, he never did make it big time, at least not as far as I know.'

'Were you surprised when he took off to Australia?' Alexi asked. 'And more to the point, do you know why he chose to go so far from everything and everyone that was familiar to him? He never told Drew why and naturally, he's curious.'

Brian looked edgy. 'Hasn't he asked his wife?'

Alexi thought that for the first time since the start of this conversation, Brian was being deliberately evasive.

'She isn't very forthcoming,' Jack replied.

'Well look, all I can tell you is that he had wanderlust. Even as a kid, he dreamed of going to far-flung places and living like a native. Geography was the only subject that held his interest. And of course, once his pockets were full of the dosh that he took in exchange for giving up on Hopgood Hall, there was no stopping him. Australia was the land of milk and honey, according to him, and he wanted part of the action. Don't ask me what action because I have absolutely no idea, but he did tell me that he had an in, an introduction, to someone with contacts.'

'You don't have any idea who, I suppose?' Jack asked, more in hope than expectation.

'Not a clue, and even if he'd told me, it'd have gone in one ear and out the other. I'd heard it all so many times before, you see.' Brian rolled his eyes. 'Like I say, he wasn't much of a realist.'

'You kept in contact after his departure, I assume,' Alexi said.

'The odd email. Frank wasn't big on communication and I... well, I'm kept pretty busy most of the time. We're not kids any more and drifting apart was inevitable, I suppose. Frank taking himself off to the other side of the world meant that was always going to happen.'

'Surely he must have got in touch when he met and married Stella,' Alexi said. 'He'd want his best friend to know that he'd found "the one".'

'Well yeah, and I'll admit I was surprised. Frank liked to play the field. I never would have pegged him as being the monogamous type.'

'She was a fair bit younger than him,' Jack remarked.

'Twenty-odd years. I think that was part of the attraction. He wanted to show the world that he could pull a fit younger woman, even if he couldn't make it in the world of business.'

'A macho thing,' Alexi suggested.

'If you like. It would fit Frank's MO.'

'What was in it for her?' Jack asked.

Brian shrugged. 'How the hell am I supposed to know?'

He looked evasive again. Alexi suspected that he did know but wasn't about to say. 'What did you make of Stella?' she asked.

'Seemed nice enough. She sure as hell didn't deserve to lose Frank so soon after tying the knot. I feel sorry for her.'

'Had you ever met her before?' Jack asked casually. 'I gather she hailed from around these parts and knows a bit about horses.'

Brian's gaze shifted to the left. 'Can't say that I had,' he replied curtly. 'And believe me, I'd remember if I had. She's a bit of a traffic stopper. But now, if you'll excuse me, there's work to be done.'

'Sure.' Jack held out his hand. 'Thanks for your time and sorry to have held you up. I hope it wasn't too painful, dredging up the past, I mean.'

'No worries. Sorry I couldn't be more help.' He was friendly and affable once again. 'Hope I've said or done something to put Drew's mind at rest.' They walked together towards Jack's car. 'Frank lived life in the fast lane and died doing what he loved. It's a tragedy but there's no great mystery about it.'

'We didn't for one moment think that there was,' Alexi assured him, 'other than that he appeared to have climbed alone, which is what's getting to Drew. He insists he would never have taken the risk, but then again, they'd lost touch and perhaps Frank had become less safety conscious.'

'It's the only explanation that fits. Frank knew that climb well. He used to do it all the time when he was still in this country.' Brian lifted a shoulder. 'Perhaps his climbing buddy let him down at the last minute, so he decided to go it alone. I don't suppose we'll ever know, not for sure.'

'You're probably right, on both counts,' Jack said easily.

But Alexi knew that wasn't what he thought. He hadn't seen Frank's phone records, and as far as he was aware, no one had any reason to check them. Perhaps Cassie would be able to hack into them, just to see who he'd been supposed to climb with that day, but at present, they didn't have sufficient reason to ask her.

'Stop by at the hotel next time you're passing,' Alexi said, 'and we'll buy you a drink by way of thanks.'

'I might well take you up on that.'

Brian stood where they'd left him, watching Jack drive away.

'A man who knows a lot more than he's saying,' Alexi remarked.

'I agree. He definitely knows more about Stella than he was prepared to let on. I think you're right; he and Stella did know one another in a previous life. The question is, did Brian encourage Frank to take his wanderlust to Australia and arrange for the two of them to meet, and for Stella to help Frank spend his inheritance? That's what we need to find out.'

4

'What possible reason would Brian have had to put a barracuda like Stella onto his best friend?' Alexi asked.

Jack smiled at her as he punched Ben North's address into his sat nav and fired up his engine. 'We won't know the answer to that one until we discover what connection, if any, there is between Brian and Stella.'

'One thing we know for sure is that our questions made him edgy, and if he is in touch with Stella then he will let her know that we've been poking our noses in.'

'Precisely! And that's what I want him to do. When she realises that we're probing, she might give up trying to con Drew and take herself off to find an easier target. Especially if she's doing something dodgy.'

Alexi twitched her nose. 'Well, we know that she is and it has more to do with simply trying to con Drew, I'm absolutely sure of it.'

'Very probably.'

Jack paused at a junction and waited for a string of race-horses to cross the road ahead of him. The rider on the final leggy equine raised his whip in acknowledgement, struggling to control a horse that was obviously keen to stretch its legs. It swung its quarters sideways and pranced on the spot, showing off as it held up traffic in both directions.

'I have a feeling that she won't be that easily deterred from whatever it is that brought her to this district,' Jack said, returning his attention to their conversation when the horses had safely negotiated the road. 'But, if she thinks we're suspicious about Frank's death, and if she was responsible for it, then she might very well cut and run, which is what we want.'

'We do, but if she killed Frank or had him killed then I want her to answer for her crime. And to explain why, so that Drew can at least find some closure.'

Silgo gave a little woof from the back seat.

'I'll swear that dog is even more attuned to our conversations than Cosmo has ever been,' Alexi said, reaching back to rub Silgo's head.

Jack chuckled. 'Nothing to do with the fact that a squirrel just darted across the road then?'

'Don't spoil my illusions,' Alexi replied hotly. 'I've decided that Silgo has psychic abilities and nothing and no one will convince me otherwise.'

'If that's the case, why not ask him which direction he'd take in this investigation?'

'Rome wasn't built in a day. I just want him to feel loved and valued before we depend upon his skills.'

'He does. How could he not after the hell he lived through before coming to us?'

'Well there is that.' Alexi allowed herself a brief pause. 'We must be able to find out where Frank and Stella were living once they returned to the UK,' she said. 'It seems highly suspicious to me that they didn't tell Drew. When we asked Stella yesterday, did you notice her deliberate prevarication? I mean, if there was nothing suspicious about their living arrangements, why all the secrecy?'

'Why indeed.' Jack slowed and indicated left. 'Hopefully, Mr North will be able to enlighten us.'

'What if Stella is living with him?' Jack glanced at Alexi and could see that the possibility worried her since the father wouldn't offer up any offending information about his daughter if that was the case. 'We hadn't considered that.'

'I rather hope that she is. That way, she can't fail to realise that we're on her case. But I doubt we'll find her here. If she had somewhere to live, why try to invite herself to Hopgood Hall? And why were none of her relations at her husband's funeral for that matter?'

'She wants to stay at the hotel to press her claim, is my guess. If Drew and Cheryl trip over her every day, they can't ignore her.'

'Hmm. Possibly, but I doubt it. She knows she hasn't got a leg to stand on. She wants free access to the hotel for some other reason. The hell if I know what that reason could possibly be but it's the only obvious conclusion to draw. She knows she's not welcome there but is brazen or desperate enough to front it out.'

'Perhaps she shared that reason with Frank and he violently disagreed with her?' Alexi suggested. 'That would be enough for her to want him out the way. If he wasn't with her, he was against her.'

'It's possible.' Jack removed one hand from the wheel and waggled it from side to side. 'But I doubt it. From what we've learned, Frank was her poodle. When she said jump, he asked how high.'

Alexi pulled a face. 'True,' she said.

'Well, anyway, this is the street,' Jack said, indicating left, 'so we're about to find out if Stella is in residence.'

They were in the suburbs of Reading. The houses were three-storey semis, older buildings with large gardens, spaced well apart. Number seventeen looked well maintained and a man, North presumably, was in the front garden raking leaves. A spaniel appeared to be hindering his progress.

'Behave!' Alexi chided, when Cosmo saw the spaniel, stood up and hissed.

Jack pulled his car up outside the house in question and told Cosmo and Silgo to stay where they were. Cosmo gave an indignant mewl and settled down, his gaze never wavering far from the spaniel, who'd loped up to the car to see who'd come calling.

'Hello.' The man stood up from his task and leaned on the handle of his rake, sending Jack and Alexi a warm yet cautious smile as they approached. He had to be in his fifties but still had a full head of hair, albeit salt-and-pepper. His features were rugged, his body a mass of solid muscle, no paunch in sight. The man had once been handsome and had aged well. Jack could see where Stella had got her looks from. 'Are you looking for anyone in particular?'

'If you're Ben North then it's you we've come to see.'

The spaniel ran up to Alexi, wagging its entire rear end. Unsurprisingly, she bent to make a fuss of it.

'That will be me,' he said, staring at Jack's car and doing a double take. 'What the hell is that on the back seat?'

'The dog or the cat?' Alexi asked smiling.

'Ah, it's a cat, is it? I thought it was a small panther, or something equally exotic. People have all sorts of weird pets nowadays.'

Jack extended his hand. 'The name's Jack Maddox,' he

said, 'and this is Alexi Ellis. She'll shake your hand too, once she's satisfied that she's given your dog enough of her attention.'

North gave a good-natured laugh. 'That might take a while.' He shook Jack's hand, and then Alexi's when she straightened up and offered it to him. 'What can I do for you?' he asked.

'Well, it's about Stella.'

North's smile faded and his expression turned wary. 'My Stella? What about her? Haven't seen her for years. Why? What's she done now?'

'She went to Australia, we're told.'

'As far as I know. We've been estranged for five years, but I'm not prepared to tell you anything more until you tell me why you're asking.'

'You're not aware that she came back to England three months ago then?' Alexi paused and Jack knew she would be studying North's reaction carefully, as was he, but the man's surprise appeared genuine.

'No, I was not but then I wouldn't expect to be. She and I will never be reconciled. Too much water under the bridge. Anyway, why do you want to talk about her?'

'If you have no contact then you probably won't know that she was married to a local man.'

'Was?' North snorted. 'Don't tell me. The marriage didn't stand the test of time. Why am I not surprised? Presumably, she came home and latched onto someone with more money than sense. Someone who'd be influenced by a pretty face and a bit of flattery. Someone who could put his money behind her ambitions.'

'Not precisely.' Alexi smiled, presumably because she could see that North was struggling to maintain his composure. For all his insistence that his relationship with Stella was beyond recall, she *was* still his daughter and the separation had to be painful. 'Unfortunately, her husband died in an accident about a month ago, here in England. Did you not read about it in the local paper?'

'Never read the papers. The news is always bad.' North put his rake aside and scratched the back of his neck. 'Stella's still in England, I take it.'

'She was as of yesterday.'

'Well, I haven't seen hide nor hair of her, so you're wasting your time with me.'

Jack sensed a seismic shift in both North's attitude and the tenor of the interview. His attitude had gone from open and friendly to wary and semi-hostile. He would now either ask them to leave his property, or curiosity would get the better of him and he'd talk more about his estrangement from his youngest child.

'I have an interest in Hopgood Hall in Lambourn,' Alexi said.

'Oh aye, I know the place. Swanky. Elegant. Beyond my budget, except for special occasions. My middle son, Simon, had his thirtieth there last year.'

Alexi smiled. 'I think I remember that. It was quite a party. Simon and his friends drank the bar dry.'

North chuckled. 'That they did. Thank goodness I wasn't paying the bill.'

'The thing is,' Alexi said, her smile fading, 'Stella was married to the elder brother of my co-owner, Drew Hopgood.'

North's eyes widened. 'Was she now.' He sighed. 'You'd better come and sit down. Seems we have stuff to talk about.'

He led them to an arrangement of patio chairs at the side of the house. Alexi and Jack lowered themselves into them.

The spaniel tagged along and flopped down at Alexi's feet, looking up at her expectantly through liquid eyes.

'You've made yourself a friend,' North said absently. 'Mind you, that ain't saying much. The stupid mutt loves anyone who shows him a bit of attention.'

'Animals are drawn to Alexi,' Jack said.

'I can see that.' North set his features into a rigid line that gave little away about his thoughts as he turned his attention to the matter in hand. 'Now then, how did my daughter's husband die?' he asked.

'In a climbing accident,' Jack replied. 'He was an experienced climber but apparently went out early one morning. Alone. Drew thinks that was out of character.'

'And you think Stella had something to do with his death?' The question was posed without rancour.

'We're not suggesting that. There was an inquest, and no one seemed to think it was anything other than an accident,' Alexi said.

'Then why are you here?'

'Because Stella is trying to muscle in on Hopgood Hall, suggesting that Frank was shortchanged when he sold out his share to Drew,' Jack said, sensing that North would be more open with them if they told him the truth.

'Sounds like Stella,' North said calmly.

Alexi certainly hadn't expected a parent to think *that* badly of his daughter without at least some supporting evidence. 'You don't seem particularly shocked.'

'I wouldn't put anything past Stella,' he replied, his features rigid.

Jack's concerns about Stella's intentions intensified. Up until that point, he hadn't seriously believed that Stella could be anything other than irritating, since her claim on Hopgood

Hall lacked foundation. But if her own father wasn't surprised by her tactics then perhaps Jack had underestimated the woman's guile.

'Tell us about her,' Jack invited. 'If it's not too personal, I'm curious to know why you're estranged. And anything else you feel willing to share.'

North's features darkened. 'I won't have anything to do with her because I hold her responsible for the death of her mother,' he said.

Jack glanced at Alexi. Whatever he'd expected the man to say, it hadn't been that. Alexi looked equally flummoxed.

'How so?' Jack asked.

'She was an ambitious little madam, right from the time that she could first walk.' He sighed. 'I suppose Molly and I were partly responsible for that. She came along a good five years after the rest of her siblings. We thought our family was complete and I'll admit that we spoiled her. And, of course, she was as pretty as a picture. Admired everywhere she went, and all that praise went straight to her head. She could be as good as gold, unless she didn't get her way, and then... well, all hell would break loose.'

'You said she was responsible for your wife's death,' Alexi said, laying a gentle hand on North's forearm. 'That must have been devastating and I can quite understand why your relationship never recovered. Tell us what happened, if you can bear to.'

North stared at his hands for a long time and at first, Jack thought he'd tell them to take a hike. The emotion clouding his features was truly disturbing. The man had clearly adored his wife and was having a tough time getting along without her. Alexi and Jack waited him out in silence. This was really none of their business. They were intruding on a man's grief, still raw after five years. Even so, it could have a direct bearing on Stella's true character, if she really was involved in some way, and Jack desperately hoped that he wouldn't clam up on them.

'They'd been arguing.' North's low voice jolted Jack out of his reverie. 'Nothing unusual about that. Stella was almost twenty at the time. She'd moved out, was living in London somewhere, working for a fancy PR company that helped to inflate her sense of self-importance because she was rubbing shoulders with the pseudo rich and famous. Gave her a taste of the life she'd always hankered after, I suppose. Swanky hotels, fabulous parties where everyone wanted to be seen... You get the picture.'

Jack nodded and assured North that he did.

'It all ended in tears, of course.' North sniffed. 'We never did get to the bottom of what happened but the long and the short of it is that Stella got the push. We assumed that also meant her living accommodation was no longer available because she dumped herself back on us.'

'Sorry to be insensitive,' Alexi said softly, 'but did you assume that she'd moved in with someone running the company?'

'We didn't assume, we knew. She couldn't stop boasting about how this influential guy was crazy about her. He ran the company. Elite Promotions it was called. His name was Nick. Never met him and don't know his surname. Don't care, either. Stella wouldn't have brought him here.' North blew air through his lips. 'That would have required her to admit to her humble origins.'

'She was ashamed of where she came from?' Jack asked.

'It wouldn't have fitted in with the image she'd created for herself. Anyway, she came home once Nick got rid of her and no one could talk to her. I'd seen her in moods over the years but never anything quite so dramatic, and nothing that lasted as long. Anyway, it all came to a head when Molly challenged her. She'd been living here for two weeks and treating Molly like a skivvy. I wanted to read her the riot act, but Molly told me to leave it to her. Like I fool I did. I'll never forgive myself for that.' North shook his head. 'If I'd taken Stella to task then Molly would still be alive today.'

'Tell us the rest,' Alexi said gently when North fell silent.

'I was at work, Molly confronted Stella, there was a slanging match and Molly fell... was pushed down the stairs.' North stared directly ahead as he spoke, all signs of emotion replaced with a blank expression.

'How can you actually know that Stella pushed her?' Jack asked. 'If you weren't there, I mean.'

'It was summer, the windows were open, and my oldest lad was working in the garden. He grows vegetables and is enthusiastic about organic stuff. The garden's big: too big for me. Although he didn't live here any more, he'd taken it over. It was his passion. Stella either didn't realise that Luke was here, or simply didn't care if she was heard screaming at her mother like a fishwife. Stella said afterwards that Molly was on the landing, talking to her, when she toppled over and fell but Luke swears that he heard a struggle and Molly crying out, telling Stella to stop pushing her around. Luke knew that this particular confrontation was more serious than usual and ran into the house to intervene, but he was too late. He found his mother crumpled at the bottom of the stairs.'

'I'm so very sorry,' Alexi said. 'How do you get over something like that?'

'You don't.' North swiped at his eyes with the back of his hand. 'Worse yet, I couldn't bring myself to tell the police that

I suspected my own daughter of murder. Stella was beside herself, probably because she realised what she'd done and that Luke, that we all, knew it. She was sweetness and light after that but we none of us wanted to know her. I told her to leave my house and never come back and I haven't seen her since.'

'The records show that your wife died of a heart attack,' Jack said.

'Stella said they were talking when she clutched her chest and toppled over. She was unable to prevent her falling down the stairs. That's what she told the police too. She was all tears and devastation. It was sickening to watch. But Molly did have a mild heart condition. Her medical records backed that up, and we let the cause of death stand, mainly because we couldn't prove otherwise.'

'Thanks for telling us,' Jack said. 'I know it can't have been easy for you.'

'I don't talk about it, not even to my other kids,' North replied, 'and I only opened up to you because if Stella married your friend, and if he died under suspicious circumstances, then it doesn't do to assume that Stella knew nothing about it.' He set his chin in a firm line. 'It's not easy to talk ill of my own flesh and blood but she's a wrong 'un. There's always been something not quite right about her and if she doesn't get her own way, or if life somehow disappoints her, then there's no saying how she'll respond. She downright dangerous when she gets into a strop and, trust me, she has a vicious temper.'

'Frank Hopgood was almost twice her age,' Alexi said. 'Did she have a penchant for older men, do you know?'

'Well, Nick, the PR guru was a lot older than her. Apart from that, I couldn't say. Stella did what Stella wanted to do.

We never knew with whom and only knew as much about her exploits as she felt like telling us.'

'When did she go to Australia?' Alexi asked.

'Soon after Molly died. Like I say, I had nothing more to do with her; couldn't even look at her. But my daughter Louise, who's the closest in age to her, ran into her just after the funeral and she mentioned that she was making a fresh start Down Under.'

'Just one more question,' Jack said, 'then we'll get out of your hair. Did Stella like horses?'

'Oh aye, she was into them almost as soon as she could walk. We bought her a pony and she went to all the gymkhanas, winning rosettes left, right and centre. She was a natural on horseback, I'll give her that, but she gave it up when she turned fifteen and became fully aware of her femininity and what it could do for her.'

'You've been very open with us, Ben,' Alexi said, once again touching his arm. 'Thank you. It's helped a lot for us to better understand the woman Frank married. We'll leave you now but if you think of anything else that might be useful, please give me a call.' She extracted a card from her bag and handed it to him.

'I'll do that,' North replied. 'You know, I never talk about Molly, especially not to the family. We all find it too painful. But talking to you guys, strangers, has felt cathartic.'

'Then I'm glad,' Jack said, shaking the man's hand.

They left North to his cogitations, armed with an address for Luke, Stella's brother.

'That is so sad,' Alexi said with a little sigh as the got back into Jack's car and Silgo smothered Alexi's face with kisses. Cosmo remained aloof for a moment or two, and then pulled rank by leaping over the seat and landing softly on Alexi's lap.

'At least he enjoyed talking about it, in a perverse sort of way,' Jack replied. 'He *knows* that his daughter pushed his wife down the stairs, deliberately or in the heat of the moment, and it doesn't sit well with him to also know that she got away with it. But at the same time, he couldn't put the accusation out there. She is, after all, his daughter, and feels partly responsible for the way she turned out.'

'At least we have two more avenues to explore now. Luke North and Elite Promotions, always assuming they're still in business.' Alexi checked the name on her phone. 'Yep. An address in Battersea, which is now the height of trendiness, I happen to know, given that I once lived there. Nick Fairburn. There's a picture.'

Jack looked over Alexi's shoulder. 'A man in late middle-age, trying to hold back time with his gelled hair and fake tan.'

'Yeah, my thoughts exactly. Anyway, what now?'

'We'll leave Fairburn until tomorrow. We need to find out a bit more about him first. Right now, we're visiting Harrisons Rock. We're expected.'

5

Alexi felt a little shellshocked by Ben North's candid revelations. She had taken a dislike to Stella North even before she'd met her for reasons she hadn't properly understood. But she understood all too well now that her instinct hadn't let her down. Be that as it may, could Stella really be *that* vindictive? So spoiled, and so determined to have her way that she would have actually pushed her mother down the stairs?

'I suppose, if Stella was involved romantically with Nick Fairburn, who sounds like he moved in the types of circles Stella wanted to be accepted in, and if he threw her over, then her feelings would be hurt, to say the least,' she mused. 'But to the extent that she'd resort to using violence against her own mother?' Alexi frowned. 'What sort of monster would that make her?'

'Let's give her the benefit of the doubt for the time being and assume that it was an accident. They had an argument, that much is beyond question,' Jack said, focusing his attention on the road, but Alexi knew that all sorts of scenarios would be playing themselves out inside his head. Unlike her, he wasn't permitting personal feelings to get in the way of his judgement. 'A better question to ask would be why she went to Australia and, more specifically, why she linked up with Frank when he got there. He was hardly in the same league as Fairburn.'

'Frank talked a good game. If he did tell her that he still had an interest in Hopgood Hall, Stella would have known the place and thought he'd make a good meal ticket. Then she was disappointed for a second time because he didn't live up to expectations. Whether that was because Frank had already run through the money Drew paid him or because it wasn't enough to satisfy Stella's ambitions is another matter. Either way, she found herself stuck in a marriage to a man twice her age who had disappointed her. She felt let down again and needed an escape clause.'

Jack nodded. 'I'd like to know what Frank did with all that money Drew paid him for his share of Hopgood Hall. I'd also like to know what attracted him to Australia in the first place, or who. It's a hell of a long way to go on a whim and he must have known that he couldn't stay there indefinitely. Did someone suggest a business opportunity, or did he just fancy a bit of guaranteed sunshine? I asked Drew but he just said it was typical of Frank to take off, chasing his latest dream, without a thought for the practicalities.'

Alexi nodded. 'I hear you.'

'Anyway, let's see what they have to say at this climbing place.'

'Where is it exactly?'

'Close to a village called Groomsbridge that straddles the Kent and East Sussex border.'

'Quite a trek then. I hope it's worth it.'

'I'm not expecting to learn much. It's just a case of being thorough. That way, things often pop to the surface.'

'Very true.'

They hit the motorway and the motion lulled Alexi to sleep. She woke only when the car slowed again and opened her eyes to find Jack driving through a town she recognised from signposts as being Tunbridge Wells.

'Sorry,' she said, stretching her arms above her head and yawning. 'Not much company, am I.'

Jack laughed. 'Don't worry about it. I've had a one-way conversation with these two while you slept.' He jerked a thumb towards the back seat where cat and dog were entwined. 'We're only a few miles away now.'

'Harrison's Rocks are owned by the British Mountaineering Council, apparently,' Alexi said, scrolling through her phone, 'but it says here that a separate group manage them. There don't appear to be any climbing schools.' She looked up at Jack, scowling. 'So how come someone from a school spoke up at the inquest? And more to the point, why haven't we questioned that aspect before now?'

'There's a group that Frank climbed with, not just at Harrison's Rock but all over the south of the country. They have rules about never climbing alone. It was their captain who spoke at the inquest and he's agreed to meet us here.'

'Oh, okay.'

They pulled into a car park a short time later. At that time of the year, there were few other vehicles about. A strong wind blew, tossing random raindrops around which would, Alexi assumed, make any climbing surface slick and more danger-ous. She opened her door and let Cosmo and Silgo out. Stand-ing, she stretched and placed her hands on the small of her back in an effort to dislodge the kinks that had accumulated there.

'It's beautiful,' she said, taking in the view, or what she could see of it through the mist.

'Yeah, but I just don't get the climbing thing,' Jack said, staring up at the sandstone peaks. 'Thrill seeking, or what?'

'I couldn't say. Better than potholing, I guess. At least you're out in the fresh air and getting exercise.'

A man dressed for the outdoors approached them from the direction of a hut. Silgo woofed and loped up to him, anxious for some attention. Cosmo sent him an imperious look and then ignored him.

'You must be Jack Maddox,' the man said. 'I'm Reg Parsons. We spoke on the phone. Didn't realise you were bringing a zoo with you,' he added, scratching Silgo's ears and sending Cosmo a curious look.

'Sorry about that. They kinda tag along and we don't have the heart to leave them behind.'

'Or the courage,' Alexi added.

'This is Alexi Ellis, my partner,' Jack said.

'Hi,' Alexi extended her hand and Reg took it in a firm grasp. 'I know that name. Didn't you used to write for the *Sunday Sentinel*?'

'In a previous life, yes I did.'

'Well, I'm pleased to meet you both, even if there's not much I can tell you about Frank's death. The jury's still out on the feline though.'

'Don't worry,' Alexi said. 'If Cosmo had taken against you then you'd know all about it by now. He's an excellent judge of character, if he does say so himself.'

Reg laughed. 'That's a relief.'

'Where did Frank fall?' Jack asked.

'Over here.'

They followed Reg to the base of an escarpment that rose almost vertically as far as the eye could see.

'Challenging,' Alexi said, shivering when it occurred to her that they could be standing in the exact spot where Frank had actually fallen. She subconsciously shuffled backwards. She glanced up at what appeared to her to be a sharp incline of slick rock, with few footholds visible to the naked eye. Even an experienced climber falling suddenly seemed more plausible.

'Not for Frank. Or it shouldn't have been. He knew what he was doing and was paranoid about safety.'

'Not paranoid enough,' Alexi said, shivering again and folding her arms across her torso in a futile effort to keep warm. The rain had intensified and neither she nor Jack were dressed to withstand it.

'If you've seen enough, come on over to the hut and we can talk in the dry,' Reg said, anticipating their dilemma.

Silgo trotted along beside them as they headed for the hut in question. Cosmo had disappeared to investigate this new territory, but Alexi knew he wouldn't stray far.

They entered a hut that was crammed full of climbing gear. Ropes, slings and karabiners were the only items that Alexi could identify but there was a plethora of other equipment lining the walls, all neatly stacked.

'You're well organised,' Jack said, voicing Alexi's thoughts.

'Only foolhardy climbers wouldn't be.'

'Did you know Frank Hopgood personally?' Alexi asked, cutting to the chase. This spot was beautiful but she found it eerie and slightly sinister and definitely didn't want to linger. Silgo clung to her legs and whined, clearly sharing her feelings. She reached down a hand and found comfort in the contact with his damp fur.

'I did know Frank slightly, before he went off to parts foreign. We climbed together a few times. I heard he was back but I never saw him myself. Others in the club did. He was a good guy. Popular. Everyone liked him. What happened to him was a tragedy.'

Alexi nodded, not sure what to make of Reg's words. It hadn't told them much that they hadn't already known. She wondered if he was trying to fob them off with platitudes.

'I gather that experienced climbers don't go out alone,' she said, deciding to press the man. 'Apparently, he told his wife that he was meeting someone here, presumably from your group, but that wasn't the case, was it?'

'Nope, but even if for some reason he did decide to go out alone, I'm really surprised that he fell. He was way too experienced for that to happen.'

'People get distracted, lose concentration, in all walks of life,' Jack said. 'Especially if they have pressing problems on their minds.'

'True, I suppose, but...' Reg spread his hands and his words trailed off.

'That's not what you said at the inquest,' Alexi said. 'About suspicious circumstances, I mean.'

'There were none, not really. That was just my personal feeling. I had nothing to back it up.' Reg shrugged. 'Besides, why would I cast doubt on what was obviously an accident and cause more grief for his widow and family?'

'You say you haven't seen him since his return to the UK,' Alexi said. 'But you mentioned just now that some others have. '

'There are a couple but there isn't anything they can add to what I've already told you.'

'Nevertheless, it would be good if we could have their names,' Jack said with an easy smile.

'I'm not sure what it is that you're trying to establish.' Reg's attitude had turned wary. 'There was an accident, an inquest, and it's all done and dusted. Why drag it all up again? What are you hoping to achieve, other than to give climbing a bad name? The sport comes with risks attached and everyone who indulges is aware of the fact.'

'We're just trying to find out as much as we can for Frank's brother's sake,' Alexi said. 'They hadn't seen one another for a long time and when he did come back to this country, his focus was on his new wife and Drew still didn't get to spend much time with Frank. He's having a hard time getting to grips with what happened.'

'So an experienced journalist and a private detective are spending time digging it all up again. Yes, I looked you up,' Reg said in response to Jack's raised-eyebrow look. 'But honestly, there's nothing to see here.'

'Very likely not, and we appreciate your time,' Jack said. 'If we could just have those names, we'll get out of your hair.'

'Bob Green and Andy Dawson. They climbed with Frank all the time before he left the country.' Reg provided them with phone numbers for both men and Alexi jotted them down. 'I'll tell them to expect a call but then, after that, I'd appreciate it if you'd let this go. People have accidents. They die. There doesn't have to be a mystery.'

'One last question. Did Frank ever climb with women?'

Reg laughed. 'Only every woman who ever joined our group. They were drawn to him like moths to flame. He simply had that effect on the opposite sex. Men too, for that matter. Frank never met a stranger.'

'Were you surprised that he married a woman who didn't climb?' Jack asked.

'Didn't think much about it. Didn't know that she wasn't a climber, come to that. All of us are obsessed with climbing but I can count on the fingers of one hand those who are married to climbers. But still, the moment I saw her picture, I could see why he'd finally taken the plunge.'

'Fair point,' Jack conceded, nudging Alexi when she opened her mouth to ask another question. 'Well, thanks for taking the time to meet with us.' He offered Reg his hand.

'No problem. Nice to meet you both.' He released Jack's hand then shook Alexi's before bending to again scratch Silgo's ears. 'Nice to meet you too,' he added.

Alexi and Jack left the hut and were greeted by Cosmo, who appeared on cue and trotted along beside them. They heard Reg chuckle as he stood at the hut's door, watching their departure.

'What did you make of that?' Alexi asked, the moment they were in the car and on the road for home. 'You picked up on his slip, I take it.'

'That he'd seen Stella's picture but claims not to have seen Frank since his return. Sure I did.'

'Then why did you stop me asking him about it?'

'Because it wouldn't have served any purpose, other than to antagonise him, or put him on his guard. As things stand, he thinks we missed it. There are hundreds of ways he could have seen her picture. He said he hadn't seen Frank in person, but they could have been in email or social media contact. Or Frank sent wedding pictures to his old friends. Something like that.'

'Even so, he was very nervous. Edgy.'

'Protecting the reputation of his group, is my guess. I can't think of any reason why he would want to kill Frank, but we'll delve into his background and see if anything comes to light, the same as we would with anyone in an investigation. If we find anything to interest us, then is the time to ask more probing questions.'

'Of course you're right.'

Jack chuckled. 'It has been known.' He paused. 'Given that Stella wasn't a climber, I really can't see a connection to Reg and his cronies.'

'But we're not going to discount the possibility, are we? After what Ben told us about his daughter, I can't rid myself of the feeling that she somehow engineered Frank's death, so she would have needed help.'

'I agree.' Jack stopped outside a pub in Groomsbridge. 'We missed lunch and I'm starving,' he said. 'Let's see if they're still serving.'

They entered the pub with the animals at their heels. The bar was sparsely populated and only a few brows were raised at the sight of Cosmo. Jack ordered pub grub and soft drinks for them both and they then settled at an out of the way table where Cosmo couldn't cause any harm and there was suffi-cient space for Silgo to stretch out his rangy body.

'What's your gut feeling?' Alexi asked a short time later, whilst tucking into scampi and chips. 'Do you think Frank was murdered and that Stella did it?'

'My instinct is that she did but our chances of proving it are almost zilch.'

'I know.'

They ate in silence for a while, consumed by their own thoughts.

'Nick Fairburn might be able to shed some more light,' Alexi eventually said, pushing her empty plate aside.

'If you want to continue chasing this thing.'

'What do you mean?' Alexi sat upright and Cosmo mewled indignantly. 'We're doing this for Drew. Of course we need to keep probing, if only to prevent Stella from going after him and Cheryl.'

Jack held up a hand. 'I wasn't suggesting that we stop. I just wanted to make you understand that we could well be chasing shadows. Just because we don't like or trust Stella, it doesn't mean there's anything sinister about her. Perhaps she genuinely loved Frank and her grief is real.'

Alexi puffed out her cheeks. 'And perhaps I'll win the lottery.'

'Yeah.' Jack chuckled. 'I tend to agree with you. She's a piece of work and probably incapable of loving anyone other than herself. But still, I needed to make sure you were aware that we could well have met our match on this one.'

Silgo rolled on his back and waved his legs in the air when a lady, on her way to the facilities, stopped to make a fuss of him.

'He's adorable,' she said, tickling his exposed belly.

'He thinks so,' Alexi replied, smiling.

Cosmo appeared from beneath the table and the lady gave a little shriek.

'Don't worry about him,' Alexi said, 'he's just posturing. He hates it when Silgo gets more attention than him.'

Cosmo proved the point by stalking up to the lady and rubbing his head against her shin. Jack watched him playing the part of the innocent pussycat that he would never be and simply shrugged. Cosmo had long since lost the ability to surprise him.

'You don't often see cats in pubs,' the lady said, rubbing Cosmo's flat ears. 'I don't know why not. They're just as amenable as dogs.'

'That's a first,' Jack said, once the lady had gone. 'Hearing Cosmo described as amenable, I mean.'

'You know he can be when it suits his purpose,' Alexi replied, draining her glass and standing. 'But there's no telling how long his mellow mood will last so shall we quit while we're ahead and hit the road?'

'Good plan. We have a way to go and a lot to think about.'

6

There was something niggling at the back of Jack's brain. Something important to do with the circumstances surrounding Frank's death that he just couldn't bring into focus. He concentrated on driving and tried to think of other things, hoping that the elusive something would pop into his head if he didn't force the issue.

But it wasn't happening.

'Let's stop at the hotel before we go home,' Alexi said. 'I want to be sure that Drew and Cheryl know we're working the case, and update them on our findings so far. I know they will be fretting.'

'Sure. We could eat there too, if you like.'

'We just had lunch!'

'True, but I'm a growing lad.'

'Outwards, if you're not careful.'

Jack laughed. 'My metabolism prevents me from putting on weight.'

'Keep telling yourself that, Maddox.' Alexi flash a smile

that quickly faded. 'I hope Drew hasn't been harassed by Stella again.'

'Stop worrying.' Jack took a hand off the wheel and placed it on Alexi's thigh. 'He would have called if that had been the case. I'm pretty sure that she *will* have another go at him, but she met with opposition from us that she hadn't expected and needs to rethink her strategy.'

'Do you think someone else is pulling her strings?'

'I wouldn't bet against it.' Jack frowned, but not because the traffic on the motorway had almost come to a halt. 'I don't like coincidences, you know that, and Frank going all the way to Australia only to link up with a woman who came from the same part of the UK as him seems like too much of a stretch.'

'When she discovered that he wasn't in a position to keep her in the style she aspired to become accustomed to, I can see her thinking that if she'd gotten away with murder once, she could do it again,' Alexi said. 'They say these things get easier with practise. Even so, I don't see Frank being murdered just because he wasn't prepared to try and get more dosh out of Drew. I know people have been killed for less, but it still seems far-fetched.'

'Yeah, we're missing something. I've been thinking so ever since we left Reg. He said something significant but I can't for the hell of me recall what it was, or why it mattered so much.' He thumped the steering wheel. 'Something that would point us towards the vital element that will make sense of all this, but I have absolutely no idea where to start looking.'

'It's not like you to be so defeatist,' Alexi replied, taking her turn to give his thigh a reassuring pat. 'We've been in situations like this before. If we keep turning rocks over, something will pop eventually and make sense of it all.'

'You're right, I guess. It's just that I don't like letting Drew down.'

'We won't,' Alexi said with determination. 'They have done so much for me, and now I finally get an opportunity to repay the favour, albeit under horrible circumstances. Even so, Stella is on borrowed time.' She turned towards the back seat. 'Isn't that right, Cosmo?'

The cat lifted his head and sent Alexi an imperious look.

Jack chuckled. 'I feel almost sorry for her,' he said, putting his foot down when the hold-up cleared, and the traffic moved freely again.

They arrived at Hopgood Hall at seven in the evening. The car park was nicely full of top-end cars belonging to clients drawn to the restaurant by the reputation of Marcel, their talented and temperamental, pseudo-French chef.

Jack and Alexi walked through reception with the animals trotting obediently at their heels. The bar was full, but Jack caught sight of Drew through the open door chatting to a few regulars. He raised a hand when he saw them, broke away and followed them into his private kitchen. Cheryl was already there, feeding Verity. Toby broke into a happy dance when he saw Cosmo and bumped his head against the cat's stomach.

'How have you got on today?' Cheryl asked, her smile failing to conceal her anxiety. She placed Verity on the floor, and she made a beeline for Cosmo and Toby, already curled up together in Toby's basket. Silgo watched her as he flopped down on the floor with a contented sigh.

Drew poured coffee for Jack and Alexi and sat down across from them. 'Come on, give,' he said. 'You've been gone all day. You must have found something out in that time. Don't keep us in suspense.'

Jack gave them an edited account of the meeting with Stella's father. He knew it would upset them to learn that she'd killed her mother, deliberately or otherwise, but decided against sugarcoating his account.

'Bloody hell!' Drew dug his fingers into his hair and vigorously scratched his scalp. 'I never saw that one coming and to be honest, I didn't think she'd killed Frank.' He glanced at Cheryl and threw his hands up in a gesture of bewilderment. 'Now I don't know what the hell to think.'

'Me neither,' said Cheryl, scooping Verity into her arms when she almost tipped the dogs' water bowl over.

'Do you think she killed my brother because he disappointed her in some way?' Drew asked after a prolonged pause, during the course of which only Verity singing to herself broke the silence.

'We both think it's entirely possible,' Alexi replied. 'He didn't go along with her plans so outgrew his usefulness, but proving it will be next to impossible, especially as we haven't yet come up with a plausible motive, other than Frank's dosh, of course, but she probably had access to that anyway.'

'And discounting the fact that Stella isn't a climber, so if she arranged an accident, she couldn't have done it alone,' Jack added.

'Perhaps Frank did arrange to climb with a friend and Stella somehow got him to do the deed. She seems to be able to wind most men round her finger,' Cheryl said bitterly. 'But why?' She shook her head. 'None of this makes any sense.'

'Has it occurred to anyone that Frank's death may not be connected in any way to Stella's supposed claim on this place?' Alexi asked after another pregnant silence.

'What do you mean?' Cheryl and Drew asked together.

'Well, just supposing that Frank and Stella were into something on the dodgy side of legal, but Frank got cold feet.'

'I see where you're going with this,' Drew said, nodding. 'Frank did like to flirt with the letter of the law but would never have flagrantly broken it. Well, he wouldn't have done when I knew him, but that was before a gold digger got her claws into him and started him thinking with an organ situated south of his brain.'

'Where are you going with this hypothesis?' Jack asked Alexi.

'I'm not sure, but one thing I do know is that we haven't been able to equate Frank being murdered over a supposed claim on this place. He knew that you wouldn't roll over, Drew, and I don't believe he would even have attempted to make you. He did have a sense of fair play. You've always said as much. You also said that you thought the gloss was wearing off regarding his relationship with Stella. Perhaps that was why. She'd got him into something illegal and he didn't want to play ball.'

'It makes more sense than anything else we've come up with,' Jack said, nodding. 'Something's been bugging me about the whole business, and you've just come up with an alternative scenario that's more plausible than a claim on the equity in this place.'

'Stella is making a fuss about Frank's claim on the hotel as a smokescreen,' Cheryl said, looking relieved by the possibility. 'Perhaps because she belatedly realised who you two are, Alexi, and also realised you'd fight our corner.'

'Which is why she raised the possibility of a claim on the hotel in front of us,' Alexi said. 'I mean, it was a private matter, and she ought to have waited until she got you on your own, Drew, but she seemed to do the opposite in the hope of sending us off on a tangent, which she's managed to do, by the way.'

'There's a guy called Luke North here asking for you, Jack,' one of the hotel's employees said, putting her head round the kitchen door.

'Stella's brother,' Alexi said, glancing at the others. 'We were planning on calling to see him tomorrow. Presumably, his dad has told him we've been asking questions.'

'Then let's see what he has to say. Show him in please, Debbie,' Drew said, looking anxious. 'He's bound to take his sister's side and is probably here to warn us off,' he added, once Debbie had disappeared.

'Not necessarily.' Jack held up a hand. 'Let's not pre-judge.'

Jack and Drew both stood as a man in his thirties with even, rugged features and a full head of light-brown hair, sporting a goatee beard walked through the door.

'Thanks for stopping by,' Jack said, shaking his hand and making the introductions. 'We were planning to track you down tomorrow.'

'Sit down,' Alexi invited. 'Don't mind him,' she added, as Cosmo stalked up to him, sniffed and then turned his back. 'Believe it or not, you just passed muster.'

Luke laughed. 'I'd hate to see how he'd have reacted if I hadn't. That must be Cosmo. Everyone around these parts is aware of that feline. He's infamous.'

'Don't say that in front of him,' Alexi said with mock terror in her tone. 'His ego is already quite inflated enough.'

Everyone laughed when Cosmo arched his back and twitched his tail. Silgo simply flapped his own tail but didn't bother to get up.

'Coffee?' Drew asked.

'Don't mind if I do.'

'You've come to talk to us about your sister,' Drew said,

once Luke had his coffee in front of him and they'd run out of small talk. 'You're aware that she was married to my brother?'

'I am now.' Luke added sugar to his beverage and stirred it vigorously. 'I've had no contact with Stella since... well, since she killed my mother.'

Everyone in the room inhaled sharply. To suspect her of being a murderer was one thing, but to hear it spoken of by her own flesh and blood held the capacity to shock.

'You have no doubt that she did so?' Cheryl asked, swallowing. 'You seem very calm about it.'

'None whatsoever.' Luke's expression clouded over. 'And believe me, I wasn't calm at the time, but I'm not going to let Stella ruin my life. Mum's gone and I have a wife and kids of my own and they're my priority now.'

'Fair enough,' Jack said easily. 'Tell us more about your sister.'

'Stella was indulged. Spoiled. Used to getting her own way as a kid. And when she got older and realised what her looks could do for her... well, her ambitions knew no bounds. Nor did her temper if she hit a speedbump in the road to success.'

'She was banking on her boss opening doors for her, is the impression your father left us with,' Alexi remarked.

'Yeah, but that was never going to happen. I met Nick a few times. Can't say as I took to him. I'm not into the world of celebrities and who said what to whom, who was seen with who, and all that malarky. I warned Stella it would all end in tears. Nick's a married man with two teenage kids. And although he's a serial womaniser, he has never left his wife for any of his conquests and was never likely to, and that's what I tried to make Stella understand. But she was having none of it. She seemed to think she had the power to manipulate him, just as she'd wheedled and manipulated her way through her entire life up until that point.'

'I see,' Cheryl muttered, sharing a look with Drew.

Luke took a sip of his coffee, returned the mug to the table and rubbed his chin thoughtfully. 'Our dad doted on Stella, and he'll be the first to admit that he was blind to her faults. He saw no harm in her flaunting her good looks, until it was too late to stop the rot. Which is one of the reasons why he blames himself for what happened to Mum. He told me once that if he'd instilled discipline and respect into Stella, as he did with the rest of us, then Mum would still be alive now.'

'You look as though you don't agree,' Alexi said.

'I don't. There was something intrinsically bad about Stella, even when she was little. She learned early on how to get what she wanted. She could be sweetness and light when it suited her purpose, but her temper... well, I've never seen anything like it when she lost it, before or since.'

'How do you mean?' Jack asked.

'Well, one example. She couldn't have been more than ten. She begged Dad for a pony. Kept on at him night and day until he agreed to taking a half share in a spirited little animal. The child she shared it with was arguably a better rider than Stella and knew how to handle the pony, which meant she'd never give up her share, which was Stella's aim. I saw her one day when she didn't realise I'd turned up to collect her. The other girl was on the pony, riding it up a lane, and Stella was following on foot. She had a riding crop in her hand and brought it down over the pony's quarters, quite deliberately. Like I say, the pony was flighty. It bucked the girl off and bolted.'

'Oh God! How could she?' Cheryl cried, clutching her face.

'What happened to the girl?' Alexi asked.

'She was badly hurt. She was wearing a helmet but still gave her head an almighty bash when she fell off backwards. She finished up in hospital for two days. She never rode the pony again, of course, and so Stella got her way.'

'Does she know you saw what she did?' Drew asked.

'I tackled her, and she denied it hotly. Went crying to Mum, who took her side, just like always. She insisted that she didn't touch the pony with her whip. She just swatted at a fly that was irritating her and the pony took flight. All a load of nonsense, of course, but it was a fight I was never going to win, so I let it go. Perhaps if I hadn't...'

'Were your parents similarly indulgent with the rest of you?' Alexi asked.

'Actually, no. We had discipline and set boundaries right from the get-go, as all kids should. But Stella... well, you might as well know.' Luke paused to rub aggressively at his chin once again. 'I'm pretty sure she wasn't Dad's.'

Alexi's mouth fell open. The others looked suitably astounded.

'Your mother had an affair?' Drew asked.

'I obviously don't know for sure, but I do recall Mum and Dad having a lot of arguments before Stella was born. I didn't understand half of what I overheard at the time, but looking back, it all makes more sense.'

'We got the impression that your father worshipped the ground your mother walked on,' Jack said. 'Were his feelings not reciprocated?'

'Oh, I think they were, but Dad lost his job, times were tough, and he hated feeling that he couldn't support his family. He went into a real downer, and I don't think Mum could reach him to offer him the support he needed. She was an attractive woman, very attractive, and so I guess she briefly looked elsewhere.'

'Your father was aware that Stella wasn't his?' Cheryl asked.

'I reckon so. It's not something that was ever discussed. All I can tell you is that Dad got another job, got over his depression, and he and Mum patched up their differences. They brought Stella up as their own and nothing was ever said about that difficult period, at least not in my hearing.'

'That would explain why she was so indulged, I guess,' Alexi said. 'Your father was over-compensating for his depression.'

'Do you have any idea who her father might have been?' Drew asked, frowning.

'Nope. None whatsoever.' Luke shrugged. 'Perhaps I've gotten it all wrong, misinterpreted the stuff I overheard. Bear in mind, I was only ten myself when Stella was conceived. But I don't think I am. Stella is different to the rest of us in so many ways. My other sister is gorgeous looking but modest with it and never uses her looks to get what she wants. Nor did any of us sulk when we didn't get our way. We knew better.'

'She inherited some of her biological father's characteristics, you're thinking,' Jack remarked.

'Perhaps. I neither know nor care. I washed my hands of her, even before she pushed Mum down the stairs.' His expression hardened. 'And she did push her. I heard that argument and know what she was like when she got into a strop. She'd lash out for no reason other than that she was hurting and wanted others to hurt too. Think of that incident with the pony if you doubt me.'

'But your mum indulged her,' Alexi said, 'so why take it out on her?'

'That's just the thing. Even Mum had had enough of her theatrics by that point and read her the riot act. Told her she only had herself to blame for being fired from a job she loved, given that she'd entered into an affair with her boss.' Luke rolled his eyes. 'Given that Stella was probably the product of an extra-marital affair, that seemed a bit hypocritical, but there you have it.' Luke sighed. 'The point I'm trying to make is that Stella could always depend upon Mum absolutely to have her back. She chose the wrong moment to adopt an attitude of tough love, is all.'

'Do you have any idea why she chose to go to Australia?' Alexi asked, feeling vindicated for taking against Stella for no obvious reason when they'd first met.

'Nope. Dad finally saw the light and turfed her out after Mum's death. She knew that there was every chance of him, or me, telling the police what I'd overheard and so she couldn't wheedle her way back into the family this time and was all out of options. That's all I can say.'

'I don't suppose you have any idea what she was doing to make a living then?' Alexi asked, more in hope than expectation.

'Sorry. But whatever it was, you can be sure it would have involved wealthy individuals. Stella simply didn't do ordinary.'

'Right.' Drew nodded resignedly.

'Look, there's really nothing more I can tell you. I only called by to say that talk of Stella reminds Dad of our mum. Not that he's ever forgotten her or stopped blaming himself for her death. He's not been the same as he was before she died but he has learned to live with his grief, so I'd be grateful if you'd come to me if you have more questions. I don't want him worried or unduly upset.'

'I hear you,' Jack said, standing to shake the man's hand.

'And I'm really sorry about your brother,' Luke said, when Drew also stood with outstretched hand.

'Well, if it's any consolation, I don't see that history could have repeated itself,' Drew replied. 'Frank died in a climbing accident, and I gather your sister is afraid of heights.'

Luke's mouth fell open. 'Who told you that?'

'She did,' Alexi replied. 'Well, she told us she didn't climb. Why?'

'She lied.' Luke ground his jaw. 'Stella climbed like a monkey. She loved it.'

'She was an experienced climber?' Drew asked, recovering first from the shock of this latest revelation.

'Absolutely. If Frank was similarly obsessed, that's probably how they met.'

7

Alexi fell back into her chair once Luke left them and fanned her face with her hand. 'Wow!' she said.

'That revelation about Stella being a climber must put her name firmly in the frame when it comes to Frank's death,' Drew said.

'It certainly brings up a load of unanswered questions,' Jack replied. 'I'm annoyed with myself for accepting Stella's word for her lack of climbing ability, given that we know she's a liar.'

Alexi nodded. 'I hear you,' she said.

'Why tell us she was afraid of heights when she must have known it would be an easy assertion to disprove? We only have her word for it that Frank intended to climb with a friend that morning. He could just as easily have agreed to climb with her.'

'Unfortunately, we don't know who that friend was and so we can't corroborate her version of events. The question was asked at the inquest but Stella, playing the grieving widow, pretended not to know,' Drew added, disgust dripping from his tone. 'I don't suppose his phone records were ever checked either since there was no suspicion of foul play.'

'Frank's car was found at the climb,' Cheryl pointed out. 'If Stella was there, how did she get home?'

'A dozen ways,' Alexi said, 'but my money's on her having an accomplice waiting in the wings to drive her back.'

'All well and good, but we don't have a hope in hell of proving our suspicions,' Drew said, throwing up his hands.

'Unless we track down her accomplice,' Alexi suggested.

'How?' Drew asked. 'Needles and haystacks spring to mind.'

'By probing. We already know a lot more than we did a day or two ago. Besides, the inquest is done and dusted and whoever's involved assumes he or she got away with it. They won't be on their guard now,' Jack pointed out.

'Even so,' Cheryl said, 'as things stand, she'll get away with murder... again! Always assuming she did the deed, of course. Perhaps I'm letting my dislike for the woman cloud my judgement.'

'We need a motive,' Alexi said, leaning back in her chair and sighing. Her friends needed her help like never before and she was damned if she'd let them down. But as things stood, the chances of getting to the bottom of Stella's machinations seemed slim. 'But right now, we simply don't have one.'

'In order to establish that motive, we need to know who Stella hangs out with,' Jack added, drumming his fingers against the tabletop in obvious frustration. 'And to do that, we really need to find out where she's living.' He turned to look at Drew. 'How do you feel about giving her a call?' he asked. 'Say you've had time to consider her request and you're happy to talk to her about it. But Cheryl is adamantly opposed to even opening discussions, so you need to meet in absolute secrecy, out of the public eye.'

Alexi nodded. 'Yep. Lambourn's a small town and someone will recognise Drew if they meet in a public place, so you need to go to hers.'

'But it will be me who turns up,' Jack said with determination. Cosmo looked up and mewled, lightening the moment and making them all smile. 'Make that *us*,' he amended. 'Or not. We'll have someone watch her movements before we decide if and when to confront her, then we won't be going in completely blind.'

'There must be something we can do in the meantime,' Cheryl said, anguish in her tone. 'All this waiting for Stella to make her next move is telling on my nerves.'

Alexi could see that was the case. Cheryl's face looked drawn and tired, as though she'd barely slept. Drew didn't look a whole lot better, and Alexi could cheerfully have throttled Stella for the problems she's caused for her friends.

'Try not to let it get to you, darling.' Drew reached across to pat his wife's hand. 'This has gone far enough, Jack.' He sent Jack a look of steely determination. Alexi couldn't recall the last time she'd seen Drew so angry. 'We need to do something, even if it's only reporting Stella to Vickery for attempted extortion. I will not have my wife upset,' he growled.

'We could go to Vickery but we don't have enough as things stand for him to be able to do anything.'

'So we simply wait for her next move, like sitting ducks,' he replied in a mordant tone.

'Calm down, Drew.' It was Cheryl's turn to pat her husband's hand. 'Let Jack work his magic. He knows what he's doing.'

Alexi smiled, sincerely hoping that on this occasion she and Jack would get the desired result. As things stood, they had precious little to go on.

'Alexi and I are going to pay Nick Fairburn a call tomorrow,' Jack said. 'He was Stella's boss. Her married boss with whom she was having a torrid affair. The end of that affair resulted in the death of her mother: the catalyst that forced Stella's relocation to Australia.' Jack rubbed his jaw. 'I can't help feeling that her rejection by Fairburn is the basis for everything that Stella did after he dumped her but, of course, unless he's willing to be candid then we may never get to the truth.'

Drew shook his head. 'He may not know.'

'Either way, he'll be able to shed some light on her character,' Jack replied.

'We also have the names of two of Frank's climbing buddies,' Alexi said. 'We'll be talking to them as soon as we can track them down. It will be interesting to learn if they've climbed with Frank since his return, and whether Stella joined them.'

'Thanks guys,' Drew said, sounding weary. 'Sorry I got a bit lairy just now, but this is really getting to me. I appreciate you're going above and beyond.'

'For goodness' sake!' Alexi jumped up and threw her arms around Drew's neck, feeling emotional and determined. Determined to stop Stella in her tracks before she did anything else to wreck the lives of those who Alexi cared about. 'You absolutely don't have to thank us. We want to know as much as you do. All I would say is don't get your hopes up. If Stella did murder Frank, then the chances of us finding any proof now are pretty slim.'

'I'll settle for you getting her off our backs,' Cheryl said with feeling.

'*That* I can promise you,' Jack replied, his tone brooking no argument. 'She doesn't have a leg to stand on regarding her claim on this place and she must know it. I think she's just hoping you'll give her something so that she goes away. That spells desperation and desperate people make mistakes.'

'I'll make that call, shall I?' Drew said, reaching for his mobile.

Without waiting for an answer, he scrolled through his contacts, dialled a number and put it on speaker. No one spoke as they listened to it ring for so long that Alexi began to think no one would answer. In the end, an abrupt, 'Yes?' proved her wrong. It sounded like Stella, but her voice was muffled, as if it was coming from underwater. Drew glanced at Jack, who shrugged.

'Stella?'

'Who is this?'

'It's Drew.'

'Oh. Hello.' She sounded normal now. Interested. Alexi wondered if the call had woken her, but it was the middle of the day. Why would she be sleeping? Perhaps she wasn't alone. They really did need to know where she lived. 'How are you?'

'Look, about what you said, I don't buy it for a moment, but we can't leave it hanging. It's wearing on Cheryl's nerves. We need to talk.'

'I knew you'd see sense.' Stella's voice sounded cautious.

'You were my brother's wife, so the least I can do is hear you out. But Cheryl doesn't feel that way. She's heavily pregnant and I don't want to upset her... She doesn't know I'm making this call.'

'She won't hear about it from me.'

'Good. Then let's meet. I'll come to you.'

'Can't we meet on neutral territory?'

'You make it sound like we're at war, when I'm actually offering you an olive branch. And no, we can't meet in public. I'm well known around this village; someone will see us and it'll get back to Cheryl. It has to be at yours, or we forget the whole thing.'

Jack made frantic hand gestures. Drew was being too insistent, and she'd smell a rat if they weren't careful.

'Okay,' Stella said, obviously reluctant. 'When did you have in mind?'

'A couple of days' time. Cheryl has a meeting with our accountant that morning. I can slip away on some pretext or another, but I can't give you a time. Keep the morning free and we'll play it by ear.'

'Fine.' She reeled off an address in Newbury. Alexi Googled it. It was an upmarket block of flats in the centre of the town.

'I'll call you when I'm leaving,' Drew said, cutting the call.

'How can she afford to live there?' Alexi asked, pointing to the flats in question on the screen of her phone. 'The rents must be extortionate.'

'I'll get Cassie to see who owns the unit she's in,' Drew said, reaching for his own phone. 'And how much rent she's paying.'

Jack conducted a short conversation with his partner.

'She's on it,' he said. 'Now to get Danny, our new investigator, watching that flat.'

He made another call and put the arrangements in place.

'He'll watch it himself some of the time, and use others to cover when he can't. We should know pretty soon who she associates with,' Jack said. 'So that's it for now. Not much more we can do today so Alexi and I will get out of your hair. We'll go up to town and doorstep Nick Fairburn tomorrow and then reconvene here to discuss progress. We'll drop Silgo off with you, if that's okay, but his lordship will expect to come along for the ride.'

Cosmo lifted his head, well aware that he was being talked about, and sent Jack one of his trademark imperious looks. Everyone laughed.

'Sure. Silgo is always welcome,' Cheryl said. 'And now that we have a plan of action, it feels as though we're being proactive. Or more to the point, you are. Thank you.'

'Will you stop thanking us,' Alexi cried impatiently. 'This, in case it has escaped your memory, is what we do, and we're not too bad at it either.'

* * *

Having dropped Silgo off with Toby for the day, Jack, Alexi and Cosmo headed for the motorway, and London.

'Remind me what precisely Cassie found out about the flat Stella occupies,' Alexi said, yawning behind her hand.

'It's owned by an Australian company but she's having trouble finding the names of the company directors, which makes me highly suspicious.' Jack frowned. 'No one can hide from Cassie for long, as well you know. But everything is channelled through a firm of Australian lawyers and every thread she's followed has turned into a blind alley so far.'

'Anyone would think they had something to hide,' Alexi replied, her voice dripping with sarcasm. 'Everything with this case seems to lead back to Australia. Can't help wondering why.'

'Well, if nothing else, it certainly gives us more reasons to suspect Stella's motives. Someone in Australia has to be paying her rent, or letting her live in that flat rent free. Why would they do that? What do they expect in return? Anyway, Cassie is continuing to dig. Danny reported in this morning while you were in the shower. No signs of life in Stella's flat. He knows which one it is and has high-powered binoculars, but it's been as quiet as the grave, almost as though no one's actually living there. The curtains haven't been opened or closed. No lights have gone on. But still, it's early days. The moment she arrives or leaves the place, or if anyone else comes or goes, we'll be the first to know.'

'The only problem is, what with it being a block of flats, there will be a lot of comings and goings. We have no way of knowing who's going in to visit Stella.'

'Our guys will take pictures of all visitors and we'll sift through them, see if anything pops. It probably will, if she's there, that is.'

'You really think that isn't her actual address and she just happens to have a high-end flat at her disposal?'

Jack lifted one shoulder. 'Truth to tell, I have no idea what to think. All I know for sure is that she's a conniving madam and I wouldn't trust her as far as I can throw her.'

Alexi fell silent for a while, mulling things over.

'I know you prefer to call on people unannounced,' she

said after a while, 'but what makes you think Fairburn will be in the office today, or that he'll see us even if he is?'

'Because I just happen to know that they have a big presentation this afternoon regarding a contract they're pitching for.' Jack nodded as he indicated and overtook a Volvo. 'He'll be there.'

'You know this thanks to Cassie, I assume.'

'True,' Jack conceded.

'Then he'll be busy and focused. All the more reason not to see anyone without an appointment.'

'Well, that's the interesting thing.' Jack shot her a sideways grin. 'If he doesn't have time to see us once I mention Stella's name, then I will think he's probably got nothing to hide.'

'Ah, I get you.' Alexi nodded and returned his smile. 'If he has a guilty conscience, or knows something about Stella's recent activities, then he will want to see us and find out how much we know.'

'Right.'

The rest of the journey was made mostly in silence. Alexi dozed, as she often did on long car journeys, and Jack used the time to think about what they knew, along with their growing raft of suspicions. With nothing more concrete to go on than gut instinct, he was nonetheless convinced that Frank had been murdered. The hell of it was, whichever way he came at things, he was unable to hit upon a motive strong enough to necessitate such a complex murder. It would be helpful to know what Frank had spent his inheritance on. Over a half a million quid, gone in just a few years. Did he start up a business that went belly-up? Did he lend it to Stella for whatever reason – perhaps to impress her – and then asked for it back? She was unable to pay and so wiped out the debt. Permanently. It seemed unlikely. They were married, so he could hardly pursue repayment through the courts.

Even so, as things stood, it was all he could come up with. He'd ask Cassie to delve into Frank's financial affairs a little more deeply once the meeting with Fairburn was out of the way. He'd also ask Drew if he had any idea what Frank might have done with so much money. There was very little in his bank accounts; that much Jack did know, thanks to Cassie's online snooping. Drew had previously said he had absolutely no idea where the money had gone, but he'd had time to dwell upon the situation now and might have recalled one of Frank's favoured money-making schemes.

Alexi sat up and blinked when the car slowed, crawling its way into London. Despite the congestion charge that made it cost a small fortune to drive in the centre of town, the roads were still clogged with delivery lorries, couriers on all forms of transport and an endless stream of private vehicles.

'My old stomping ground,' she said, as they approached Battersea Park Road, the home of Fairburn's PR empire. 'To think, all this hustle was once so familiar, and I thrived on it. Now it makes me feel uncomfortable.'

Cosmo sat up on the backseat, looked out the window and made a sound that could have been anything from a growl to a howl of recognition.

'He knows where he is too,' Jack said, laughing. 'Seriously though, do you ever miss it?'

'I sometimes miss the cut and thrust of the newspaper world, but mostly not. I like my life much better now.'

'Glad to hear it.'

Jack found a car park, took out a second mortgage to make use of it, and left Cosmo in charge of the car. He and Alexi then set off on foot for the offices of Fairburn and Farlow –

glass and steel vying for space against old terraces of houses, the reinvented power station and the constant sound of trains in and out of Victoria.

'This area used to be almost derelict,' Alexi said, glancing at all the designer outlets and trendy coffee spots. 'Now it's the height of chic.'

'So it would seem.'

The pavements were crammed with a sea of people, all rubbing shoulders without a problem. A taxi did a reckless U-turn directly in front of them when it was hailed by someone on the other side of the road. Bicycle couriers darted in and out of the traffic, somehow managing to get where they were going without mishap. One lady in four-inch stilettos walked a tiny dog on the end of a pink, diamond-encrusted lead.

'Only in London,' Alexi muttered.

Jack pushed open the door to Fairburn and Farlow and stood back so that Alexi could enter ahead of him. Together, they crossed a marble foyer and headed for the reception desk which was manned by an impeccably groomed twenty-something who looked as though she had stepped straight from the pages of a magazine.

'Can I help you?' she asked, her smile zeroing in on Jack and remaining fixed there. Alexi might as well not have existed. It had happened before, and Jack knew it would irritate her.

'Jack Maddox, Private Investigator, here to see Nick Fairburn,' he said, handing the girl, whose name badge identified her as Crystal – *of course it did!* – his card. 'And this is Alexi Ellis, Journalist, here for the same reason.'

Alexi dutifully handed over her own card. If Alexi was surprised by Jack's direct approach, she gave no sign and instead remained silent whilst the girl absorbed that information.

'Nick doesn't see anyone without an appointment,' she said, glancing at their cards and looking uncertain. 'Especially not today.'

'He will still want to know we're here, to give himself the opportunity to tell his side of the story.'

'What... what story?' Crystal had lost her professional poise, such as it was, and now looked as though she should still be in school.

'We're here about Stella North,' Jack said in a conversational tone. 'Before Alexi takes the story further, we thought Nick would like to comment.'

She blinked at Jack. 'I haven't been here for long. I never knew Stella.'

'But you know the name,' Alexi said, speaking for the first time.

The girl set her jaw and nodded.

'Just give Nick a call,' Jack said. 'If he doesn't have time to talk to us, we'll understand and will also know what we have to do next.'

'Yes.' She nodded. 'Yes, that's probably the best thing to do.'

She picked up a phone, turned her back to them and spoke in a muted voice.

'Nick will be down in a couple of minutes,' she said, looking relieved. 'Take a seat over there.'

Jack thanked her and turned towards an array of trendy but not especially comfortable-looking chairs arranged around a hexagonal, glass-topped table littered with artfully arranged glossy magazines.

'This place is about as genuine as that girl's smile,' Alexi said, glancing around and shuddering, 'and yet, not so long ago, I would have taken it for granted.' She stood a little straighter. 'I am a much better person now.'

'Have a word with her,' Jack replied in an undertone. 'See what gives. I'll sit over there.'

Alexi nodded and lingered beside the reception desk. Jack took the chair closest to them and picked up a magazine at random. Since the area was relatively small, he assumed he'd be able to hear whatever Alexi said to the kid, especially since there was no one else around and it was deadly quiet.

'This is quite some place,' he heard Alexi say in a gushing tone. 'You're lucky to work here.'

'I know. I never thought I'd get the job. I mean, I have no experience and not many qualifications, if I'm honest, but Nick believes in giving people a chance.' Jack could hear the pride in her tone and had no difficulty guessing why Nick was being so philanthropic. He already didn't like the guy and had yet to meet him. 'He says that someone saw something in him when he was young and helped him get onto the career ladder. He believes in giving back.'

I'll just bet he does!

'You didn't know Stella then.'

'No, but I've heard her name mentioned. She made trouble for Nick, so he had to let her go. Sometimes, he's too kind-hearted. Everyone says so.'

'What sort of trouble?'

'I don't know and anyway, I probably shouldn't say anything to you. Nick is big on confidentiality.'

'Of course. Sorry. I didn't mean to make you feel uncomfortable.'

'It's okay. It's just that we're doing a pitch today for a children's clothing line. It's a new line, very upmarket and there's another person in the running. Everyone's a bit anxious.'

'Gosh, that sounds glamorous. Lucky you.'

'Yeah, Kids Unlimited is a big deal. If we get the contract, then there will be no stopping Nick. He deserves it. He works so hard.'

'I'm sure he puts in long hours.'

'Nick says the next time we pitch for an adult clothing line then I might be able to model some of the outfits.'

'Wow!'

'I know. It's surreal.'

Jack did a quick search on his phone. He found Kids Unlimited's range and a write up about its Australian owners suggesting that Nick's company were the forerunners in the scramble for the PR contract. He inhaled sharply when he saw the name of the company he was up against. *Stella.* Nothing else, just the one name, but that and the fact that the company was Australian owned was enough to convince Jack who Nick's competitor must be.

The sound of feet tripping rapidly down the wide, glass, spiral staircase in the corner of the reception area caused Jack to glance in that direction as he pocketed his phone. A man in his late forties approached them wearing chinos and a white shirt hanging loose outside his waistband. Hair that was too long and thinning on top had been slicked back with gel. A precise length of designer stubble adorned his chin and Jack was absolutely convinced that he was wearing foundation.

He wore deck shoes without socks and, to Jack's mind, looked as though he was trying a little too hard to hang onto his youth.

'Nick Fairburn,' the man said, approaching Jack with hand outstretched. 'And I assume this is Ms Ellis,' he added, giving

Alexi's person a swift once-over as she joined them. 'I can't give you long. Busy day. What's this about?'

'Do you really want to talk here?' Jack asked, his tone passive aggressive.

'In here.' Nick's friendly manner dissipated in the face of Jack's abrupt opening salvo. He opened the door to a small meeting room and stood back to let Alexi and Jack enter it before him. 'See we're not disturbed please, Crystal.'

'Of course, Nick.' Crystal followed Nick's every move with a devoted gaze.

'Okay, I'll ask you again, what's this about?' Nick leaned against the window ledge, his arms folded defensively across his chest. 'You've chosen the worst possible day to come here unannounced so let's not waste any more of my valuable time.'

Jack knew better than to put himself at a disadvantage by sitting and having to look up at Nick, so he remained standing too, as did Alexi. Jack had a good couple of inches on Nick and enjoyed staring down at his bald patch. Without saying a word, Nick pulled out a chair and sat at the head of the table. Jack and Alexi then took the chairs on either side of him.

'Stella North,' Jack said. 'You had an affair with her.'

Nick blew air through his lips. 'In her dreams.'

'You think she dreamed about you?' Alexi asked sweetly. 'A red-hot babe like her lusting after a man twice her age. I somehow doubt it.'

'Not twice her age,' Nick shot back.

'Ah, hit a sore spot, did we?' Jack taunted.

'Look, Stella and I worked closely together. The kid had talent and knew how to put a pitch together. She had a way with the clients, as well, especially the men. A mix of professional expertise and old-fashioned coercion. A hundred years ago, she'd have been accused of using her feminine wiles. Despite the equality movement, nothing's really changed, other than the labels we put on things. I encouraged her to be hands-on, metaphorically not literally, and it worked. We won a couple of decent contracts thanks to her ingenuity.'

'What else did you encourage her to do?' Jack held up a hand to prevent the interruption he sensed Fairburn formulating. 'Don't bother to deny it,' he added wearily. 'We know you had an affair with her. She read more into it than she should have, wanted you to leave your wife and family for her, made all sorts of threats and it got to the point where you had to cut her loose.'

Fairburn dropped his head into his splayed hands and shook it from side to side. 'Yeah, okay, we had a thing going. It was casual. You must know how it is,' he added, lifting his head again and glaring at Jack. 'You work long hours, speak the same language, have the same aspirations. It gets intense. You find yourself eating late at night, stuck in hotels far from home.' He shrugged. 'It happens. I thought she knew the score. And, for the record, I never told her that I'd leave Meg. It's not happening. It had never been on the agenda, but she chose to believe otherwise. When I put her straight, she went to my wife with pictures she'd taken of us together. Caused real problems for me.' He glanced at Alexi. 'I can sense your disapproval, but these things happen. I thought she understood the score and didn't read too much into it. Obviously, I misread her.'

'And now you're up against her for the Kids Unlimited contract.'

Jack sensed Alexi's surprise.

'Yeah, I didn't realise it was her. Not at first. Then I got a sneak peek at the opposition's campaign and knew at once.'

He let out a long sigh. 'I recognised her style. She's good, and cheaper than us, so we're up against it. Not sure where she found the funds, but I can imagine. Anyway, the company's Australian and I gather that's where she took herself off to after her mother died.'

'You know about that?' Jack asked.

'I heard. Anyway, I've not seen or heard from her, but I know it has to be her, leaving aside the fact that the company is called *Stella*. Not exactly subtle. Besides, someone dropped her pitch outline in my mailbox.'

'She wanted you to know she was coming after you?' Alexi suggested. 'She doesn't strike me as the type to take rejection well.'

'Yeah, I guess. But I haven't seen or spoken to her since she left my employ and that is the God's honest truth.' Fairburn sat upright again, attempting to reassert control. Not that he'd had any control of the interview in the first place. He was here under duress and everyone in the room knew it, but that insignificant fact didn't appear to deter him. 'Now then, why are a PI and respected journalist so interested in my admittedly sordid love life?'

Jack and Alexi shared a glance. Jack gave an imperceptible nod and left the floor to Alexi.

'I have shares in a hotel in Lambourn,' she said. 'My principal owner and friend has... had a brother, Frank, who took himself off to Australia. He met Stella and they married. Like you, he was old enough to be her father.'

'With you so far,' Nick said, glancing at his watch.

'A month ago, Frank died in a climbing accident.'

'Ah!'

'But we're not convinced that it was an accident,' Jack

added, 'especially since Stella told us she'd never climbed in her life and was afraid of heights.'

'She's an avid climber,' Fairburn said slowly.

'Yeah, that's what we've subsequently discovered,' Alexi said.

'Her mother died falling down the stairs. It was deemed an accident, but her family believe Stella pushed her.'

'Christ!' Fairburn ran a hand through his gelled hair. It didn't move.

'And now her husband has died in an accident too.' Jack's expression turned severe. 'One accidental death I can just about believe, but two...' He shook his head. 'You can see why we're suspicious.'

'Our problem is that she's now trying to get money out of my friends,' Alexi explained. 'Frank inherited half the family home when his parents died. He didn't want to know about the hotel that his brother converted it into and so Drew bought him out. The hotel struggled at first but is successful now and Stella's claiming that Frank wasn't given enough to reflect his half-share.'

'She's a ball-breaker,' Nick said, rubbing his chin. 'No question about that. I've been wondering where she got the money to set up her own company and pitch for such a rich contract. The people behind Kids Unlimited don't deal with amateurs.'

'And we've been wondering where Frank's inheritance went,' Alexi said. 'I guess we now know.' She paused. 'The question is, would she have killed Frank to prevent herself from having to pay it back? It seems extreme.'

'And impossible to prove,' Jack added.

'I think it's more probable that he'd served his purpose,' Fairburn said in a reflective tone. 'If she'd used all his funds she'd have no further use for him. I don't know how much money the guy had, but I can tell you that running a PR company and launching successful pitches is not something that can be done on the cheap. That could explain why she's going after your hotel. If she were to win Kids Unlimited then she'd need working capital. The contract would pay in arrears.' Nick pulled a wry face. 'Well in arrears. Trust me on this. But if her primary objective is to steal the contract from me then she'll sign off on terms that disadvantage her, just to get one over on me. She's *that* vindictive.'

'You haven't expressed surprise at the possibility of her killing a man,' Jack said.

'That's because the scenario doesn't surprise me.' Fairburn fixed each of them in turn with a look of candid appraisal and Jack suspected that they were seeing the real man beneath all the gloss and spin for the first time. 'She had a temper on her that scared the hell out of me when she didn't get her way. Look, I know I didn't behave well, but it takes two. I never pretended not to be married and she was the one who made the first move.' He held up a hand when Alexi opened her mouth. 'I didn't try very hard to resist, but it really didn't mean much to me and I thought it was a casual fling from her perspective too. Ha! How wrong was I.'

'Okay.' Jack stood up. 'Thanks for your time. We'll let you get back to your pitch. One thing you can do for us though, please, if you want to help.'

'Name it.'

'Don't tell Stella that we've been here, asking questions.'

'I'm doing my level best to keep well clear of her,' he replied with a shudder, 'and have no intention of talking to her any time soon.'

'She has no idea that we suspect her of killing Frank and

unless or until we can gather enough evidence, that's the way we'd like it to stay. We don't want her going to ground.'

'Stella won't hide away, no matter what you think you have on her. She's too self-assured for that.'

'Even so.'

'Okay, mum's the word. Not that I'll see her. We're doing our pitch at Kids Unlimited headquarters on the other side of town in...' He glanced at his watch. 'Less than two hours. I think she's on tomorrow morning.'

'Fair enough.' Alexi managed a smile that Jack could see wasn't genuine. She'd taken against the man, and so had he. 'You have our cards. If you think of anything else that might help, please call. Oh, and good luck with the pitch.'

8

Alexi's brain struggled with information overload as she walked with Jack in a dazed silence. Cosmo leapt onto her lap the moment she got into the car, clearly of the view that she needed a little uncomplicated feline company. Well, as uncomplicated as things ever got with her cat. She gently stroked his back as he set up a rattling purr and settled down, making himself comfortable in a way that only cats seemed able to manage so effortlessly.

'Well,' Jack said, starting the engine and moving slowly out of his parking space, 'at least we now know where Frank's money went.'

'She really was determined to get one over on Nick Fairburn, wasn't she,' Alexi replied. 'I'm just having trouble deciding how she did it, or more to the point, who made it happen for her. Well, I assume she used Frank's money but how did a start-up company even get to pitch for such a big contract? There must have been lots of competition. It's all to do with the Australian connection, isn't it?'

'Very likely. As to Fairburn's relationship with Stella, I

think we both know that we just heard one sanitised version of events. Fairburn made her wild promises he had no intention of keeping. He's likely done it before and gotten away with it, but Stella wasn't about to be cast aside and was holding him to his word, probably thinking they'd make an unbeatable duo in the PR world.'

'No doubt they would have done too,' Alexi agreed. 'Fairburn clearly regrets leading her on. She's made a hell of a lot of trouble for him, and they parted on bad terms but even he admitted that she had a flair for the business, and an edge that he couldn't counter, at least not when it came to dealing with men.'

'She used a combination of brains, solid preparation, femininity and flirtation to get her point across.' Jack nodded. 'Yeah, I got that part,' he said, pulling out into heavy traffic and stopping at a red light. 'He probably turns it on for his female clients but I'm betting that with the bigger contracts, it's the men who have to be sold. It's still very much a man's world at the sharp end of big businesses.'

'How did you know? About her company and being his competitor, I mean?'

'When I heard Crystal mention that he had a strong competitor for the Kids Unlimited gig, I got curious and did a check on my phone. When I saw that his competitor was called *Stella*... well, it didn't take a genius to join the dots, so I put it out there and Fairburn confirmed my suspicions.'

'So, presumably we get Cassie to see who set the company up. Stella surely must have a partner, don't you think?' Alexi asked, frowning at the stalled traffic in front of them without really seeing it. 'This is bigger than we first thought and Frank's half a million wouldn't have gotten her far.'

'I agree with you. Working practises have changed. People

can do their business remotely online and there's no longer the need for flashy offices, the type of which we just enjoyed.' Jack chuckled at Alexi's affronted expression. 'Or not.'

'But PR is all about perception. If you can't sell yourself then presumably you can't sell a client's product, so you have to have somewhere to do the type of pitches that Fairburn and Stella are setting up.'

'Exactly. Stella's website doesn't mention her by name, other than in the company's name, obviously, and doesn't show her picture anywhere. Now that does surprise me. She doesn't strike me as the type to be camera shy. But it does give a London office address and I'm betting that Cassie will find that office is owned by the same company that holds the lease on the flat in Newbury where Stella is expecting to entertain Drew.'

'What does it all mean, Jack? I can understand a woman like Stella who thinks so well of herself balking at being cast aside when she'd served her purpose, become too demanding, or whatever. But to go to such lengths to get her revenge, even murdering her own husband.' She shook her head. 'There has to be more to it than a simple desire to get her own back.'

Jack kept his gaze focused on the traffic ahead of him as he lifted one shoulder. 'She had visions of her and Nick being the dream team in the PR world, which is probably what he promised her. That didn't work out, so she's set out to eclipse him. As to the rest, Frank's death and so forth... well, that's what we need to ask her about when we've gathered enough ammunition to force her hand.'

'Right. What I don't get is why she couldn't have just put it all down to experience and moved on.' Alexi shifted her position, producing an indignant mewl from Cosmo, who did not appreciate having his repose disturbed. 'Instead, she's clearly recruited someone with the power to finance her ambitions. Someone who even stood aside while she married Frank, presumably to extract working capital from him, and then aided and abetted when Frank had served his purpose.' She shook her head. 'What the hell?'

'The better question to ask would be, "who the hell?". And I'd bet my pension on it being someone in England, or more specifically centred around Lambourn. Someone who knew about Frank's windfall and deliberately pushed him in Stella's direction. It's the only thing that makes any sense.'

Jack cleared the outskirts of London, joined the motorway and put his foot down.

'It must be someone connected to a person we've already spoken to,' Alexi said, after a long pause taken to mull the matter over. 'But none of the guys we've seen appear to have two pennies to rub together. And as for Stella's family... well, none of them have given her the time of day. And even if they had, they're not nearly wealthy enough to have helped her build a PR company from scratch.'

'How about Frank?'

Alexi's head jerked round. 'What do you mean?'

'Well, we're assuming that a connection of Stella's set her up with Frank but what if, for the sake of argument, someone who Frank had hacked off and who knew about his windfall decided to take an extreme form of revenge?'

'Hmm, it's possible, I suppose. Frank was known for ducking and diving which, presumably, didn't always end well. His madcap schemes to make money never did, at least not according to Drew. He was also a lady's man and didn't much care if his conquests wore wedding rings and had husbands waiting in the wings, so there could be some angry husbands out for revenge somewhere.'

'We need to ask Drew. We'll be back in Lambourn soon and that's the first thing we'll do.'

* * *

Silgo greeted them as though they'd been gone for weeks, rather than hours. He wagged his entire body, knocking into legs, furniture and poor Toby, who almost got trampled on.

'Hey, big guy, we've missed you too,' Jack said, rubbing the dog's ears and sending him into a state of near delirium.

'He has abandonment issues,' Alexi said, bending to kiss her dog's head.

Cosmo, tail aloft, ignored the commotion and made his way directly to Toby's basket, much to the little terrier's delight. Cat and dog curled up together, their backs turned disdainfully away from Silgo's antics.

'How did it go?' Drew asked. 'Hang on, I can see you've got news and Cheryl will want to hear it. I'll give her a shout.'

By the time Jack had poured coffee for Alexi and himself, Drew returned with his arm thrown around Cheryl's shoulders.

'Verity's asleep.' Cheryl rolled her eyes. 'For now.' She sat down across from Alexi and inhaled the fumes from her coffee. 'That's what the life of a pregnant woman is like,' she said. 'We thrive on what others take for granted. God, I'd kill for a strong, black coffee! Anyway, Drew says you have news.'

Drew and Cheryl listened to Alexi's precis of their meeting with Fairburn, their jaws occasionally dropping. But they asked no questions until Alexi ran out of words.

'Bloody hell!' Drew scratched his head. 'What a piece of work that Stella is.'

'She and Fairburn deserve one another,' Alexi replied. 'I Did Not Like Him.'

Cheryl chuckled. 'We got that part.'

'Even so,' Drew said, 'if they had an affair and Fairburn gave her certain assurances he had no intention of living up to, then I kinda get why she was pissed off. We also know from what her father told you that she was accustomed to getting what she wanted, so at a stretch, I can also see why she decided to play Fairburn at his own game.' His expression hardened. 'But what I will never understand is why she had to pull Frank into her scheme. Well, obviously I realise she needed his money and at least we now know what he did with it, but why kill him?'

'And she did kill him,' Cheryl added quietly. 'Didn't she? Poor Frank. He was a dreamer and didn't always play by the rules. He made things tough for us when he insisted upon being paid off, but we thought in the long run it would be better than him part-owning the hotel and interfering with its running. He didn't have a practical bone in his body, and it would have definitely failed if that had been the case. But he didn't deserve to die because he was a chancer.'

'That's what we wanted to talk to you about,' Jack said, leaning his forearms on the table and drilling them both with a look. 'Stella obviously has someone payrolling her new company but working capital was needed and Frank was a convenient patsy.'

'He would have been putty in her hands,' Drew said, looking both disgusted and distraught.

'That's what we figured. The question is, who directed him towards her? We haven't come across anyone in her back-ground sufficiently devoted and wealthy enough to do her bidding, especially when it comes to aiding and abetting with

Frank's murder. Sorry!' Jack held up a hand when Drew winced. 'I could have phrased that more sympathetically. It's the policeman in me. Unlawful killings are part of the day job and you're trained to switch off your emotions.'

'Don't worry about my finer feelings,' Drew replied, waving aside Jack's apology. 'I'm more interested in what we do to stop Stella.'

'What we're exploring now,' Alexi said, taking up the story, 'is the possibility of someone in Frank's background looking for revenge. An investment that went wrong, or a husband whose wife cheated on him with Frank. Something of that nature. But we have no idea where to start looking. We thought you might have some idea.'

Drew rubbed his chin. 'It's more than three years since Frank and I saw much of each other. Once Ma died, that was it. He got his share of the inheritance and was out of here with a head full of plans.'

'So if we're on the right track then someone who knew Frank from that time, someone with a long memory, patience and money to burn could be the person backing Stella?' Jack said.

Cheryl and Drew exchanged a look.

'Where to start?' Cheryl let out a long breath. 'Frank was in and out of here all the time before Ma died, always full of stories, bursting with excitement about the next big opportunity that couldn't possibly fail. He had a wide circle of friends, but I think they all realised his schemes were pie in the sky, unlikely to succeed and they learned to steer well clear of the investment opportunities he tried to sell them.'

'Can you think of anyone who he was particularly close to?' Jack asked. 'Anyone who he might have shafted in the worst possible way?'

Once again, Cheryl and Drew exchanged a prolonged look.

'There's Angus Daventree,' Drew said. 'He and Frank were friends since their school days. Angus inherited a big pile on the edge of the village from his grandfather. He doesn't have horses and uses it as a retreat of some sort.'

'Did he send you condolences or attend the funeral?' Jack asked.

'Actually, no.' Drew frowned. 'Now you come to mention it, we haven't seen or heard from him for months. Years even. And I don't recall seeing him at the funeral. Stella took centre stage, of course, but all of Frank's old buddies made a point of having a word or two with me.'

'In my old line of work, we reckoned that if there'd been foul play, then the culprit always attended the funeral, if only to congratulate himself on being too clever to get caught.' Jack smiled to soften the effect of his words. 'Harsh, I know, but true for all that. So, who else might fit that description?'

Drew shook his head. 'I'm all out of ideas.'

'What about Emily Pearson?' Cheryl asked, glancing speculatively at Drew. 'She and Frank had quite a thing going for a while. We really thought he'd found "the one",' she added, making quote marks with her fingers around the two words, 'and would settle down. But he dumped her for reasons that we never understood. She's a lovely person. A bit older than him and worth quite a bit. She has a converted barn on the edge of the village, quite a lot of land and several horses. She was at the funeral and seemed genuinely distressed. She also appeared to take against Stella. I noticed her watching the grieving widow during the wake, clearly wasn't taken in by her performance and didn't try and hide her disdain. I didn't see the two of them exchange a single word, but of course, they might well have done when I wasn't watching.'

'Has she moved on?' Alexi asked. 'Linked up with anyone else?'

'Not as far as I'm aware,' Cheryl replied. 'She comes into the restaurant occasionally, often with female friends, but I have seen her once or twice with the same guy. Not recently though. Whenever our paths have crossed, she's always asked after Frank.'

Jack quirked a brow. 'So she knew he'd gone to Australia then?'

'Yes. I told her that. She said it was probably the best place for him. The UK wasn't big enough to absorb his personality. We laughed about it.'

'Was she bitter about the breakup with Frank?' Alexi asked.

'I think more bewildered,' Cheryl said in a considering tone. 'But I also think she'd put it behind her and got on with her life.'

'I can't see a woman being Stella's benefactress insofar as she's been set up with her own PR company,' Alexi said. 'She isn't fond of her own sex but that works both ways and women aren't drawn to her. Even so, I'm sure you'll tell us, Jack, that you saw stranger things during the course of your career with the Met.'

'Right. I agree she's an unlikely suspect, but we'd still best have a word with her. She might have been back in contact with Frank for all we know.' Jack paused. 'Can you think of any more of Frank's old sparring partners who might bear a grudge and have the wherewithal to get even?'

Cheryl and Drew shook their heads simultaneously.

'Sorry, but no,' Drew said.

'Okay, not to worry. We have enough to be going on with. No chance you have phone numbers for Angus Daventree and Emily Pearson by any chance?' Jack asked.

'Probably.' Cheryl got to her feet. 'They both come here to eat so will have phoned to book tables. Like I say, I haven't seen Angus for years but I did notice his name on the reservation list a few months back. Their numbers will be in the system.'

She grabbed her work phone, scrolled through it and reeled off the requested numbers. Jack punched them into his phone, put it on speaker and called Angus.

'Hi,' he said when the call was answered with an abrupt *yes*. 'Am I speaking with Angus Daventree?'

'Who wants to know?' A note of suspicion entered the deep voice echoing through the airways.

'Jack Maddox. Private Investigator and friend of Drew Hopgood.'

A long sigh. 'Is this about Frank?'

'In a roundabout sort of way. Any chance I could pop and see you sometime tomorrow?'

'Why?'

Jack withheld an irritated tut. 'Because Drew's trying to make sense of his brother's death.'

'Nothing to make sense about as far as I'm aware. He died doing what he loved, so I hear. Tragic, but not suspicious. Accidents happen.'

'Even so.'

'Look, there's nothing I can tell you about the guy. We lost touch years ago and went our separate ways. End of...'

The line went dead.

'That went well,' Alexi remarked into the ensuing silence. 'I suppose we give up on him.'

'Nonsense.' Jack sounded upbeat. 'That's the first positive break we've had in this investigation.'

'Because he doesn't want to talk to you?' Drew shrugged. 'If he was involved, surely he would want to know what you know.'

'We'll find out when we doorstep him tomorrow, Alexi.'

'Yes dear,' she replied, sharing a smile with Cheryl.

Jack called Emily next. She was far more amenable, and they agreed a time to meet the following day. She reeled off her address and Alexi noted it down.

'I haven't forgotten about Frank's climbing buddies, Bob Green and Andy Dawson.' Jack said. 'I might as well try and fix up meetings with them tomorrow, just to be thorough, but I have no idea if they're wealthy enough to be in league with Stella. Still, there's only one way to find out.'

Jack made the calls. He was greeted with muted surprise on both occasions and the two men agreed to see him the next day.

'They'd been warned to expect your call, Jack,' Alexi said, when he hung up. 'Their surprise was not genuine.'

'Yeah, I thought they would have been. Reg Parsons protecting the integrity of his club members, I have no doubt, even though he agreed not to give them advance warning.' He sighed and stretched his arms above his head. 'Anyway, let me get Cassie onto tracing the origins of Stella's company, then I think our work here is done for the day.'

Alexi was surprised. It was still only four o'clock. Even so, there wasn't much more they could do until they'd spoken to the people Jack had arranged to see the following day, she supposed, and they could use the ensuing time to do more research into their fledgling case.

'At least we know Stella will be out of harm's way until

after her pitch tomorrow, which will take place in town,' Alexi said. 'She's probably up there now, fine tuning her presentation. That could have been where she was when you called her, Drew, given that there's been no activity at her flat.'

'That's probably why she was happy enough not to have me under her feet until the day after tomorrow,' Drew replied.

'Our discoveries today make it clearer why she was coming after you,' Alexi remarked.

'They do?' Drew's eyebrows disappeared beneath his hairline.

'Tell him, Jack,' Alexi invited. 'I bet we're thinking the same way.'

'Okay,' Jack said. 'I'm guessing that she convinced her partner in crime that she could land the Kids Unlimited contract, which is probably worth a king's ransom. Fairburn mentioned a TV ad campaign, nationwide press coverage, interviews, VIP receptions, fashion shows, the works. He couldn't help showing off and I'm betting the thought of all that exposure had Stella wetting herself. But what if she failed and he got the gig instead of her? The partner would be heavily out of pocket and Frank's inheritance would be long gone. Stella would be broke and in need of some spare cash to fall back on in case the worst came to the worst. She thought that if she worked a number on you, Drew, played on your grief, you'd be an easy touch. She simply didn't bargain on Alexi and me fighting your corner.'

Jack stood up and naturally, Cosmo unwound himself from Toby's basket, dislodging the dog's head from his belly in the process. He stretched and trotted towards the door, closely followed by an expectantly wagging Silgo.

'He thinks it's walkies time and I guess he's right,' Alexi said, tugging Silgo's silky ears.

'We'll keep in touch and let you know what we find out,' Jack said, hugging Cheryl and shaking Drew's hand. 'Let us know if there are any developments your end but, like I say, I doubt whether you'll hear anything from Stella. She has other things on her mind right now.'

They all piled into Jack's car. He drove a short distance to a turnoff near the river, parked up and they all wandered along the riverbank. Cosmo made frequent forays into the river, failing to catch any fish. Silgo splashed through it in his wake, probably frightening away any fish stupid enough to come anywhere near Cosmo.

'This spot always has a calming effect,' Alexi said, slipping her hand into Jack's. 'It was a good idea to stop here.'

'Happy to oblige,' he replied, bending to throw a stick for Silgo, who woofed once and bounded after it with his ungainly gait.

They laughed at Cosmo when he vaulted up a tree in pursuit of a squirrel who easily evaded his claws.

'I think we're probably right about Stella's reasons for leaning on Drew,' Jack said, after they'd walked on for some way without speaking. 'It will be interesting to see whether or not she wins that pitch.'

'We also need to find out how long her company's been running, and as much else about it as we can, or rather as Cassie can. It can't be a start-up operation, or like you said earlier, it's hard to imagine how it can be in the running for such a big contract.'

Jack whistled to Silgo, who'd trotted off to investigate a clump of reeds, and turned back to retrace their steps.

'Let's go home, have something to eat and try to relax. We'll come back at this fresh tomorrow.'

'Good thinking,' Alexi replied.

* * *

They had only just eaten and cleared away when Jack's phone rang.

'It's Drew,' he said, checking the screen. He shared a concerned look with Alexi and took the call. 'Hey buddy, what's up?'

'Christ, Jack.' Drew's voice sounded near hysterical, increasing Jack's concerns. 'She's dead.'

'Whoa!' He held up a hand, even though Drew couldn't see the gesture. 'Take a step back. Who's dead?'

But Jack had an uncomfortable feeling that he knew the answer to his own question and so was not surprised when an audible gulp echoed down the line.

'Stella.'

9

The call was on speaker. Alexi jumped to her feet and gaped at Jack, her jaw literally falling open as feelings of abject horror gripped her. *This simply cannot be happening*, she thought, totally flummoxed.

'Where are you?' she asked.

'At Stella's flat.'

'What the hell...' Jack shared a bemused look with Alexi.

'She called me an hour ago, in a right old state. Said she didn't want anything from me now, other than my help. She'd been misled and now had a serious problem. I said I couldn't help her and made it clear I wanted nothing more to do with her. I thought it was some kind of low trick to get me alone, but she was crying and begged me to go over. She sounded frantic and said she had no one else to turn to.'

'So you went?' Jack fixed Alexi with an incredulous look.

'I wish to hell I hadn't. I got in through the street door that someone held open when Stella didn't answer her bell. I took the stairs to the first floor. The door to her flat was ajar.' The

words came out in a jumbled rush. Alexi struggled to understand them. 'I pushed it open and knew from the smell that
something wasn't right. She's... she's spreadeagled on the
lounge floor, and she's been stabbed. There's blood everywhere.' Drew choked. 'It's terrible.'

'I know, Drew, but I need you to try and stay calm,' Jack
said in a placating tone. 'Have you called the police?'

'Yeah, they're on their way.'

'Okay. So are we. Stay outside in the corridor and don't
touch anything in the flat until we get there.' He paused. 'I
assume you didn't touch anything.'

'Don't think so. I certainly didn't touch Stella. There's no
question that she's dead.'

Alexi grabbed her jacket. Jack did likewise as he cut the
call and picked up his keys.

'Not you guys,' Jack said to Cosmo and Silgo, who had
roused themselves and headed for the door. 'Can't have you at
a crime scene.'

Cosmo appeared to understand, gave Jack a haughty look
and returned to the spot on the window ledge where he'd
been sleeping. Silgo looked confused, flapped his tail and
seemed disappointed.

Alexi jumped into the passenger seat of Jack's car and he
sped away before she'd even closed her door.

'What the hell, Jack?' she asked, shaking her head. 'I've
never heard Drew half so shaken up before.'

'Finding a murder victim would have that effect,' Jack
replied, his jaw set in a grim line.

'What does it all mean?'

'What it means is that I'm probably responsible for Stella's
death,' he replied shortly. 'This is on me.'

'How do you figure that one out?'

'We knew she probably had a powerful accomplice, bankrolling her ambitions. And those ambitions appear to have had something to do with the Hopgoods. Perhaps not just Frank but Drew as well. I was aware of that but blithely called them all and set up appointments, letting them know that we're looking for answers.'

'And you think that person blamed Stella somehow and decided to shut her up.' She sent Jack a sceptical look. 'That's a bit of a reach, isn't it?'

'Until we know more about Stella's activities, it's the best I can come up with. Anyway, it makes sense.'

'Possibly.' Alexi took his point but wasn't about to make him feel worse by saying as much since she could see that Jack was seriously disturbed by the possibility of inadvertently getting the woman killed.

'Almost certainly,' Jack replied curtly.

'Even if you're right,' Alexi said, 'you're not responsible for Stella's actions. She clearly had something to hide and the person pulling her strings was determined that we wouldn't get to the truth. This whole thing is bigger than we realised. Frank was murdered when he ran out of funds and was no further use to them. The mastermind probably had the same fate in mind for Stella once she'd played her part. It's just that her own greed brought that fate forward. Besides, I can't help wondering why she was in Newbury when she has the pitch of her life to make in London tomorrow.'

'I honestly didn't think that we'd unearth any evidence to prove that Frank had been murdered,' Jack admitted. 'I was going through the motions, apart from anything else, simply to appease Drew and get Stella off his back.'

'Stella was responsible for her own actions, Jack.' Alexi leaned across to touch his knee. 'If you dance with the Devil and all that...'

'Yeah, I know.'

They reached the end of the street where Stella's flat was situated. The flashing blue lights halfway down it and the crowd of curious onlookers confirmed that they'd gotten the right place.

'Game time,' Jack said, with a grim nod as he opened his door.

They were immediately stopped by a uniformed constable, who asked them their business.

'Here with Drew Hopgood,' Jack replied with authority.

Alexi didn't think that would be enough to get them past the cordon, but it worked. They found Drew sitting on a wall, his big shoulders hunched and covered with a blanket. He was talking to a uniformed sergeant but looked up when Jack called his name.

'How you holding up, bud?' he asked.

Alexi moved straight in to hug him. 'It must have been horrible for you,' she said. 'Have you been seen by a medic?'

'On their way,' the sergeant said in a reassuring tone. 'So is the doctor, to confirm life extinct.'

'Not much doubt about that,' Drew said, shuddering.

'Yeah, but there are procedures,' Jack told him.

'Mr Hopgood was just explaining what happened.'

'I don't know what happened. All I can tell you is that Stella called me. She is... was my late brother's wife. She sounded in a state and asked for my help. So I came over and found her the way she is. I called 999, then called my friend here, and that's all I can tell you.'

'Came from where?'

'Can't this wait for the detectives?' Jack asked. 'You can see that Drew's pretty shaken up.'

'Just need the basic facts.'

'You have them,' Jack replied. 'Drew lives in Lambourn. He's the proprietor of Hopgood Hall.'

'Ah, beyond my means, I'm afraid. I've heard the restaurant is something else. Anyway, to business. Did you touch anything in the flat, sir?' the sergeant asked.

Drew shook his head. 'The door was ajar. I pushed it open, but I don't remember touching anything else.'

'We won't find your DNA or prints inside then?'

'Nope.' Drew sounded a little more in control.

'Okay. Just hang on for a while longer, if you wouldn't mind. You do need to be checked by a medic. You're obviously in shock. God knows what's keeping them.' The sergeant looked down the road, as though expecting to see an ambulance approaching. 'The lead detective will want a brief word too.'

Left alone with Drew and Jack, Alexi clasped her friend's large hand. It was cold and trembling.

'Honestly, Jack,' Drew said, shaking his head. 'I don't know how you stuck to a career that involved violent death on a daily basis. What I just saw turned my stomach and I'm not sure how I managed not to throw up. It was horrible. Stella was bad news but didn't deserve such a grisly end.'

'I know,' Jack said.

Before anything further was said, a familiar presence loomed over them.

'Ah, Mark. I'm glad it's you.' Jack straightened up and shook the hand of DI Mark Vickery, an old friend and also the officer who had investigated the recent spate of murders in and around Lambourn.

Alexi knew that Mark would be fair and not jump to obvious conclusions. He knew Drew well enough to accept that he was a gentle giant, incapable of hurting anyone no matter what the provocation. But facts had to be faced. When he learned that Stella had been leaning on him, hoping to extract money and threatening legal action that would have an adverse effect on his business if he didn't cough up, and when he also learned that Drew had found the body, he would become the obvious suspect.

'You're the harbinger of violent death, Maddox,' Vickery replied, shaking Jack's hand. 'Glad you're no longer one of us. No one would want to work with you. Good evening, Alexi.'

'Evening, Mark.'

Vickery glanced at Drew and blinked. 'Good heavens!'

'That about covers it,' Jack said, the brief smile he conjured up at Mark's banter abruptly fading.

A paramedic bustled over and took charge of Drew, who went with him to his ambulance like a docile lamb.

'What happened?' Vickery asked Jack.

Alexi knew that he would already have gotten the bare bones from the sergeant who'd taken control prior to his arrival. It was a testament to his belief in Jack that he was prepared to ask him for his take in an informal manner. Jack knew it too and proceeded to give him a concise account of what little he knew.

'How long has she been dead?' Alexi asked.

'Very recently,' Vickery said, rubbing his temple as though warding off a headache. 'It's a nasty one. Very personal, if you ask me. That flat is unlived in. We'll need to check Drew's phone, obviously, to confirm the incoming call. Presumably, he told Cheryl where he was going, and why?'

'We haven't had a chance to ask him anything much.' It

was Alexi who replied. 'Besides, he's in no state to answer questions.'

'No, I can see that. Once he's been checked over, take him home, Jack. Don't let him drive. I'll call in early tomorrow and talk to him then. Have the coffee ready.'

'It always is.' Jack shook Vickery's hand. 'Thanks, Mark.'

'Does she have a next of kin that you know about?'

'Her father, but they're estranged.' Mark flexed a brow when Jack explained about Ben North and his conviction that Stella had killed her mother.

'Nothing's ever straightforward with you guys, is it?'

Jack gave a mirthless chuckle. 'Where would be the fun in that?'

Vickery responded with a grunt.

'Later,' Jack said, waving over his shoulder as he and Alexi walked towards the ambulance and smiled at Drew, who seemed a little more together.

'He can go,' the paramedic said. 'I've given him a little something to calm him down. So as long as he doesn't drive, he'll be okay.'

'Thanks,' Alexi said, taking Drew's hand in much the same motherly way that she would have clasped his daughter's. 'Come on, big guy, let's get you home. Jack'll drive your gas guzzler and I'll take you back in his old banger.'

'Hey, a little less of the old banger, if you don't mind!' Jack protested.

The exchange didn't even raise a smile from Drew. Instead, he walked obediently beside Alexi, hands still entwined, and slid passively into the passenger seat of Jack's car when Alexi opened the door for him. She sent a worried look towards Jack as she slid behind the wheel and fired up the engine.

Having relieved Drew of his keys, Jack walked to the

Range Rover that the hotel used as a runaround and drove away from the scene in Alexi's wake.

'What on earth is going on?'

They had driven for ten minutes with neither of them speaking. Alexi figured that Drew needed time to come to terms with what had happened without her offering him empty platitudes. He would talk when he felt ready, or when the full implications hit him, which appeared to be happening about then.

'That's what we aim to find out, obviously,' Alexi replied, slowing at a junction and indicating right.

'Stella clearly was very worried about something and feared for her life, which is why she called me. I didn't really believe her. I just wish now that I could have got there sooner and perhaps saved her.'

'Or risked being killed yourself,' Alexi pointed out briskly. 'Despite Stella being an unpleasant person who manipulated your brother, probably killed him, or had him killed, and who tried to then play on your emotions and extort money from you, we none of us wanted her dead.'

'Yeah, I hear you.' Drew lowered his head until his chin touched his chest, his words barely audible.

'She'd gotten herself involved with something or someone dangerous and *that* is what got her killed.' Alexi flashed her lights at a car waiting to pull out and it did so, thanking her with a similar gesture. 'Jack and I think that by putting the squeeze on you and therefore getting us on her case, she drew the sort of attention to herself that this mystery person objected to, and that is what got her killed. Frank had outlived his usefulness and by stepping out of line, so too had Stella.'

'Who though?' Drew had brightened up a little as he pondered the question.

'Who indeed? Jack thinks it's one of the people he phoned to set up appointments with and is blaming himself for Stella's death.'

'That's ridiculous!'

'Is it though? He could well be right actually, but the fault is not his. Don't worry about Jack. He's a sensible guy, accustomed to these sorts of investigations. He won't waste energy blaming himself for long.'

The conversation brought them back to Hopgood Hall. Drew got out of the car with newly determined energy. Aware that he would have to face his pregnant wife and tell her what had occurred, he was obviously pulling himself together for her sake. Jack parked beside them, locked Drew's car and tossed the keys to him. He glanced at Alexi, a question in his eyes, and she nodded to confirm that Drew had gotten his act together, after a fashion.

'Hey, guys.' Cheryl glanced up from the kitchen table, where she was feeding Verity. Toby jumped from his basket, yapping with excitement, but the furious wagging slowed when his friend Cosmo didn't materialise. 'I didn't expect to see you here again today. And where did you disappear to?' she added, fixed Drew with a curious look. 'Oh God, something's happened, hasn't it? You all look so sombre.' She abandoned feeding Verity, lifted her from her highchair and placed her in the playpen in the corner of the room where she happily settled down to play with her toys. 'What is it then?' she asked, sitting heavily down again.

Drew sat beside his wife, took her hand in his and gently explained what had happened. Cheryl's face turned chalk white as she gasped and stared up at Drew in abject disbelief.

'It's not possible,' she said, slowly shaking her head. 'The police will think you did it.' She started to cry, and Drew pulled her into his arms. 'I can't bear it.' Her voice sounded weak and muffled as she rested her face on Drew's shoulder.

'Don't get upset, darling. No one will blame me.'

'You shouldn't have taken that call or gone running to her when she asked you to. And you definitely ought to have told me before you went.' Cheryl sat up, pulled a tissue from her pocket and blew her nose.

'I knew you'd try to stop me.'

'Too right!'

'I just thought by the way that she sounded so frightened and contrite that I could get her out of our lives once and for all,' Drew said, sounding distraught. 'I guess I didn't think it through.' Drew splayed his legs, rested his elbows on his thighs and dropped his head into his hands. 'I know you'll say she didn't have a leg to stand on with her stupid demands, Jack, but she could still have created a shit storm of bad publicity for this place, given the contacts she must have made in her line of work, so I figured, why make an enemy out of her?'

'What did you think when your phone rang, and her name flashed up?' Jack asked. 'I know you have her in your contacts, and I'm surprised you took the call.'

'Actually, now that I think about it, her name didn't show.' Drew glowered at the opposite wall. 'It was an unknown caller, but I get a lot of those: suppliers and what have you. My personal phone is also a business line, so I always answer.'

'So she didn't call you from the number you have for her?' Alexi clarified, thinking that could be a problem.

'No. But I'm sure the police will find the phone that she did call me from.'

Alexi wasn't sure of any such thing but decided against voicing that view.

'What time did you leave here?' Jack asked.

'About six o'clock. It was dark, I know that.'

'The cameras in the car park will confirm that much,' Jack said, glancing at Alexi. 'And when did you arrive at Stella's road?'

'About six forty-five. There was an accident on the Newbury Road that held me up.' Drew tapped his fingers on his thigh. 'If it hadn't been for that, I might have got there in time to save her.'

'The police will be able to confirm the accident. Hopefully, there will be cameras in the vicinity of Stella's flat that show you arriving,' Alexi said, 'then you'll be in the clear. Not that you're a suspect, but you know how these things work, Drew. You found Stella, had issues with her, and so will have to be eliminated from the enquiry, so to speak.'

'The police don't actually know that we had issues with Stella,' Cheryl said in a speculative tone. 'And if they don't find out then Drew has absolutely no motive to kill the wretched woman.' Cheryl tilted her chin defiantly. 'And if that makes me sound cold-hearted, not speaking well of the dead I mean, then I simply don't care. I don't subscribe to the view that anyone who dies must be eligible for a sainthood. Horrible people die too, and Stella was most definitely not a nice human being.'

'You're right,' Jack said softly, 'but I think it's best to level with Mark when he comes to see you tomorrow. I'll make sure we're here and since you're not officially a suspect, Drew, I'm sure he'll let us sit in. Tell him the absolute truth. We don't know who else, if anyone, Stella mentioned her intention of extorting money from you to, and if he hears it from another source then you *will* look as guilty as hell.'

'Yeah, I would have told him. I know why you said what

you did, darling,' he added, turning to Cheryl, 'but I won't lie because I have no reason to. I didn't kill the woman.'

'Good point,' Alexi said. 'I'm sure we'll be able to pick up your car somewhere along the way to prove your time of arrival as well, so you really have nothing to worry about, Drew. You wouldn't have had time to arrive, kill the woman and then call it in. It's totally implausible.'

'Give me the number Cheryl called you from, Drew,' Jack said. 'I'll have Cassie run it down, although I'd put big money on it being a pay-as-you-go.'

Drew extracted his phone from his pocket, unlocked it and handed it to Jack. 'It's the last call I received before I called the emergency services and then you.'

'Right.' Jack jotted down the number.

They chatted round the subject for another half an hour and Alexi was pleased to see that by the end of that time, her two friends appeared a little less fraught with anxiety. Verity started to grizzle, so Cheryl got up, extracted her from the playpen and sat down again, bouncing the child on her knee.

'I'd best put this one to bed,' she said, when Verity didn't settle. 'It's not like her to be difficult. I guess she's picked up on the tension.'

'Either that or she's tired,' Alexi said, laughing and ruffling Verity's hair.

'I'll be through in a minute, love,' Drew said, watching his wife and daughter leave the room with a devoted gaze.

Jack reached for the brandy and poured the three of them decent measures. 'Didn't want to do that in front of a pregnant woman,' he said, grinning, 'but I think we've all earned this.'

Drew drained his brandy in one long swallow and reached for the bottle. No one tried to stop him.

'You realise, I suppose, that there is one far more likely suspect,' Alexi said into the ensuing silence.

'Who?' Drew asked.

'Nick Fairburn,' Jack said at the same time.

'Precisely.' Alexi nodded emphatically. 'Not only did Stella try to wreck his marriage, but when that ploy failed, she went after his most lucrative contract and there's no saying that the financial backing of her mystery supporter wouldn't have been sufficient for her to pull it off. I got the impression that Nick has put all his assets into pursuing that gig and would be in deep trouble if he failed.'

Jack pulled out his ever-present notepad. 'I'll have Cassie look into the state of his company's finances.'

'Presumably,' Alexi said, 'there's no one to push Stella's bid ahead. Her pitch died with her.'

Jack made another note. 'That's something else we need to check out.'

'I don't suppose Nick would have come down here and done the deed himself,' Drew said.

'I wouldn't rule it out,' Jack replied.

'But why would Stella have been so afraid of Nick?' Drew asked. 'And her fear was genuine. I'd put good money on it.'

Alexi sent Drew a speculative look as a thought occurred to her. 'Are you absolutely sure it was her who called you?'

'Well... yes. She said who it was immediately, and it sounded like her. That high-pitched Australian twang she'd picked up. I certainly didn't have any doubts.'

'Sounded like her, even though she was in a right old state?' Jack asked, catching on to Alexi's point. 'You assumed it was her because whoever called you said it was and we all believe what we're told unless we have reason not to. So it may very well not have been her. She could already have been dead, and someone deliberately lured you to the scene in order to set you up.'

'A woman?' Drew shook his head.

'Someone lured you there so you could discover the body. Someone who knew what she was trying to do to you and how guilty it would make you look,' Alexi said. 'That person didn't even need to be there. That's the beauty of mobile phones.'

'It's possible, I suppose.' Drew shook his head. 'I really couldn't say.'

'Look, if you're okay, we'll leave you and Cheryl to come to terms with what's happened,' Jack said, standing because he could see, as Alexi could, that Drew had recovered from the initial shock. Further reaction would set in later. 'Call any time if you need us between now and the morning. We'll be back first thing.'

Alexi stood too and bent over Drew to kiss his cheek. 'Stay strong, big man,' she said. 'We'll get this sorted.'

'Thanks, you two. I'm not sure what it is about Hopgood Hall. We've finally got ourselves profitable, but that profit is coming at a heavy price. We seem to be murder central.'

'Any publicity is good publicity,' Alexi said, her voice sounding artificially bright even to her own ears.

'Later, mate,' Jack said, opening the door for Alexi.

'Will we?' she asked, once they were reinstalled in Jack's car. 'Get it sorted, I mean?'

'We're sure as hell not going to let Drew take the blame for something he didn't do,' Jack replied with determination. 'This crime was hastily put together, no real thought put into framing Drew. He assures me he didn't touch anything in that flat and we know he's never set foot in it before.' Jack removed a hand from the wheel and placed it on Alexi's thigh. 'Try not to worry. We've got Vickery working the case and we know he won't jump at the easy option.'

'True,' Alexi replied. 'Are we still going ahead with the interviews we have arranged for tomorrow?'

'Absolutely! One of those people could have been spooked into killing Stella and if that's the case, we now have a pressing need to discover which one.'

10

Jack, Alexi and their menagerie were in the car and on the way to Hopgood Hall before the sun was up. He knew that Alexi hadn't slept any better than he had but also knew that it would be pointless telling her not to worry. Hell, Jack was worried too but more determined than ever to find out not just who'd murdered Stella and Frank, but who had it in for Drew.

Someone sure as hell did.

Jack wasn't nearly so optimistic about Drew's situation as he'd led the others to believe. No sense in them all worrying, he'd decided, opting to keep his reservations to himself. He wondered about calling Ben Avery, the local solicitor with a shabby appearance and sharp brain who'd successfully defended more than one local person wrongfully accused of criminal acts. He decided against it, at least for the time being. Even if Mark seriously suspected Drew, he wouldn't act precipitously, and it would look more suspicious if Drew jumped the gun and got himself legal representation.

'Don't lose sight of the fact that we have several alternative, more viable suspects to point Mark in the direction of,' he told Alexi as they negotiated narrow lanes heavily populated by horses heading for the gallops – rush hour, equine style. It was a situation they had become accustomed to and one they now much preferred to the alternative type of morning hold ups they'd once accepted as inevitable.

'Nick Fairburn, you mean,' Alexi replied, snapping out of a reverie.

'Nick, and Stella's family members, of course.'

'Surely they wouldn't...' Alexi blinked. 'Would they?'

'Unlikely, but we both know there's a lot of anger still simmering away there. They all think she got away with murder. All the time she was on the other side of the world, out of sight, they could just about live with what they knew. Then she came back, not only to England but right back to their home territory. It must have seemed like a taunt. Then her husband died in suspicious circumstances.' Jack stopped for another string of horses and looked directly at Alexi. 'In their situation, wouldn't you wonder if your silence had cost a man his life?'

'Yeah, I guess, but it seems cruel to make the suggestion when we have no concrete proof. Stella's dad was still grieving the loss of his wife and struggling to come to terms with the fact that his own daughter was responsible for that death, deliberately or otherwise.'

'I'm not going to tell Mark that I think any of them did it. It's merely an avenue that needs to be explored and that will take some of the heat off Drew.'

'Finding Stella's mystery benefactor will be the most efficient means of doing that,' Alexi replied with conviction as the last of the horses crossed in front of them and Drew was free to move on. 'I assume we're going to tell Mark about our investigations?'

'Absolutely, especially since any of the people we've made appointments to see today could have been spooked into silencing Stella.' He smiled at her. 'You see, we've got a dozen directions to point Mark in and something's bound to pop if he, and we, delve deep enough.'

Their conversation had taken them to Hopgood Hall. The car park was almost empty on a cold October early morning and Jack drew his car up close to the entrance. Cat and dog leapt out the moment the door opened and went off to investigate only they knew what. Jack smiled as he watched the large dog trotting dutifully off in Cosmo's wake, nose to the ground, tail wagging ceaselessly. Silgo had been neglected all his life up until the time when Alexi had recently adopted him and now thought all his Christmases had come together. Jack envied him his simple existence.

Jack took Alexi's hand as they climbed the steps and entered the hotel. Cosmo appeared from nowhere to lead the way, followed by his canine devotee. The small party entered the kitchen, unsurprised to find Drew and Cheryl already in occupation of it, with a sleepy Verity throwing her breakfast all over the tray of her highchair. Jack could see that neither of their friends had slept well.

'Morning,' he said cheerfully, smiling as Verity recognised Alexi and raised her arms, wanting to be picked up and fussed over by her favourite auntie. Alexi duly obliged. It was the first time that he'd seen a spontaneous smile from Alexi that morning and was glad for the innocence of the baby's diversion.

'Help yourselves to coffee,' Drew said, his voice gruff.

'Cheer up guys,' Jack replied, doing just that and setting a mug of steaming java in front of Alexi, well out of Verity's probing reach. 'Alexi and I were just discussing all the possible people who could have killed Stella. Mark's going to be busy, looking them all up and getting them to account for their whereabouts at the time of the murder.'

'Besides,' Alexi said, picking up a wipe and removing the gunk from Verity's fingers, 'it will be the work of a moment to account for your own movements, Drew, so stop looking like you have an appointment with the hangman.'

'Yeah, I know.' He let out a long breath. 'It's just one bloody thing after another. It wears a guy down.'

They barely had time to touch their coffee before Mark Vickery and DC Hogan arrived. Without saying a word, Drew got up and poured coffee for them both. They'd visited his kitchen so often recently that he knew how they liked their drinks without having to ask.

'Greetings,' Vickery said, sitting down and helping himself to one of Cheryl's legendary homemade biscuits. 'How are we all today?'

'About as you'd expect.' It was Cheryl who responded. 'We've just dealt with Drew's brother's death, and now his widow has followed him to the hereafter. We didn't like her, but that's not the point.'

Jack suppressed a smile. Yesterday, she hadn't wanted to tell Mark about the problems they'd had with Stella. Today, she'd clearly seen the futility of denial and decided upon the direct approach.

'This is an informal interview,' Vickery replied, placing his coffee mug back on the table and nodding at DC Hogan, who already had her notebook at the ready. 'I wouldn't normally interview the person who'd found the body in a hotel kitchen in front of his family and friends, so don't make me regret being so lax.'

'We certainly don't intend to lie to you, Mark, if that's what you mean to imply,' Drew said, an edge to his voice.

'No one does, not intentionally, but there can be degrees to untruth or misdirection. People put a spin on stuff and draw erroneous conclusions. Anyway, it's too early to get philosophical, but you get my drift.'

Drew nodded. 'Loud and clear. And to save you asking, I'll tell you everything relevant about my relationship with my late brother, and his subsequent marriage to Stella.'

Drew proceeded to do just that, clearly and concisely. Jack could tell that he had recovered from the initial shock of stumbling upon a murder victim and was now intent upon clearing his name and protecting his family. The frequent glances he sent Cheryl's way, presumably to ensure that she was holding up, was all the evidence Jack needed in that regard. Drew wasn't thinking about himself but about the well-being of his pregnant wife, reinforcing Jack's determination to find Stella's killer and free Drew from the weighty and debilitating burden of suspicion.

DI Hogan made notes as Drew spoke in a controlled manner. Vickery showed no reaction whatsoever, but Jack knew he would be taking it all in, and processing what he heard.

'So,' Vickery said, when Drew ran out of words. 'Let's see if I've got this straight. Frank took his half share of his inheritance and scarpered off to Australia, confident of increasing his fortune. He met Stella North there, a woman half his age who actually came from this neck of the woods and married her.' He sniffed. 'A bit of a coincidence, wouldn't you say?'

'Absolutely.' Alexi nodded decisively. 'She's got a PR

company, and we think she persuaded Frank to invest all his worldly wealth in it. His half a mil is certainly all gone, as far as we can tell. By the time they came back to England, which we think they did because Stella reckoned there were more opportunities for her here and because she was pitching for a big Australian kids' clothing contract that was out for tender in the UK.'

'I'm listening,' Vickery said, when Alexi paused.

'Frank had run out of funds. Perhaps he'd led her to believe that he had more available than was actually the case. We don't know for sure,' Jack said, taking up the story. 'Either way, if he couldn't bankroll her ambitions then he became surplus to requirements. He subsequently mysteriously died in a climbing accident when he was an experienced climber and never went out alone.'

'You think Stella did for him?' Vickery asked. 'Did he fall or was he pushed? Sorry,' he added hastily when Drew winced. 'Force of habit. I should know better than to think out loud in front of civilians.'

'You're not saying anything that we haven't already thought,' Drew said. 'I was never happy about his death. He was too experienced a climber and too careful to have had such a stupid accident. But there was an inquest, and no suspicious circumstances came to light. And leaving aside the fact that Stella insisted he was climbing with an old buddy, we have no name and haven't been able to find that person.'

'We're still looking,' Alexi added.

'I'm sure you are,' Vickery said with a grave nod. 'So will I be now.'

DC Hogan looked up from her note taking but made no comment.

'Stella also told us that she's petrified of heights,' Jack said, 'but her brother told us that she loved climbing. Lived for it, in fact. Perhaps that's how she and Frank met in Australia. Perhaps she knew he was coming and contrived that meeting. The question is, why lie to us about something that would be so easy to disprove?'

'Why does anyone lie about anything?' Vickery asked with another dramatic eyeroll. 'You get used to it in my line of work, as well you know, Jack.'

Jack inclined his head. 'Ain't that the truth.'

'Anyway,' Vickery said. 'You and Alexi got involved, Jack, and decided to look into Frank's death. Am I right?'

'Spot on,' Jack told him. 'We spoke to Stella's father, who was less than enthusiastic about his daughter's return to the UK. He said he didn't know she was back, hadn't seen her and had no desire to. Her eldest brother came to see us and told us pretty much the same thing.'

'Did you believe them?'

Alexi and Jack nodded. 'Possibly,' they said simultaneously.

'There's a lot of suppressed anger there, as you can well imagine,' Jack explained. 'They know Stella pushed her mother down the stairs, either deliberately or in the heat of the moment. In their eyes, she got away with murder but they couldn't bring themselves to turn her in. The next best thing was banishment. Out of sight but not out of mind. Anyway, they were not best pleased to learn that she was back.'

'Then there's her ex,' Alexi said with a sweet smile.

'God give me strength!' Vickery shook his head and let out a world-weary sigh. 'Go on then. Let's hear it.'

Alexi told Mark about Nick Fairburn and Stella's determination to steal the Kids Unlimited contract from him.

'Geez!' Mark said.

'The bottom line, Mark,' Jack said, 'is that someone was bankrolling Stella. Someone with a strong motive to see Frank dead and that person has a connection to this area. I don't have any actual proof of that... yet, but all the evidence we've so far gathered points in that direction.'

'So why would that person want Stella out of the way, especially before she'd secured the contract?' Vickery scratched his head. 'Help me out here. Either I'm being slow, or I'm missing something.'

'Because Stella was muckraking,' Drew said. 'She insisted that Frank had been shortchanged when it came to his share of his inheritance in this place. He hadn't been, of course; the probate valuation was fair, based on the house's condition at the time. But she insisted that Frank had been in touch with me, and that we'd agreed to re-evaluate. It's all a load of cobblers. She has no paperwork to back up her allegations because none exists.'

'And she didn't have a leg to stand on legally,' Jack added. 'I made Drew aware of that and I believe his solicitors have confirmed the fact.'

'She must have known that,' DC Hogan said, speaking for the first time. 'So why come after you?'

'I think she wanted to scare us,' Cheryl said in a reflective tone. 'Now that I know she was after that clothing contract, I wonder if she had plans to use this place to do fashion shows, hold swanky PR receptions and what have you. We wouldn't have agreed if she'd asked us because she would have wanted it for free so there wouldn't be anything in it for us other than publicity. But I think, knowing more about her methods now, that she had something to prove to the part of the world where she was brought up. I certainly recall her, on the one occasion she came here with Frank, sizing the place up and muttering what could be done for it with the right marketing. I basically told her that we were doing very nicely thank you and didn't need outside interference.'

'Or the person backing her gave her direct orders to make life uncomfortable for Drew for reasons we have yet to fathom,' Jack added.

Vickery scratched his head and then shook it from side to side. 'Why do you lot always manage to give me a headache?'

'Life ain't that simple,' Jack replied, chuckling. 'Anyway, it will be interesting to learn if Stella's pitch went ahead this morning without her. We have no idea who was working on it with her. But if it didn't then presumably Fairburn will get the contract. And we think he put everything he had into gunning for it. He would not have taken kindly to a vengeful ex playing him at his own game, is all I'm saying.'

'We'll talk to him, obviously,' Vickery replied.

'I've got the names of a couple of Frank's climbing buddies and we have appointments to speak with them today,' Jack said. 'It will be interesting to know if they had heard from Frank after his return and what they made of Stella.'

'That doesn't really form a part of my investigation into Stella's death,' Vickery replied, 'so I can't waste resources on that avenue as things stand, but let me know how you get on.'

'There's more,' Jack said.

Vickery groaned. 'Of course there is!'

'It's this mystery person who backed Stella,' Jack said. 'Someone funded her and that person has, we think, connections to this part of the world, and more specifically to the Hopgoods. It's made me wonder if Drew was the actual target of this vendetta and Frank just got in the way. Or perhaps it was both of them.'

'But I don't have a clue who it could be,' Drew added,

spreading his hands in a gesture of supplication. 'I don't have any serious enemies, current or past. The odd disagreement along the line, like everyone else, but that's about it. I'm an easy-going guy and tend to get along with everyone. You have to in this business, otherwise the smallest scrap gets talked up, exaggerated. Then, before you know it, you have a reputation to compete with Freddie Kruger's and your business suffers as a consequence.'

'Drew gave me the name of two of Frank's old friends,' Jack said, 'and I've made appointments to see them both today, as well as the two climbers.' He paused, his expression grave. 'My concern is that I inadvertently alerted the person behind Stella to her going rogue. She wasn't supposed to make waves, is my guess,' he added, feeling the weight of guilt sitting heavily on his shoulders. 'She wasn't supposed to hit Drew up for access to this place either, thereby setting Alexi's and my investigative noses twitching. I could be to blame for Stella's death.'

'It sounds to me as though Stella was in bed with the Devil.' Vickery sat forward. 'Let's clear up your involvement, Drew, before we move on. As I understand it, Jack wanted to know where Stella was living so he had you phone her and make conciliatory overtures. You were going to call on her the day after tomorrow and discuss terms, only it would have been Jack who turned up.'

Drew nodded. 'That's about the size of it.'

'It sounds pretty tenuous, I know,' Jack said, 'and in retrospect, I wish I hadn't set that particular ball in motion, but hindsight is bloody irritating.'

'We wanted to find out where she's living in the hope that would lead us to the owner of the property in question,' Alexi added.

'No one was living in that flat,' Vickery said. 'Certainly not the victim. There's no clothing or personal items, no food in the fridge, no pictures on the walls. It was like a show home but obviously, we'll look into that aspect.'

DC Hogan made a note.

'Anyway, Drew, you say Stella called you. Our problem is, her phone, laptop and all other communication devices were taken. We know she had them there. There were chargers. And the call you received didn't come from the number you had in your contacts for her. Am I right?'

'Yes, but I didn't realise it at the time. Like I told Jack last night, I always answer calls because a lot of them are connected to the business. I recognised Stella's voice, or thought I did, and when she said it was her, I didn't have any reason to disbelieve her.'

'I find it hard to believe that you went off like that, on your own, when you were at odds with her,' Vickery said mildly.

'I wish to hell that I hadn't but what can I say.' He shrugged. 'She sounded genuinely terrified and I'm a gentleman deep down. When a lady's in distress, even if I don't like her much, then I will help her. Besides, I hoped I might be able to thrash out our disagreement and come to a resolution.'

'Okay, so we know what time you left here and that will be verified by the cameras in your car park. I also know what time you said you arrived but that's longer than it ought to have taken you at that time of the day.'

'There was a crash on the Newbury Road. It held me up for a good ten minutes.'

'We checked, Drew, and there's no report of an accident.'

Drew's face paled. 'What can I tell you. It happened. A blue Fiat and a four-by-four were in collision, blocking the road. It didn't look that serious. The drivers and a few others were pushing the vehicles clear. I was going to help but by the time I got out, they'd almost done it. I wasn't needed. I wish now that I had been, then there would be people to confirm that it happened.' He ran a hand through his hair. 'Geez! Why don't people report accidents nowadays like self-respecting, law-abiding citizens?'

'Making up a ten-minute delay wouldn't have given Drew enough time to get there, park up and murder Stella, then calmly call it in,' Jack pointed out.

Vickery fixed Drew with a penetrating look. 'If you're telling me the truth then you have nothing to worry about. And, obviously, as Jack well knows, he's given me plenty of other avenues to explore.'

'Presumably, the phone she used to call Drew is a pay as you go,' Alexi said, 'but I assume you'll be checking the records of her official phone.'

'I dare say we would have thought of that eventually,' Vickery said in a mildly castigating tone.

Verity, who had remained quiet and occupied in her playpen up until that point, decided to make her presence felt. Cosmo stretched and sent Vickery a languid look that implied it would be a mistake to try and pin the crime on Drew.

'I hear you, big guy,' Vickery said, laughing as he stood. 'Right, I'll get out of your hair for now. Someone will come and take your prints and DNA for elimination purposes, Drew. I take it you have no objections.'

'None whatsoever and thanks for giving me the benefit of the doubt,' Drew replied, offering Vickery his hand. 'I appreciate the vote of confidence, if that's what it is.'

'Nah, nothing like that.' Vickery jerked a thumb in Jack's direction. 'It's just that I know better than to get on the wrong side of this one. The paperwork he could generate for me if he decided to be vindictive doesn't bear thinking about.'

'Hold that thought,' Jack said, laughing.

'Besides, he has an annoying habit of being right.'

'Well, there is that,' Drew said, shaking Vickery's hand.

'Later,' the detective inspector said, opening the door. 'And let me know what you find out, Jack. I'm serious. Don't go off alone and screw up my investigation.'

'Far be it from me to remind you that I usually solve your investigations for you,' Jack replied.

11

Alexi watched the detectives leave, feeling deeply unsettled. And helpless. Incapable of aiding her closest friends in their hour of need. She glanced at Drew, who simply threw his hands in the air, as mystified as she herself was by the turn events had taken and no doubt blaming himself for taking Stella's call and rushing to her rescue without telling anyone what he intended to do. It was typical of Drew's natural inclination to help anyone who needed it but his generosity of spirit had now come back to bite him on the backside.

'Cheer up, guys,' Jack said, his upbeat tone sounding forced. 'Alexi and I have got this. We're going to head off out now and get on with the interviews we've arranged. We'll be back later to let you know what we find out but if you need us in the meantime...' He lifted his phone in the air and waggled it about.

'Yeah, get out of here,' Drew said with forced joviality. 'You're making the place look untidy. And take that motley collection of animals with you before the health inspectors get on my case too.'

Cosmo stalked up to Drew and rubbed his big head against his shin, as intuitive as ever. Drew laughed and bent to scratch his ears.

* * *

'Are you as worried as I am?' Alexi asked Jack, once they were on the road with cat and dog occupying the back seat of Jack's car.

'Yes and no.' Jack removed one hand from the wheel and jiggled it from side to side. 'There's no chance of Drew being arrested because we know he's telling the truth, so his car will be picked up on a camera somewhere. Mark will have someone looking for it as a matter of urgency. Even so, I can see that the stress is getting to them both and they won't feel vindicated unless we identify the killer. That's obviously what we were attempting to do in respect of Frank's death before Stella got herself bumped off. Her murder has ultimately opened a whole new can of worms. But it will also force Vickery to take our suspicions about Frank's death seriously.'

'Well, there is that, but in the meantime, Drew being a suspect will find its way into the papers and damage the hotel's reputation.'

'Unless we do find the actual culprit and do it fast.'

'I can imagine what will be said in the meantime, about Drew, I mean.' Alexi laced her fingers together in her lap and frowned at nothing in particular. 'No smoke without fire, and all that, especially given all the other suspicious deaths indirectly linked to Hopgood Hall.'

'Whoever killed Stella miscalculated,' Jack replied. 'Instead of taking the heat off him or her, it's turned up the thermostat.'

Alexi raised a brow. 'You think it could have been a woman?'

'Why not? It doesn't take physical strength to stab a person, especially if that person trusts you, and isn't expecting an attack. She let her killer in, never expecting that it would be the last thing she did.'

Alexi nodded. 'You think it was a crime committed without proper planning.'

'I do. Stella took matters into her own hands insofar as she put the squeeze on Drew and whoever's pulling her strings wasn't about to let her direct the heat their way. He or she also couldn't let Stella's pitch go ahead, just in case it was successful.'

'Because Stella had outgrown her usefulness. Crossed a line, or whatever.'

'Yep.'

'You could well be right. Especially if that person has a long memory and endless patience insofar as he or she has waited years to exact revenge upon the Hopgoods for reasons we have yet to fathom.' Alexi let out a long breath. 'So, where are we going first?'

'To Southampton. Both of Frank's climbing buddies are down that way today and have agreed to meet us in one of those fancy hotels opposite the docks.'

'Wouldn't it be better to see them individually?'

'No point. If they do have anything to hide, they've had plenty of time to get their stories straight.'

Alexi nodded and fell silent, her mind going into overdrive as she tried to figure out all the possible scenarios, the most pressing of which was the identity of Stella's backer. She was no nearer to having decided who it could be, when Jack pulled his car up in the parking area in front of a glass and steel hotel. Cosmo and Silgo both looked up expectantly when he cut the engine.

'Stay here, guys,' Jack said. 'There's a park across the way. We'll go over there afterwards.'

'You do realise that you're talking to them as though they can understand you,' Alexi said, smiling.

'Well, they can, can't they? That's what you're always telling me. Anyway, look. They're settling back down again.' Jack grinned at her. 'I rest my case. Either that or I'm losing my mind.'

'Very likely,' Alexi agreed, as she opened her window a few inches before leaving the car. 'Are we crazy, roving round the country, asking questions in a murder investigation and having a dog and cat riding shotgun?'

'I never thought to hear those words leave your lips,' Jack replied, as he slid from behind the wheel, and they walked together towards the revolving door that protected the entrance to the flashy hotel. 'And for the record, I wouldn't want you snooping around dangerous situations on your own without them. I know!' He held up a hand to cut off her protest. 'You can take care of yourself as a general rule but when we're crossing swords with dangerous, unpredictable people then those rules go out the window. I'd back Cosmo against a ruthless killer any day and so I feel much better knowing he has your back.'

Alexi smiled. 'It makes me feel much better too.'

They entered the hotel's foyer and glanced around. Several of the tables, spaced well apart, were occupied by people clearly having business meetings. Only one, at the far end, had two men seated at it, heads together, deep in conversation. Jack headed in that direction.

'Bob Green and Andy Dawson?' he asked.

'That's us.' Both men stood. 'You must be Jack Maddox.'

'Right first time.' Jack shook their proffered hands. 'This is my partner, Alexi Ellis.'

'Good to meet you,' she said, sizing both men up as she too shook hands. Bob was short, stocky and probably in his early fifties with a receding hairline, workworn hands and an open, friendly expression. Andy was tall and muscular, with smooth hands that implied a desk job and shrewd, sharp, brown eyes that subjected them to a protracted appraisal. He was moderately handsome but obviously wary of their presence.

Seated around the table and with coffee ordered, Jack wasted no time with small talk and got right down to business.

'We're here about Frank, as I mentioned on the phone,' he said.

'Yeah, it was tragic what happened to him,' Bob replied with a sad little shake of his head. 'He was one of the good guys. Always chasing the next big thing that couldn't possibly go wrong and would make him a fortune. It never did, of course, but what the heck? We all have to dream.'

'Had you known him for long?' Alexi asked, thanking the waitress when she delivered their coffee.

'Yeah, more than twenty years,' Bob told them. 'The three of us met on a climbing holiday in Wales, found out we were from the same neck of the woods and hit it off right away. We lost contact when he took himself off Down Under, but he got in touch when he returned, and we met up with our respective other halves to have a catch up.'

'What did you make of Stella?' Jack asked.

The two men exchanged a prolonged look. Andy had yet

to say a word, but Alexi still felt that he was in control of the interview.

'We both thought Frank was punching above his weight,' Andy said. 'We could also see that she ran the show. We didn't like what he'd become, truth to tell. He was always a man's man but now this admittedly attractive woman had him dancing to her tune and it was like he needed her permission to sneeze.'

'She didn't like other women much either,' Bob added, glancing at Andy first, as though seeking permission to express his view. 'Our wives were no threat to her, but she treated them as though they didn't exist. Andy and I decided afterwards that we wouldn't meet up with them again as couples. No way will I have my wife made to feel inferior.'

'You didn't take to Stella then?' Jack asked.

Both men shook their heads.

'She was fiercely ambitious and used her looks and femininity to get what she wanted,' Andy said. 'It didn't take me five minutes in her company to figure that much out and frankly, I didn't trust her an inch.'

'I hear you.' Alexi nodded, not in the least surprised to hear it. 'Did either of you climb with Frank once he came back?'

'Yeah, we did, both of us a week before he died, but that was the only time,' Bob said. 'We had a weekend in Snowdonia, but Frank's phone never stopped ringing. It was like she was checking up on him all the time. I heard him placating her on several occasions.'

'Did he mention that Stella climbed?'

They shared a glance, appeared surprised and again, both shook their heads.

'What's this all about anyway?' Andy asked. 'Frank's death

has been investigated, we've mourned the loss of our friend and have moved on.'

'We know that,' Alexi said, 'but like Jack explained on the phone, we're close friends with Frank's brother and he isn't entirely satisfied with the results of the inquest.'

'Grieving relatives seldom are,' Andy replied. 'It's only natural.'

Alexi smiled. 'Don't you think it odd that a climber with Frank's experience would fall on what was probably an easy climb for him?'

Bob nodded. 'Yeah, we did think it odd, but accidents happen. A moment's inattention is all it takes, and Frank *did* appear to be distracted on both occasions when we met him.'

'Probably due to Stella's constant demands,' Andy added. 'Instead of using the time as an escape, his mind was full of Stella's expectations. Stupid bugger!'

'Did either of you agree to climb with him on the morning that he died?' Alexi asked. 'Stella insists that he'd arranged to meet someone.'

'And she doesn't know who?' Andy shook his head decisively. 'I don't buy it for a moment. Like I already said, Frank couldn't sneeze without her permission.'

Jack shared a glance between the two men. 'Would he climb alone?'

'Possibly, if he was stressed, or wanted to clear his head. Climbing is in our DNA. It's what we do when things get on top of us, and we need to get away from all the stress of modern life,' Bob replied.

'I get that you think he was deliberately killed,' Andy said, 'but isn't it a bit late to start asking questions?'

Jack sent him a speculative look. 'You don't seem surprised that our thoughts are veering in that direction.'

'Stella was a piece of work,' Andy replied in a vicious tone. 'She had her claws well and truly into Frank and if they'd had a falling out, if the blinkers had come off from Frank's perspective... well, I wouldn't put anything past her, but good luck proving it.'

'That won't be so easy,' Jack said, his expression sombre. 'Stella was found dead yesterday. Murdered.'

'Bloody hell!' Bob cried. He and Andy both looked astounded.

'So you're looking into her death, too?' Andy said accusingly.

'We think the two might be connected and need your help.' Alexi spoke quietly, careful to keep the accusation out of her voice. 'Anything you can remember about that one meeting with Stella, or anything that Frank said to you subsequently that might shed some light would be greatly appreciated. To be honest, we're floundering a bit here.'

'Leave it to the police then,' Andy said. 'It's what they get paid for.'

'We are. They're all over it. We're just helping out a bit,' Jack said. 'Frank's brother needs answers and we're trying to find a reason for this madness.'

'I had a chat with Frank on the phone not long before he died,' Bob said. 'I got the impression that he was on his own, that *she* wasn't hovering over him, because he sounded more like his old self again. He was upbeat, said he'd made a decision. Come to his senses, as he put it, but he didn't say in what respect. We arranged to meet the following week for a beer, but in the meantime... well, he died.'

'Do you know anyone who didn't get on with Frank?' Jack asked.

Both men shook their heads.

'Frank was a Walter Mitty,' Andy said, 'but harmless, never met a stranger and we all liked him. We just steered well clear of any business opportunities that he tried to push on us because they never worked out.'

Alexi smiled, frustrated that this interview was producing so little. 'Are you aware of anyone who actually went into business with him?' she asked.

'Someone who lost their money and decided to murder him years after the event?' Andy shook his head. 'You're barking up the wrong tree. If he was deliberately killed, then Stella either did the job herself or had someone do it for her. Then that someone turned their attention to her. Don't ask me why because I have absolutely no idea. But now, if you'll excuse me.' He glanced at his watch. 'I have to be somewhere.' Andy stood. 'See you at the weekend, Bob.'

They all waved Andy off, but Bob didn't seem to be in any hurry to leave. Alexi was glad of the opportunity to have a few words with him alone, still convinced that Andy was the driving force in their friendship. Andy seemed satisfied that Bob couldn't say anything to upset the applecart, always assuming there was anything to upset, and had been happy to leave Bob with them.

'Is there something you want to tell us?' Jack asked.

'Look, I don't want to tell tales out of school but if you keep probing then you'll probably find out anyway, so I might as well give you the low down.' Bob paused, in no obvious hurry to dish the dirt. 'Just before Frank went to Australia, he hit on Andy's wife.'

Alexi gulped. 'Blimey,' she said. 'We'd heard he was a womaniser but...'

'I don't think he instigated things. It was Sarah. She's attractive, not in Stella's league, but still pretty hot and Andy neglects her. Between you and me, I think his money was the attraction. He's a successful builder, worth a few bob, and treats her a bit like a chattel. Anyway, they had words, Frank apologised and promised to keep his hands off Sarah. Then a few weeks later, he took himself off to Australia. I think Andy was pleased to see the back of him.'

'You think the previous attraction between Frank and Sarah was partly responsible for the atmosphere when the six of you met up?' Jack suggested.

'Could have been. Sarah was certainly sending Stella death looks and I reckon Stella would have picked up on it. But still, it's old news and can't have had anything to do with Frank's death. After all, Frank was fully invested with Stella and even Sarah couldn't compete with her in the looks and style department.'

'You think Sarah Dawson still had feelings for Frank?' Alexi asked.

'Hell if I know! It just seemed that way. I get the impression that she's not happy with Andy but has no escape clause. If she divorced him, she wouldn't walk away with much. He hides his money away. Always has. Always been the last up to the bar as well, even though he's better off than any of us.'

'And yet he's your friend?' Alexi flexed a brow as she posed the question.

'More a climbing buddy. Climbing glues our friendship together. It's the only thing we have in common. We mix in different circles other than that.'

'Your wife and Sarah don't link up?' Alexi asked.

'Not really. Andy keeps her on a tight leash. My Jan on the other hand has a whole load of friends, she's very outgoing, and can't be arsed to deal with Andy's jealous tirades, so unless Sarah calls her, she leaves her more or less alone.'

'What's your take on Stella?' Jack pushed his empty coffee cup aside. 'You didn't say much about her when I asked earlier.'

'I thought she was a trophy wife and that Frank had made a right prat of himself. He'd always been the life and soul, guaranteed to liven up any party, but now, here he was acting like Stella's poodle. I figured she'd married him for his inheritance. I could also sense that the gloss had worn off from Frank's perspective and that he regretted his decision to marry her. Did she kill him?' He turned his hands, palms upwards and shrugged. 'Hell if I know, but now that she's no longer with us, there doesn't seem much point in flogging a dead horse, no disrespect intended.'

'You're very likely right.' Alexi extracted a card from her bag and handed it to Bob. 'But we're like terriers. Once we get our teeth into something, we're reluctant to let go. Unless I get to the truth, I will know no peace. Anyway, thanks for your time. If you think of anything else at all that might help us, please get in touch.'

Bob stood and shook both their hands. 'I'll do that,' he said.

'Just one more question,' Jack said. 'Whose idea was it for you to meet us here together? We'd already said that we'd come to you individually.'

'Andy's, as a matter of fact. I'm a chippie, working on a site here at the docks. Andy said he had appointments in the area today and it would make sense for us to see you together.'

'I see.' Jack paused. 'And Frank absolutely didn't talk to you about meeting him for a climb on the day he died.'

'Not me,' Bob replied without hesitation.

'Okay, well, thanks again for your time.'

'No worries.'

'Well,' Alexi said, as they left the hotel and returned to the car in order to drive the short distance to the park. 'That was a waste of time.'

'I wouldn't say that exactly,' Jack replied, speaking only once they'd reached their destination and released cat and dog.

'What did I miss?' Alexi sent him a speculative look. 'Surely you don't think Andy bumped Frank off because he made a pass at his wife, or vice versa, more than three years ago?'

'I think there are a lot of things that were off about that interview. For starters, why was Bob so anxious to tell us about Frank's dalliance with Andy's wife? How can that be relevant?'

'Andy's definitely a control freak. He said a lot less than Bob but didn't miss a trick. You think Bob has issues with Andy and wants to cast suspicion his way for some obscure reason?'

'It's one possibility.' Jack bent to throw a stick for Silgo, who woofed and bounded after it. Cosmo had disappeared somewhere, declining to participate in such mundane activities. 'But there's definitely tension between those two. Andy keeps tabs on his wife and clearly does the same with his friends. Perhaps Bob resents that.'

'Perhaps.'

'Anyway, let's hit the road again. We need to get back to Lambourn and speak with Frank's old sparring partners there. If we don't get the feel that one of them was behind Stella's games, then it'll be back to the drawing board. We can stop somewhere for lunch on the way.'

12

The ride back to Lambourn was largely uneventful. Both Jack and Alexi were consumed by their individual thoughts as they digested what the interview with the two climbers had thrown into the mix. Their ruminations were disturbed only by the sound of Silgo's snuffling snores from the backseat as he chased rabbits in his dreams.

'Who's next?' Alexi asked, stretching her arms above her head as they reached the outskirts of the village.

'Emily Pearson is expecting us,' Jack replied, using one hand to grab his phone and pull up the address he'd already programmed into his sat nav.

'Frank's first love. Well, first serious love, at least the way Cheryl tells it. The woman he shacked up with for quite a while. As far as I'm aware, she's the only one who got to wash his socks on a regular basis so I guess she must be special.'

Jack chuckled. 'It takes a special kind of gal to wash a man's socks.'

'Well, don't look at me that way. Ours is a quid pro quo

relationship. You do the lion's share of the cooking and I'll throw the laundry in the machine. That works for me.'

'Good to know.'

Jack let out a low whistle when they pulled up at tall, wrought-iron gates that protected a sprawling property set a long way back from the lane, horses grazing in a field to one side. The ultimate des res. The gates in question were firmly closed, presumably to discourage casual callers. Jack lowered his window and pressed a button on a brick pillar. Upon giving his name, the gates swung smoothly open.

He drove up a gravel driveway, no weeds in evidence, and parked in front of an imaginatively designed modern house.

'This was once a barn?' Alexi asked, gaping out the window. 'It's not like any barn I've ever seen.'

Jack chuckled. 'I think there might have been one or two additions made to the old cow shed over the years.'

Two lurchers bounded up to the car, barking but with tails spiralling. Cosmo stood up, indulged in a feline stretch, then pressed his face against the window and hissed at the dogs. They whimpered and backed off, tails between their legs. Silgo gave a friendly woof and wagged his tail.

'Cosmo!' Alexi burst out laughing. 'How many times have I told you that it's bad manners to intimidate.'

The cat sent her a disparaging look and, duty done, settled back down to his slumbers.

'You've hurt his feelings,' Jack said, laughing as well. 'Best leave these two in here, under the circumstances.'

The dogs had recovered a little of their courage and trotted beside Jack and Alexi as they headed for the front door. It opened before they could press the bell and an elegant lady, dressed in jeans and a loose, white top, smiled as they approached.

'My early-warning system would have advised me of your arrival, even if pressing the gate bell hadn't,' she said, tugging one of the dog's ears. Emily's hair touched her shoulders and had been carefully and expensively coloured. She wore minimal makeup and although probably in her early fifties, or even older, she had aged well. 'Anyway, sorry about these two and their mixed messages. They seem to think they should show everyone around, even those who are not invited.'

'No worries,' Jack replied with an easy smile.

'You must be Jack Maddox. We spoke on the phone.' Emily offered Jack a slender hand to shake. Her grasp was firm, belying the fragile femininity Jack recalled seeing at the funeral.

'Thank you for seeing us,' he said. 'This is my partner, Alexi Ellis.'

'Lucky girl,' she said in a loud aside to Alexi as she shook her hand, sending Jack an appreciative look.

Jack laughed. 'I'm the lucky one, or so Alexi insists upon reminding me at every opportunity.'

'That's the spirit! Treat 'em mean and keep 'em keen.' Emily transferred a warm smile to Alexi. 'I can see you give him a run for his money. Anyway, come along in, both of you. I'm in the kitchen and the coffee's on.'

'You have a lovely home,' Alexi said, glancing around as they followed Emily into a modern kitchen – all granite surfaces and hidden appliances – with a large island in its centre, upon which a formal array of china had been set out for their coffee.

'Thank you,' Emily replied. 'It suits my purposes. Now do take a seat.'

She indicated the tall stools at the island and Alexi dutifully climbed onto one that gave her a spectacular view over the surrounding countryside. The smell of freshly brewed coffee assailed Jack's senses and he thanked Emily when she placed a delicate cup and saucer in front of him.

'Help yourselves to cream and sugar,' she said, seating herself across from them and pouring cream into her own coffee. 'Now, I gather you want to talk to me about Frank. I'm not sure how much I can tell you after all this time, but fire away.'

'He's only been dead for a month,' Alexi said.

'Oh, I'm aware of that, believe me.' She closed her eyes for an expressive moment and Jack sensed her genuine grief. 'But our friendship... make that affair, was over a good three years or more ago and I've barely laid eyes on him since then.' She stirred her coffee. 'Anyway, why all the questions, and why now? If you thought there was anything off about his death then the time to be asking would have been then.'

'Drew can't accept what happened to his brother,' Alexi replied. 'I assume you know that I'm an investor in Hopgood Hall?'

'How would I know that?' Emily asked, smiling at Alexi, but there was steel beneath the mild tone and Jack sensed that she was now on her guard, perhaps because she assumed they suspected her of having a hand in Frank's demise. A woman deserted after she'd financed a man's dreams, which Jack imagined she'd done, was likely to bear a massive grudge.

'I simply assumed,' Alexi replied. 'It's a small village and Hopgood Hall hasn't exactly been flying beneath the publicity radar lately.' She raised her cup to her lips and gently blew on the liquid's surface. 'But anyway, it's not important.'

Jack thought Alexi was right to labour the point. She was modest to a fault but her high-profile career on the *Sentinel* had made hers a household name. Add that to all the publicity the hotel had received, not always for good reasons, and it was hard to imagine a local resident *not* recognising Alexi's connection to the place.

'We're simply trying to get a handle on Frank's background,' Jack said, leaning towards Emily and treating her to his most ingratiating smile. 'Drew is finding it hard to accept that Frank would have fallen on what was for him a relatively straightforward climb. We're talking to everyone who knew him, including his climbing buddies, to see if they can throw any light on his activities. Did you think it was odd when you heard how he'd died?'

'Well yes, I suppose... now that you mention it, Frank was like a monkey when he was younger. He treated any climb as a challenge and had plans to turn professional at one point. Dreams of conquering Everest and all that. Mind you, Frank had plans to do a lot of things, but he never stuck to anything for long enough to see it through. He bored easily. Climbing was his only enduring love.' There was a tinge of bitterness to her tone now. 'No one and nothing were more important to him than that. He enjoyed pitting his wits against the elements, the tougher the better.'

'You and he were together for a long time, Cheryl tells me,' Alexi said.

'We've known each other since we were kids,' Emily replied. 'I was a little older than him.'

More than a little, Jack knew, but it would be impolite to draw attention to the disparity in their ages. Besides, it was irrelevant.

'We both grew up in Lambourn, mixed with the same crowd. Our ways parted for a while. I married. He was running all over the place chasing his dreams.'

A soft smile touched her lips and Jack knew then for a

certainty that she'd never stopped loving a man whom she'd been unable to tie down, even though she'd probably thrown a lot of money his way attempting to do so. It was impossible to buy a person's affections, he could have told her. Jack felt a moment's sympathy for her situation.

People always wanted what they couldn't have, he knew from bitter experience. He'd come across that situation more times than he could recall during the course of his career. The worm eventually turned, love became resentment and then hate and the desire for revenge overrode all other considerations. Emily appeared to be harmless, but Jack would not permit appearances to deceive him, and her name remained very much on his list of suspects.

'He didn't leave the village, but he came and went all the time.' Emily's voice recalled Jack's wandering attention. 'Drew said he wasn't living at home all the time, but he kept a room there. He was very close to their mother and never went too long without seeing her. He was her favourite son and she lived for his visits but then, didn't we all.'

'How did you and he finish up together?' Jack asked.

'There had always been an attraction between us. Frank would have flirted with a doorpost if there was nothing else available, but I knew that what we had would endure. You can always tell, can't you? He lived here with me for about five years, and I helped him to get a business enterprise up and running.'

'What type of business?' Alexi asked.

'He was starting a climbing school and promoting it.'

'Where?' It was the first Jack had heard of a climbing school and was sufficient to reignite his mild suspicions regarding his climbing friends.

'In Wales.'

Wales? Andy and Bob had mentioned meeting Frank in Wales. They had made it sound like a chance encounter, which it could well have been. Wales was popular with climbers from all over the country. Even so, Jack didn't like coincidences and half hoped they were onto something.

'Why are you so interested in old history?' Emily asked. 'It never took off and Frank lost his investment. The Welsh wouldn't give him the necessary licences. Something to do with risk assessment but Frank hadn't done his research properly, assumed the licencing would be a formality and went ahead with purchasing climbing rights.' She shook her head. 'He was in such a hurry, the idiot! Anyway, I can't remember all the details, but it was a long time ago and can't possibly have anything to do with Frank's death.'

Alexi's expression displayed both surprise and sympathy at this revelation, but Jack knew her mind would have gone into overdrive and that she would have connected the dots too. 'Did he have a partner in this scheme?' she asked.

'Yes, me. I lost my investment but I'm not stupid. I knew that with Frank, there was always a chance that it wouldn't work out, so I only invested as much as I could afford to lose. I loved the man and had faith in him, even though he didn't have much of a track record when it came to business acumen, or monogamy, come to that.' She looked reticent and suddenly every year of her age. 'Anyway, my husband left me well provided for and so I could afford to give the man I adored an opportunity to prove himself.'

'Were you surprised when he took himself off to Australia?' Jack asked.

'I always knew that he'd take his half of his inheritance in Hopgood House and run when the time came. I told him to stick with Drew, convinced that he'd make a success of the hotel, which he has, and Frank would now be reaping the rewards, if he'd displayed a little patience.' She shook her head. 'But patience wasn't built into his DNA. He was always a man in such a hurry.'

'Why Australia? Do you have any idea?' Alexi asked.

'None whatsoever. When we separated, I had nothing more to do with him.'

'I saw you at the funeral,' Alexi said. 'You were very upset.'

'You don't stop loving someone just because they let you down,' Emily replied. 'And, ridiculous as it sounds, I'd never given up hope of his coming home to me. Eventually.' She brushed impatiently at an errant tear as it trickled down her cheek. 'Pathetic, or what? I knew that if he did come back, it wouldn't be because he realised he loved me, but for more practical reasons. But still, what's the point of having all this,' she added, waving a hand airily, 'if you don't have someone you care about to share it with?'

'Of course you're not being pathetic.' Alexi reached across the table and gently touched her hand in a gesture of feminine solidarity. 'Your heart feels what your heart feels and there's not an awful lot you can do to change that situation. Anyway, what did you make of Stella?'

Emily's expression shut down. 'A gold-digger,' she replied without hesitation. 'Frank had finally made a complete prat of himself by marrying her. Everyone who knew him that I've spoken to felt the same way.'

'Perhaps they were in love,' Jack suggested mildly.

Emily rolled her eyes. 'And perhaps I'm a twenty-year-old supermodel.'

'Did you meet Stella, with Frank I mean?' Jack asked.

'No. I heard that he was back with a trophy wife in tow, but he didn't have the decency to get in touch and tell me the news himself. She probably didn't allow him to. The first time I met her was at the funeral, but I didn't speak to her, or pass on my condolences either, since I don't believe she was upset.'

'But you were,' Alexi said softly. 'I noticed you crying quietly to yourself at the back of the church.'

'I always cry at funerals. Besides, despite what happened between Frank and me, all the arguments, his wandering eye and our acrimonious separation, I still cared deeply for him. I simply couldn't help myself. One's head and one's heart aren't always on the same wavelength in such situations, as you yourself just pointed out. Frank was bad for me. He played upon my partiality for him, used me if you like, but part of me still didn't care and if he'd returned to Lambourn alone and came to see me...' Emily waved one hand in a wild circle. 'Well, who knows. I'd have probably taken him back again.' She shared a defiant look between them. 'In fact, there's no probably about it. There. Is that what you wanted to hear?'

Jack decided it was cards on the table time. Emily knew a lot more about Frank than she'd let on and wasn't likely to open up to them unless Jack made the first move.

'We think that Stella either murdered Frank or arranged his accident,' he said starkly.

'I see.' Emily showed no surprise, or emotion. 'And what has drawn you to that conclusion?'

'We think she milked Frank for his inheritance.'

'Even I can see the irony in that one,' Emily replied with a chuckle.

'He helped her to finance a PR company and she came to the UK to pitch for a big Australian kids' clothing company contract. You said yourself that Frank wasn't a stayer. We think he called a halt on financing her ambitions when the going got tough and he didn't see instant results. He was almost flat broke again anyway so his inheritance had gone somewhere and the only place that could have been is into Stella's company. In other words, he'd served his purpose.'

'It's a little late to go raking it all up now, isn't it?' Emily said thoughtfully.

'It would be but for the fact that Stella was found dead yesterday,' Jack said, watching closely for Emily's reaction.

'Really?' A tight smile tugged at Emily's lips. 'I hope you don't expect me to express regrets.' She folded her hands in her lap, as though to stop herself from fiddling with a teaspoon, which she had been doing periodically throughout their conversation. 'How did she die?'

'She was murdered,' Alexi replied. 'There's no doubt in her case.'

'What did she get Frank involved with?' Emily asked in a speculative tone.

'That is what the police are trying to discover,' Jack told her. 'And they will get to the bottom of things, especially since we're helping them. We think that the two deaths are linked. It's too much of a coincidence for it to be any other way, so we're leaving the police to investigate the murder they know about whilst we probe deeper into the one that we think flew below the radar.'

'Now your presence here makes more sense.' Emily nodded. 'I'm told that Stella originally comes from around these parts. That seemed like another improbable coincidence to me when I heard. Frank going to the other side of the world to meet a woman from his own back yard, I mean.'

'We're in agreement there,' Alexi said. 'So we're wondering if someone local had a grudge against one or both of them. You and Frank go way back. Can you think of anyone who might fit the bill?'

'About a hundred cuckolded husbands,' Emily replied with a smile. 'But I doubt whether any of them would have waited this long to exact revenge. Or gone to such drastic lengths to achieve it for that matter. A punch on the nose would have put Frank in his place. And anyway, why bump Stella off? She was arrogant, self-obsessed and annoying, and those are just her good characteristics, but they aren't grounds for murder.'

'Fair point,' Alexi conceded.

'Frank went through a stage of being horse-obsessed,' Emily said after a reflective pause. 'Well, it's hard not to when you live in this town. He was never going to be a jockey, or anything like that. He was far too big, not nearly dedicated enough, and liked his food and drink too much to make the sacrifice anyway.'

'I didn't know that about him,' Alexi said. 'Was it another of his phases?'

'Until he discovered serious climbing, it was more of an obsession. My dad ran an eventing yard from here.'

Emily remained in a reflective frame of mind, which was precisely where Jack wanted her to stay. Who knew what gems she might throw into the mix, deliberately or otherwise.

He still wasn't entirely sure that Emily was being straight with them. But then again, if she'd had a hand in Frank's death, why emphasise that she'd never stopped loving him? She wasn't unintelligent and must realise that admission made her appear suspect. She'd waited patiently for Frank to realise which side his bread was buttered, only for him to return to England with a younger, prettier woman as his wife. It was easy to imagine Emily finally running out of patience and taking the ultimate form of revenge. He didn't think she was a climber, but she had sufficient resources to arrange accidents, given enough provocation.

'This was a barn then, believe it or not,' Emily said, referring to her grand living accommodation. 'Dad sold the original house off once he retired along with a lot of the land and moved in here. It had been a struggle to make ends meet and he wanted to end his days without financial restraints. Anyway, I had it extended once I was widowed and moved back to the village. Frank used to come here as a gangly teenager and muck out, groom, do all the heavy lifting in return for rides. He was a good eventer too, but then so was I, which is how we became such good friends. I think he knew that if he befriended me, I'd make sure he got to ride the best horses. Frank was never slow on the uptake in that regard. He was only fourteen but already knew how to flirt, using his charm to get what he wanted.'

'Who did Frank hang out with back then, besides you?' Jack asked.

'I really couldn't say. He always had a lot of friends because he was good company. He never took life too seriously and always seemed to have money in his pocket. Not that it stayed there for long. But still, the girls were drawn to him like flies to you-know-what.'

'Is there anything else you can tell us, Emily?' Alexi asked in a friendly, woman-to-woman manner. 'Anyone you can think of who held such a massive grudge against Frank that they'd plan a complicated murder?'

She shook her head. 'Frank could be exasperating, unreasonable, demanding. He'd drive me crazy with his wild ideas or thoughtless behaviour, but then he'd turn on that smile of his that made me feel as though I was the only female on the planet and all my resentments would fade away. It happened time and time again. He knew precisely what he was doing to me. I knew it too and told myself that I wouldn't fall for it the next time, but I always did.' Her lips formed a moue of distaste. 'Pathetic, or what?'

'Not pathetic at all,' Alexi assured her. 'I'd much prefer to be guided by emotion than cold, hard logic. At least that means you're still capable of genuine feeling. Hold that thought.'

'Thank you.' Emily flashed a genuine smile. 'I'm so glad you understand.'

'Well,' Jack said, pushing his empty cup aside, cautious about the delicate china that probably cost a fortune. 'If you can't think of a way to point us in the right direction, we'll get out of your hair.'

'Have you seriously considered that Stella might have been the actual target all along?' Emily asked. 'After all, it sounds as though no attempt was made to disguise her murder. Perhaps Frank needed to be disposed of so that he didn't get in the killer's way.' She shrugged. 'It's just a thought off the top of my head.'

'And one that we've already considered,' Jack replied, standing. 'Thank you for your time and for helping us.'

'How well did you know Drew when you were growing up?' Alexi asked as she too stood.

'Not that well. He was a good five years younger than me, and five years is more like a generation gap when you're a teenager. But I do know that he and Frank got along well, and that Frank was very protective of his little brother. How Drew felt about being second best in their mother's eyes, I wouldn't care to speculate. Anyway, why do you ask? Is it relevant?'

'I have absolutely no idea,' Alexi replied, 'but I'm a journalist and I've discovered during the course of my career that throwing out wild, unrelated questions can bring surprising results.'

'Drew was always the steady one,' Emily said, 'but I don't suppose I'm telling you something that you don't already know. Just look at how he persevered with the family home, determined to restore it to its former glory. Everyone thought he'd have no choice but to eventually sell up. That's what Frank pushed him to do, sell I mean, but Drew was having none of it, and the results have proven him right.'

'Well, you have a lovely home and thanks for taking the time to chat with us,' Alexi said, impulsively giving Emily a brief hug. 'And I'm really sorry for your loss. I can see that your feelings were engaged, and I don't suppose anyone else has offered you their condolences.'

Emily looked surprised by Alexi's empathy, as evidenced by the tears that flooded her eyes. 'Thank you,' she said softly. 'That means a lot.'

Alexi pushed one of her cards into Emily's hand. 'Give me a call if you think of anything helpful, or even if you just want to chat. I'm always around.'

'Well,' Jack said as they returned to the car. 'The plot thickens.'

'You think she was lying through her teeth too, I take it,' Alexi replied.

'Yep. She was playing us. No doubt about it. She knows more than she was willing to let on. The question is, is she Stella's backer?'

'I wouldn't bet against it,' Alexi said, as Jack paused at the gates, waiting for them to open. 'Which is why I befriended her. If she thinks we don't suspect her then she's more likely to call me, if only to probe into our investigation.'

'Clever girl!'

'I have my moments.'

Jack's phone rang and Mark Vickery's name flashed up on the screen.

'Hey, Mark,' Jack said, using the hands-free button. 'News?'

'Not the sort you're going to want to hear.'

'I don't like the sound of that,' Jack replied, glancing at Alexi, concerned by Mark's sombre tone. 'What is it?'

'A baseball bat was found at the scene of Stella's murder. It's been tested for prints and is covered in Drew's.'

13

Alexi gasped. 'That's simply not possible!' she cried.

'Fingerprints don't lie,' Mark replied.

Jack touched Alexi's knee when she opened her mouth to respond. 'Let's not panic just yet,' he said. 'We all know there could be a dozen different explanations. Someone, possibly Stella but not necessarily, called Drew to Stella's flat for a reason. Someone who knows him well enough to accept that he'd go, even though he didn't like Stella, because she needed his help.'

Alexi nodded. 'Right,' she said. 'Drew would never ignore a desperate plea of that nature, no matter who it came from.'

'I tend to agree with you,' Mark said. 'I wouldn't say this to anyone else, but why would Drew go to the trouble of taking a bat with him to that meeting and then leave it behind, covered in his prints?' Mark's chuckle echoed over the airwaves. 'I know you'll get Ben Avery to have his back and I know that's the first point Ben will make. Especially as there was no sign of Drew's prints anywhere else in the flat. Besides, a man of Drew's size could have bludgeoned Stella to death with that bat and taken it away with him. There was no need for stabbings.'

Alexi breathed an audible sigh of relief.

'Was the actual murder weapon left at the scene?' Jack asked.

Alexi glanced at him, proud that Jack could remain so emotionally detached and think like the policeman he'd once been when her own mind had turned to mulch.

'Nope.'

'Well then, it's a set-up,' Jack replied in a tone of absolute certainty. 'You know it as well as I do, which is why you've told me so much.'

'I wouldn't bet against it, but I have to go through the motions, Jack, and play by the rules. You know that.'

'You'll be interviewing Drew under caution, I take it.'

'I have no choice. Besides, if I don't then any subsequent arrest will be deemed unsafe because I didn't interview Drew. Stella was clouted over the head, presumably with the bat, to render her unconscious before she was stabbed.'

'Okay, we're heading for Hopgood Hall now. We'll tell him the glad tidings and send him down to the station. We'll get Ben to meet him there to have his back.'

'Fair enough. Make it in an hour.'

'One thing, Mark. Did you pick up Drew's car on any cameras?'

'Yeah, we did, and he was where he said he was at the approximate time.'

Alexi let out another long breath.

'Okay,' Vickery said. 'We need to talk face to face. I want to know everything you know, or suspect, so we can get the bastard who did this and save Drew from more angst.' He paused. 'But you didn't hear that from me.'

'Thanks, Mark, I appreciate your going out on a limb for Drew,' Jack replied. 'Come and see us at Hopgood Hall once you've spoken with him. We have plenty of hypotheses right now but might have something more solid for you by then.'

'Did you speak with Nick Fairburn?' Alexi asked.

'Yep. Not me personally but I sent someone I trust, and I'm told he seemed genuinely surprised to hear of Stella's demise.'

'But not unhappy about it,' Jack said.

'She was a massive thorn in his side, so it'd have created suspicion if he pretended to be,' Vickery said. 'And her death wiped out the competition. The Australian's gave him the contract he pitched for because their campaign is time sensitive apparently and they couldn't afford to waste said time casting their net further.'

'Well, there's an alternative suspect for you,' Alexi said. 'He got rid of the woman who tried to wreck his marriage *and* got the contract that will save his company from going under.'

'Believe it or not, we *are* checking his alibi for the time of the murder with a fine-tooth comb. This is not our first rodeo.'

'Just keeping you on your toes, Inspector,' Alexi replied, grinning.

'Got to run,' Vickery said. 'Play nice without me.'

Jack cut the connection and swore profusely. 'This is just what Cheryl and Drew don't need,' he said, stating the obvious. 'Drew won't be arrested, but word will still get out and tongues will wag.'

'I know.' Alexi's chin dropped to her chest. 'Why do these things happen to us? It's almost as though the fates don't want Hopgood Hall to succeed.'

'Don't let it get to you, darling. The murderer made a mistake in killing Stella so clumsily, without forward planning, and hopefully we will be able to coax him or her into further indiscretion.'

'How?'

'By doing what we do best,' Jack replied grinning.

'Which is?' Alexi cocked her head to one side and sent Jack an impatient look. 'Remind me.'

'We get creative.'

Without explaining further, he called Cassie and reeled off Emily Pearson's number. 'See if you can find out who she's been calling over the past couple of months. I especially want to know if she called our murder victim, Frank Hopgood.'

'On it,' Alexi heard Cassie reply. 'What's going on, Jack? What else can I do to help?'

'Are you any nearer to getting into Frank's phone records? And Stella's too? That mystery number that Stella called Drew on needs delving into as well, although it's probably a pay as you go.'

'Sorry, not yet. We had a drama with the Dawlish case. Didn't want to bother you, knowing what you've got going on down there. Danny's on it and he doesn't need me right now, so I'll make all three a priority and get back to you by the end of the day.'

'Thanks.'

'Was that Cassie's way of making you feel guilty for neglecting the day job?' Alexi asked, once Jack had cut the connection.

'She's welcome to try. Dawlish was Danny's case and he's more than capable of handling it. I was simply advising.'

'Okay, so why have you asked Cassie to check Frank and Stella's phone records? Mark will have done that and you know he'll share.'

'Unless he finds a connection to Drew.' Jack took one hand

off the wheel and waved it in a placating manner. 'Not that he's likely to but still, I want to know what Mark does before he decides to share that information with me. Especially if it's bad news for our side.'

'Okay, I get that, but Emily's phone records? You've asked Cassie to break the law.'

Jack grinned. 'Only if she's caught and she won't be. She knows how to cover her tracks. She has previous in that regard. As to why, I think we both know that Emily was holding something back. She was nervous and on edge the entire time we were talking to her, even though she covered it well. Her hands gave her away. She couldn't stop fiddling with things and on the rare occasion when she did, her fingers were trembling.'

'I didn't notice that she had the shakes, but I did catch onto her anxiety. I put it down to grief over Frank's demise. And she *is* grieving, Jack. That's the one thing that seemed entirely genuine.'

'Yeah, but that doesn't mean she didn't kill him. Everyone has their limits.'

'It's funny, don't you think: the last murder victim in Lambourn was a lady's man who played upon his looks and popularity to get what he wanted, until his luck ran out. There are a lot of similarities with this case. Why are so many women prepared to act like doormats? Emily seems like the strong, independent type and yet she was putty in Frank's hands.' Alexi shook her head. 'I just don't get it.'

'*Lurve*,' Jack replied, rolling his eyes. 'Emily had invested a lot of time and money in Frank. He then scarpered, only to return to the UK with a young, very young, and very gorgeous wife in tow. Not only that but he delivered her right to Emily's doorstep, rubbing her nose in it if you like. I think that would be enough to push anyone over the precipice.'

'Yes, I suppose... when you put it like that.'

'I don't believe she didn't contact Frank when she heard he was back. Perhaps they even met. Her phone records will give us a clue but since Mark has no grounds to even speak to her, much less look at her phone, we shall just have to do the leg work for him.'

'I like the way you think, Mr Maddox,' Alexi replied, leaning over to place a kiss on his cheek.

'All part of the service, ma'am.'

'God, how are we going to break this to Cheryl?' Alexi asked aloud, drumming the fingers of one hand restlessly on her thigh.

'Come on.' Jack pulled into the hotel's car park. 'Let's impart the glad tidings to Drew. Hopefully, we'll catch him alone at this time of day and then it will be up to him to tell Cheryl.'

They trooped into Cheryl's kitchen with dog and cat at their heels. As Jack had predicted, Drew was there alone, working through a pile of invoices and punching figures into a spreadsheet on his laptop.

'Hi guys.' He looked up but his welcoming smile quickly faded when he caught their sombre expressions. 'What gives?'

Jack succinctly outlined the nature of the call he'd just taken from Vickery.

'Bloody hell!' Drew seemed confused rather than concerned. 'How did my bat get there?'

'You have a baseball bat?' Alexi asked, resisting the urge to throw her arms around her bear of a friend and offer him sympathy. Jack was remaining professional and so too at that moment was Drew. Either the full implications had not yet occurred to him, or Cheryl's absence meant he didn't have to worry about her finer feelings and could instead attempt to reason the thing through in a rational manner. It wouldn't take long, Alexi suspected, for the full implications to strike home.

'Yeah, but I haven't seen it for a while. I used to keep it by the bed when the house was being renovated and wasn't properly secure. It's lived behind the bar since then. I think, anyway. Not sure why. I guess I thought in the early days it would be a deterrent. You know, wave it about a bit if anyone got lairy.'

'Let's go and check,' Jack said.

Alexi remained where she was, watching Toby and Cosmo jockeying for space in Toby's basket as she gently tugged at Silgo's ears, trying desperately not to worry. Jack would get to the bottom of things, and she would help him with every fibre of her being. If ever her friends needed her support, it was now, and she was damned if she'd let them down. Cheryl couldn't be kept in the dark for long and she was worried what effect this latest setback would have, both on her and the wellbeing of her unborn child.

'It's gone,' Drew said, coming back into the kitchen and scratching his head. 'The bat, that is.'

'Phil behind the bar can't remember the last time he saw it,' Jack added. 'But he does remember seeing it over the past month.'

'Anyone could have slipped behind the bar and taken it,' Alexi said. 'They didn't even need to be looking specifically for it. They just needed to take something with a connection to this place and hope it would implicate Drew.' Alexi crossed her arms and tapped the fingers of one hand restlessly on her opposite forearm. 'And that's what all this is about, I'm now convinced of it. Someone bears a grudge, not just against Frank but you as well, Drew. You need to have a good think and try to decide who that someone might be.'

'I already have, but I've come up blank.'

'Then think harder. I don't want this business to besmirch your good name. You know as well as I do how people like to gossip in this village. Is there some old grievance connected to your parents, perhaps? People do harbour grudges that remain dormant for decades and then something happens to resurrect them. Like Frank swanning back into Lambourn with a trophy wife on his arm.'

'Drew will give it some thought but right now, he needs to get himself down to the station to see Vickery. He's on your side, Drew, but has to go through the motions. I've called Ben Avery and he'll meet you there but do not say anything to anyone, not even Vickery, without Avery there to hold your hand.'

'I hear you.' Drew looked grim, pale and determined. 'I'll just go and impart the glad tidings to Cheryl.'

Alexi wanted to go with him but Jack's hand on her arm held her back.

'Let him do this alone,' he said. 'The time for you to comfort Cheryl will come later, once he's gone.'

Alexi nodded. 'Yeah, I guess.'

Drew reappeared a comparatively short time later with Cheryl and Verity.

'The fun never stops,' Cheryl said, rolling her eyes. 'Someone really has got it in for us, it seems.'

'Cheryl says she recalls seeing the bat behind the bar quite recently.'

'It was early morning, we were stocktaking, and I noticed one of our two cleaners moving it to dust the shelf it sits on beneath the bar,' she said. 'It's been there forever, like a permanent fixture.'

'Okay, that's good,' Jack said. 'Mention that to Ben when you see him before Vickery interviews you. It will help. One more question before you go. Emily mentioned something about Frank starting a climbing school in Wales. Do you recall anything about that?'

'Actually, yes. I remember him getting quite excited about the prospect, just as he always did at the start of any new project. But this was something else. He was bursting with ideas and enthusiasm.'

'Emily payrolled it,' Alexi said. 'She just told us so.'

'I think our mum made a hefty contribution as well,' Drew said, a slight edge to his voice. 'Frank could do no wrong in her eyes.'

'Don't tell Vickery that,' Jack warned, holding up a hand. 'It gives *you* a reason to bear a grudge.'

Drew laughed. 'If I'd wanted to kill Frank because he was the favoured son, I'd have done it years ago. Besides, I was our dad's blue-eyed boy and he left me a legacy in his will. He didn't do the same for Frank, perhaps because he could see him for the chancer that he was and knew it would slip through his fingers. Mum was just evening up the score.'

'Can you remember where in Wales the school was to be?' Alexi asked.

Drew shook his head. 'No idea, but I do know he had a partner. Don't know his name either, so don't bother to ask, but I think they registered their enterprise at Companies House.'

'That gives us a starting point,' Jack said. 'Thanks.'

'Not sure how. It was years ago. Anyway, I'm off to face the inquisition,' Drew said, kissing the top of Cheryl's head, and then Verity's. 'If I'm not back soon, send Cosmo round.'

His attempts at a joke fell flat and Alexi noticed his shoulders slump even before the kitchen door closed behind him.

'Try not to worry,' Alexi said, smiling at Cheryl even as she realised how hollow her words must sound.

'I'm not, not really. I just want to know who's doing this to us. And why. God, I could do with a drink! What a time to be pregnant and on the wagon.'

'Emily mentioned that Frank was a keen equestrian back in the day,' Jack remarked.

'He was, actually. I'd forgotten about that. It was before I knew Drew, but he's talked about Frank's talent in that regard. He said horses and Emily had a steadying influence on him. He said as well that it was a shame he gave it up for climbing, but that's Frank for you. He never stuck to anything for long, other than climbing, that is.'

'Have a good think, trawl through your memory banks, and see if you can come up with something that might help us. Anything. It doesn't matter how off the wall,' Alexi said.

'Okay, I'll try.' Cheryl straightened her shoulders as she watched Verity tottering about the kitchen, watched by two dogs and an indifferent cat. 'What are you going to do?'

'Well, we were going to talk to Angus Daventree, the person Drew said was once tight with Frank. He hung up on us the first time we spoke and I had to call back and twist his arm to make him agree to see us,' Jack said. 'In view of subsequent events though, I feel we should stay here with you until Drew gets back.'

'You're sure Drew won't be arrested, Jack, or charged with anything?'

'Absolutely, at this point in time,' Jack replied without

hesitation. 'As things stand, it's the clumsiest set up in the history of set ups but Vickery has to do things publicly by the book. Besides, even if it can be proven that Drew took a base-ball bat to meet his sister-in-law for some obscure reason, Vickery has picked Drew's car up on camera so there's abso-lutely no possibility of Drew having had the time to subdue and kill Stella and then call it in. The time frame is simply too tight.'

Cheryl let out an audible sigh of relief. 'Well then, in that case, take yourselves off to see Daventree. He's a funny chap, a bit eccentric really, who won't take kindly to your not keeping your appointment and probably won't give you another chance. You're more use to me trying to find out who did this. I really don't need my hand held. I have plenty to keep me occupied here, as well as Verity to look out for. Susie's called in sick again,' she added, rolling her eyes. 'Anyway, I also need a bit of space to think about buried vendettas.'

'If you're sure.' Alexi squeezed Cheryl's hand.

'Totally.' She snatched her hand free and made shooing motions. 'Just go!'

'Okay,' Alexi said, 'but if you need us for any reason, our phones are always on.'

14

Jack, again depending on his sat nav for directions, drove quickly to Daventree's address.

'Phew!' Alexi let out a low whistle when a massive house came into view. 'How the other half live.'

'It's not uncommon around these parts.'

'What do we know about Daventree?' Alexi asked, peering at a sign on the gateposts that advertised health, wellness, spirituality and detoxification, amongst other apparent benefits that she didn't understand and had no idea she needed. 'I've driven past this place and seen it advertised but I have no idea what he strives to achieve.'

'Inner peace and relaxation, I guess.'

'Ha! Good luck with that one in this day and age. I could certainly do with a little de-stressing at this point though. I'm really feeling the heat that's being put on Drew. I know you're convinced he won't be arrested, at least not yet, but what if he is? If Vickery's lords and masters insist upon it, Mark will have to do what they want.'

'Try not to worry about what hasn't happened,' Jack said quietly.

'Yeah, I know. Stay focused. I just had a wobble but I'm fine now.'

'Cheryl told us just now that Daventree's eccentric, and judging by what I've seen so far,' Jack said, nodding towards a cluster of people wearing towelling gowns gathered on the lawn, despite the fact that there was a howling wind and persistent drizzle. Jack lowered his window and the sound of chanting greeted them. 'I think she got the eccentric bit right. It's hard to imagine him and Frank being tight, but then again, that was a while ago. Presumably, Daventree has found his true vocation in the interim.'

'Now, now, Mr Maddox, sarcasm doesn't become you.'

Jack grinned and blew her a kiss. 'But you know I'm right.'

'Well yeah, these people probably pay an arm and a leg for the privilege of freezing to death, so perhaps you are,' Alexi conceded. 'Doesn't sound too relaxing to me. Why open up his house like this, I wonder. It looks to be well maintained, so I don't suppose he needs the dosh.'

'Let's ask the man himself and find out,' Jack said, parking up in a gravelled courtyard already full of high-end cars.

'Good job we left Cosmo and Silgo with Cheryl. I don't think they would have been welcome here,' Alexi remarked. 'There's such a thing as lowering the tone.'

'Don't let Cosmo hear you say that.'

A slim female wearing a white uniform – the entire place appeared to be obsessed with white, from what little Alexi had seen of it – stepped forward when they walked into the reception hall, offering them a wide smile.

'Peace,' she said, offering them a half bow.

'Er, quite.'

'Are you here to register for the course?' she asked. 'You're a little late but just in time. Time has no concept here, you see.'

Alexi didn't bother to point out that she'd defeated her own argument.

'We're here to see Mr Daventree,' Jack told her. 'The name's Maddox. We have an appointment for... well, I guess it doesn't matter what time it was for, given that time has no meaning here.'

The girl's smile faded. 'Take a seat. I'll tell our guru that you're here.'

'Guru?' Alexi whispered, stifling a giggle as they retreated to a seating area that looked decidedly uncomfortable. The chairs appeared to have no legs and sat awkwardly on the ground, rather like inflated beanbags. They both decided to remain standing. Several more people clad in white robes wandered into view and were directed by the receptionist to some sort of assembly point.

'Why is it so quiet in here?' Alexi asked, feeling the need to whisper. 'It's like being in church.'

'Put your phone on silent,' Jack said, pointing to a sign of a phone with a red cross slashed through it. 'Modern technology is clearly unwelcome and I don't have any intention of being parted from mine.'

The last of the robed believers wandered out of view, leaving just a tall, thin man with a neatly trimmed beard standing in the centre of the reception hall, sending Alexi and Jack a shrewd look. He too wore white. White jogging trousers, a white shirt, a white band holding back thinning grey hair that was too long. His feet were bare and Alexi, repulsed, noticed that his toenails could do with a trim.

'Mr Maddox, Ms Ellis, this is indeed a pleasure.' Angus

Daventree stood before them but instead of offering his hand, he inclined his head in an old-fashioned bow. 'It is a pleasure to meet you both. Your reputations precede you. I am a great admirer of your journalistic acumen, Ms Ellis.'

'Thank you, Mr Daventree,' she replied, resisting the urge to offer him a responding bow.

'Just Daventree, please. We don't deal in titles in this place.'

'Very well,' Jack said. 'Is there somewhere we can talk in private? I don't suppose you want your clientele to hear us discussing murder. It will mess with their chakras.'

A brief frown troubled Daventree's wrinkle-free brow, almost as though he couldn't decide whether or not Jack was mocking his set-up. Alexi knew that he was. It was unlike Jack to be so aggressive. He was a firm believer in each to their own. Presumably, he'd decided that his sarcasm would shake Daventree out of his almost trancelike state. Time would tell.

'Come this way.'

Daventree's bare feet appeared to glide across the marble floor. He opened a door which led to a pristine office. The walls were white, as was the deep-pile carpet. Alexi felt tempted to remove her shoes but since Daventree hadn't asked them to, nor surprisingly had he asked them to turn off their phones, she kept her footwear in place and her phone on vibrate, just in case Cheryl needed them. There were more low seats that Daventree gestured them towards.

'Thanks, but I'll stand if it's all the same to you,' Jack said easily. 'Getting into one of those will likely bugger my back.'

'You really need to let all that suppressed tension out, then your body won't let you down,' Daventree replied.

Alexi knew that Jack could easily occupy one of the chairs without damaging his spine, but it looked as though Daventree intended to remain standing. He certainly hadn't shown an inclination to occupy the regular chair behind his white desk. A desk that was totally empty. No phone, no computer, no papers. Nada. Jack, Alexi knew, would not want to put himself at a disadvantage by having to look up at the man. Alexi didn't intend to do so either and instead perched her backside against the window ledge.

'You wanted to talk to me about Frank Hopgood but also mentioned murder in a crude attempt to manipulate me,' Daventree said in an irritatingly calm, almost nasal whine. 'You will not succeed, of course. Better men than you have tried to break through my spiritual calm and failed miserably.' When neither Jack nor Alexi showed any reaction, Daventree seemed momentarily confused. Very momentarily. 'Now then, what's all this talk of murder?'

'Drew is plagued by the manner in which his brother died,' Jack replied. 'And our initial enquiries have led us to believe that it was not the straightforward accident it was deemed to be.'

'I have no doubt. Frank was an accomplished climber, but accidents do happen when people become distracted by the pace of modern-day life and neglect their body's foundation. That is what we concentrate on here and why our courses are always fully booked. However, I kept myself informed when I heard of Frank's death, and it seems there was no question of murder.'

'Tell us about your friendship with Frank,' Alexi said, offering Daventree a smile that it was a problem for her to summon up for such a pompous individual. 'I understand you and he were once close friends.'

'In a previous life,' Daventree replied. 'We evolved in different directions and had nothing in common by the time we parted ways. Frank was as scathing as you appear to be, Mr Maddox, about what I intended to do with this property when the inheritance came my way.'

'You argued?' Alexi asked.

'I rose above his pettiness.' Daventree sighed when neither Jack or Alexi responded and as Alexi knew would be the case, he felt compelled to fill the ensuing silence. To overexplain. 'I will admit that before I saw the light and realised what I was supposed to do with my life, I ran as wild as Frank. We enjoyed female company, and it was never in short supply.'

Alexi nodded, well able to believe it. For all his pomposity, Daventree was still a reasonably good-looking man and had probably been even more so in his younger years. Alexi cynically supposed that he could still have his pick from the female clients who registered for his courses and very likely took advantage of that fact.

'I saw the error of my ways and was no longer comfortable with that lifestyle. The only way to put it behind me was to sever all connection with Frank. He was a disruptive influence, and I was easily led by him. Far too easily, I will admit that much. We all have to grow up at some point.'

'How long ago did you go your separate ways?' Jack asked.

'Oh, twenty years or thereabouts.' Daventree waved a long-fingered hand elegantly. 'I can't recall precisely. It was, as I say, a previous life that I don't care to look back upon. I am sorry that he's left this world but am confident that he's passed to the next, where he will enjoy the opportunity to reflect upon the error of his ways.'

Alexi didn't know how she refrained from telling the man not to be so damned pretentious.

'I'm told that your parting from Frank was the result of a violent quarrel,' Jack remarked.

Once again, Alexi's acting skills, such as they were, were called upon. It was the first she'd heard of a violent dispute, and she knew that Jack had made the remark instinctively. He had seen beneath the man's arrogance and was doing his level best to rouse him to anger.

'Who told you that?' he asked, raising a brow disdainfully.

'I'm told you were the aggressor.'

'We had a disagreement, certainly, but that was twenty years ago. I fail to see how that can be relevant now.'

'Even so,' Alexi said, using an almost subservient tone that she knew would make it difficult for Jack not to laugh. 'As a man dedicated to inner peace, spare a thought for Drew's turmoil and help us out here. We're convinced that Frank was murdered and that the person responsible got away with his or her crime. Drew won't achieve the inner peace that's so important to us all if he can't get to the truth.'

'My dispute with Frank has no bearing on his ultimate demise, but since you insist upon knowing then I will tell you.' Daventree then allowed a long pause, clearly in no particular hurry to unburden himself.

Once again, Jack and Alexi remained silent, content to allow the pregnant pause to continue for as long as Daventree felt the need to hide behind it, gathering his thoughts and obviously deciding how much to reveal.

'It was over a young lady. She and I had been seeing one another for several weeks. It was unusual for either of us to remain with just one member of the opposite sex, I'm ashamed to say, but Judith... well, there was just something about her, something spiritual I have subsequently thought, that resonated with me. I was already tiring of the chase by then. We were both in our mid-twenties and I liked the idea of settling with Judith. This place was just a pipedream at the time. I wasn't serious about it, but I think on a vicarial level, I imagined myself running it with Judith.'

'Frank took her from you,' Alexi said into the ensuing silence.

'He did, simply because he could. He knew how I felt about her. I'd made the mistake of confiding in him, and he didn't like the idea of me settling down and the two of us no longer hunting as a pack, to use a vulgar vernacular. He said he did me a favour by demonstrating her flighty nature.'

'That must have hurt,' Alexi said, her voice loaded with sympathy that she didn't really feel for a man she'd taken an active dislike to, and whom she wouldn't trust an inch.

'It was a long time ago.' Another flap of that long hand in dismissal of Alexi's compassion. 'Of course, we were just as flighty as Frank accused Judith of being. She told me nothing had happened between them, but she missed the point. She'd gone on a date with him and neither of them had told me about it beforehand, which made them seem duplicitous and so was impossible for me to forgive. I found out purely by accident and the trust was gone. That was it. Frank and I were reduced to a physical brawl, I'm ashamed to say, but in a way, he did me a favour because not long after that, my grandfather died, I inherited this place and my life changed for the better.' He stood a little straighter. 'I am no longer the person who brawls in the street, or who disrespects women.'

'What happened to Judith?' Alexi asked. 'Do you ever hear from her?'

'I have absolutely no idea. I haven't seen her from that day to this.'

Perhaps not, Alexi thought, *but you certainly haven't stopped thinking about her.*

'What was her surname?' Jack asked.

'Judith Farlow,' he replied without hesitation, further proof if any was necessary that he'd never recovered from what he looked upon as her deception. 'But now, if there's nothing else...'

'You didn't hear from Frank when he returned to the UK, I'm assuming,' Jack said.

'No I did not, nor would I have expected to.'

'But you knew he was back?' Jack persevered.

'Despite this being a retreat, local gossip still gets through.' He sighed. 'Yes, I heard he was back, with a wife in tow. I was unsurprised to hear that she was half his age. Some people never change.'

All things considered, Alexi preferred the sound of fun-loving Frank to this sanctimonious creature. 'You will be surprised though, I imagine,' she said, 'to learn that Frank's wife was violently murdered yesterday.'

For the first time, Daventree's reaction appeared genuine. 'Yes, that does surprise me and also explains, I suppose, why you've come to me asking questions. What help you think I can give you however is another matter entirely. I never laid eyes on Frank's wife and had no reason to bear her ill will, if that's what you suppose.'

'You must now see why Drew's suspicions have been aroused,' Jack said. 'We're wondering, you see, if the murderer bore a grudge against his family and Stella somehow got caught in the crossfire.'

'Which is why you've revisited the cause of Frank's death.' Daventree nodded. 'I can indeed see that but still fail to understand how I can be of any help. I have told you everything of relevance that happened between Frank and myself. I'm sorry he's dead, and sorry too that his young wife met the same fate, but there's not much else I can add, I'm afraid.'

'Just one last question and we'll leave you to your clients,' Jack said. 'We gather that Emily Pearson and Frank were tight for a long time. Did you know Emily?'

'Oh yes.' A feint smile touched Daventree's thin lips. 'She was quite a girl in her younger years and had a definite thing for Frank. He played upon it, of course, and led her a merry dance. I gather they coinhabited for a while.'

Coinhabited? Who used that sort of language nowadays? Alexi wondered.

'Do you yourself keep in touch with Emily?' she asked.

'Whyever would I?' Daventree's eyes darted to the left. He huffed impatiently and Alexi got the impression that he would have consulted his watch, had he been wearing one. 'But now, you really must excuse me.'

'Thank you for your time,' Jack said. 'Sorry to have held you up.'

15

'Everyone in this case appears to be carrying a torch for someone unattainable,' Jack remarked as they returned to his car. 'Stella for Nick, Emily for Frank and now Daventree for Judith.'

'We all crave what we can't have. It's human nature.'

Jack shrugged. 'True.'

'What did you make of Daventree, leaving aside the fact that he's a pompous prat who wouldn't recognise the truth if it jumped up and bit him on the backside?'

Jack smiled. 'And leaving aside the fact that he was lying through his teeth.'

'Yeah, that too.'

'I don't think he's nearly as detached from the world as he wanted us to think,' Jack remarked. 'There was no modern-day technology on show in his office, but did you notice the computer cable tucked on the back of the shelf that he spent most of the time standing in front of, trying to hide it from view? Someone will get it in the neck for not putting it away.'

'Can't say that I did. I did pick up on the fact that he's still hung up on Judith though and I don't believe for a minute that he's lost touch with her. He knows where she is and what she's doing. My guess is that she ditched the guy and that demonstrates a lot of good sense in my book.'

'Agreed.'

Jack used the gravel circle in front of the house to turn his car back towards the gates, quelling the desire to do it at speed and send gravel shooting all over the flower borders. 'What I'd love to know is whether he's in touch with Emily as well. There was something in his reaction when we mentioned her name that got me wondering.'

'You think something happened twenty years ago that involved him, Frank and Emily? And perhaps Judith too. Something that fractured their friendship that had nothing to do with a fight over Judith.'

'It's probable. It sounds as though Frank and Daventree were tight. Free spirits ready to conquer the world, and any females who happened to catch their collective eye. Daventree admitted as much, which given the clean cut, spiritual image he's now attempting to project, implies that his reputation is akin to Frank's, and easy to corroborate.'

'We need to ask Drew to trawl his memory banks then,' Alexi replied, jutting her chin in a starkly determined manner. 'We've already asked him to think about potential grudges but now we have a direction to point him in. Apart from anything else, it will take his mind off police interviews and the discovery of dead bodies.'

'Hopefully, he'll be back from the nick by the time we reach Hopgood Hall.'

'You'll get Cassie looking for Judith Farlow?'

'Of course.'

Jack pulled Cassie's number up on the in-car display and

did precisely that. 'See if you can find a mobile number for her,' he added, once he'd given Cassie Judith's name, 'and cross check to see if she called Frank or Emily. Oh, and this is a longshot, but see what you can find on Angus Daventree. He runs a spiritual retreat centre in a big house outside Lambourn.'

'On it.' Cassie's voice echoed through the car's speaker system.

'I get the feeling that we've found our link,' Alexi said after Jack had cut the connection. 'Daventree, Emily and Frank go back a long way and I sense unresolved issues.'

'Possibly.' Jack fell momentarily silent. 'I think, even though I have nothing to back it up and I'm running on pure instinct in saying this, that Frank was forced to leave the country for reasons I have yet to fathom. His coming back was not supposed to happen, which is why he was killed.'

'Possibly. But what could he have done that required a self-imposed banishment?' Alexi shook her head. 'What did Frank do that was so terrible? If he committed a crime, was he given the choice of facing the music or scarpering? Did someone pressurise him to go or did he take himself off and allow time for the heat to die down?'

'We'll ask Drew if he can shed any light,' Jack replied, pulling his car into Hopgood Hall's car park.

They entered the kitchen to find it devoid of human presence. Two dogs were however delighted to see them. Even Cosmo deigned to twitch his tail and submit to having his ears rubbed. They had barely finished greeting the animals when Cheryl bustled into the room.

'Verity's sleeping,' she said. 'Finally. She senses the tension, I think, and has been grizzling non-stop. She's worn herself out.' Cheryl plopped herself down onto the nearest chair. 'And me too. What a day for Susie to go sick.'

'How are you holding up?' Alexi asked, sitting beside Cheryl and giving her a hug.

'By keeping busy. Well, Verity leaves me no choice in that regard but for once, I'm not complaining. Drew called about half an hour ago. He's on his way back. Should be here at any moment.'

'We've found out a few things but if Drew's almost here then we'll hang on and tell you both together.'

Jack busied himself making fresh coffee. He produced a plateful of Cheryl's famous biscuits but no one had much of an appetite and they remained untouched. Time hung heavily on their hands. Alexi made upbeat small talk, but Jack could see that it wasn't really distracting her from her worries. He felt great sympathy for Cheryl. If any sort of shadow hung over Alexi's activities, no matter how improbable, he'd be beside himself too.

'Ah!' Cheryl cocked her head to one side. 'That sounds like Drew's car now.'

The moment Drew walked through the door with Ben Avery, Cheryl stood and threw herself into his arms.

'Did they use thumbscrews?' she asked, clinging to her husband.

Drew smiled as he gave her a hug, the gesture hampered by her baby bump. 'Only the whiplash, darling.'

'Sit down, Ben,' Jack said, shaking the solicitor's hand, 'and tell us how it went.'

'Alexi and Jack have news for us,' Cheryl said, almost bouncing on her chair like Verity on a sugar rush.

'Speculation, more like. You go first, Ben.'

'Okay, well, it was pretty much as you warned me to

expect. Vickery went through the motions, but it was a soft interview. A box-ticking exercise. Drew explained about the bat, where it was kept and what have you, and that anyone could have slipped behind the bar and helped themselves. Be that as it may, I won't pretend this isn't serious. Unless we can come up with a viable alternative suspect, or preferably the actual murderer, and a confession would be nice in that respect, then Drew's name will remain firmly in the frame. The CPS can build a strong circumstantial case against him.'

Drew squeezed Cheryl's hand when she gasped. 'It's okay,' he said, probably well aware that it wasn't. The platitude sounded hollow. Unconvincing.

Jack knew that Drew had motive and, at a pinch, opportunity.

'Cheer me up, Jack,' Drew said. 'What have you found out?'

Jack and Alexi between them recounted the essence of their interview with Daventree.

'He always was a queer fish, even as a kid,' Drew said. 'He and Frank really were joined at the hip during their teens and early twenties and created a storm wherever they went. As to this spiritual business...' He spread his hands. 'I didn't see that one coming but can imagine him reinventing himself and conning people. I seem to recall that Daventree inherited a house with similar problems to ours but was determined to hang onto his home by whatever means necessary. I remember him using those exact words. Seems he found a way, a bit like us.'

'The place looks as though it's been totally refurbished now,' Alexi said. 'And it wasn't done on the cheap.'

'Well, there you are then. There's obviously a thriving market for stressed individuals searching for inner peace, or whatever,' Drew said. 'Daventree was always quick on the uptake and has obviously identified a gap in the market in this neck of the woods. He has great charisma and always been a hit with the ladies. He and Frank were never without a date.'

'Yeah, about that,' Jack said. 'What can you tell us about Judith Farlow, the lady who supposedly drove a wedge between them?'

Drew scraped his hands down his face and gave the matter some thought. Everyone else in the kitchen waited him out in silence. Even the animals became motionless, as though they too realised that it was a defining moment.

'I'm sorry, the name rings a vague bell, but honestly, I lost track of Frank's women. None of them lasted for long. I can't conjure up an image of Judith, but I do recall him mentioning her name, now that you've jogged my memory.' He shook his head. 'Sorry, but I can't tell you any more than that.'

'No worries,' Jack replied easily. 'I have Cassie trying to find her. She won't be able to hide from Cassie, unless she's changed her name, or died.'

'I find it really hard to believe that Frank and Daventree fell out over a woman,' Drew said. 'They simply weren't the monogamous types. She must have been quite something, this Judith. But even if she did come between them, it was a long time ago. No one died so why would Daventree, Judith, Emily, or anyone else who was around at the time still bear a grudge strong enough to justify murder?'

'That's what we're attempting to establish,' Jack said. 'I know it sounds unlikely. This could have nothing to do with Frank, and Stella could have been the actual target all along. We're exploring all avenues.'

'Daventree made no secret of the fact that he'd fallen hard for Judith,' Alexi added, 'and still clearly carries a torch for her. He thinks Frank got worried that he'd settle down and that he'd lose his sparring partner, so he deliberately hit on her and made sure that Daventree found out about it.'

'That sounds mean,' Cheryl said.

'But not something I'd put past my brother,' Drew added with a sigh. 'He really did like the world to do his bidding.'

'We're working on another outlandish assumption,' Jack said, 'in that Frank left the country against his will, for some reason. He agreed to do so in penance for some crime or other and his coming back is what got him killed.'

'And got Stella killed too?' Ben asked with a cynical flex of one brow, making his first contribution to a conversation he'd been following avidly.

'We're working on that part.' Jack stood up and leaned against the work surface. 'Can you think of anything cataclysmic that arose just before Frank went off to Australia? That's only a few years ago. Did anyone from his past show their face? Was he worried about anything?'

Drew and Cheryl shared a prolonged look.

'He was living here off and on,' Cheryl said. 'But don't ask me where he lived when he wasn't here because he never said, and we never asked. There was a lot of tension because he was pushing us hard to sell the house, but Drew was having none of it. Things were said in the heat of the moment that I think they both later regretted.'

'I got the impression that he was more than usually strapped for cash,' Drew added in a reflective tone. 'He seemed very stressed and said he was being pressed.'

'Could he have run off when he got his inheritance in order to avoid paying debts?' Cheryl asked.

'It's one possibility,' Jack replied, 'and something we'll look into. But debtors don't usually get bumped off because that way, the debt will never be repaid.'

'Perhaps he borrowed against his inheritance in order to finance one of his latest schemes,' Drew suggested. 'Frank was always in a hurry. Patience was not one of his strong points.'

'Now that's another avenue to explore,' Jack said, 'but if he did borrow, I'm not sure where to start looking.'

'Presumably, Vickery can get access to his bank records,' Alexi suggested.

Jack snapped his fingers. 'Of course he can now that Stella's been murdered. It gives him a legitimate reason to resurrect a case that's been supposedly resolved. I'll mention it to him.'

'We have Daventree still lusting after Judith and Emily feeling the same way about Frank,' Alexi said. 'All this unrequited love is giving me a headache.' She paused, her effort at light relief appearing to have little effect upon Drew and Cheryl. 'I suppose we could ask Emily about Judith but since we're not convinced that she didn't have something to do with Frank's death, or Stella's either for that matter, I don't suppose we'll get an honest answer. All asking her will achieve is to show our hand for no good reason.'

'You're thinking that Emily was Stella's secret backer?' Ben asked, looking up from nibbling at his third biscuit.

'Either her or Daventree. One of them had a compelling reason that we haven't yet uncovered to get rid of Frank,' Jack replied, 'which is possibly why he took himself to the other side of the world.'

'And then came back again?' Ben's expression didn't change but heavy sarcasm underscored his words.

'Stella wanted to come back,' Alexi reminded them all. 'She had to be here to pitch for that contract and we know that what she wanted, she got. Perhaps Frank was depending upon her winning so that he'd be flush with cash again and could buy himself out of debt, or trouble, or at the very least, buy himself some time.'

Jack could see that Drew and Cheryl remained to be convinced. Ben's expression gave little away about his thought process, but Jack knew he'd seen it all in his time and that it would be hard to surprise him.

'Cheer up, Drew.' Jack slapped his friend's shoulder. 'No charges will be brought against you. Don't forget you were picked up on camera going into Newbury. You'd have to be superhuman to have committed the murder, and then called emergency services within the few minutes available to you. Vickery will have had someone timing it. You can count on that much.'

'You're missing the point,' Drew replied, addressing his comment to the table's surface. 'Unless my name's cleared, which means finding the guilty party, then people will believe it was me, especially when my reasons for wanting rid of Stella find their way into the public domain, which I dare say they will. Some zealous reporter will root them out, make connections to all the murders that have happened around us and go for the sensational. No offence, Alexi.'

'None taken, and you're right. I know you'll find no peace until your good name is cleared, which is why you're so lucky to have Jack and me fighting your corner.'

'Yeah, but it's all so speculative.' Drew let out a long breath. 'All these what-ifs and digging up the past. We don't even know if the murderer was after Frank or Stella.'

'I still think Stella killed Frank because he'd started asking questions about her business. Who was backing her and what had happened to his dosh? Stuff like that,' Cheryl said. 'And since he appeared to have run out of funds, the last thing she needed was a jealous spouse clipping her wings or claiming a share of her profits. He'd served his purpose and was expendable, from her perspective.'

Ben nodded. 'Makes sense. But whoever backed her didn't want the spotlight focused on her so when you started asking questions, Jack, it sealed Stella's fate.'

'Okay, so...' Jack paused when his phone rang. 'It's Cassie,' he said checking the screen and putting the call on speaker. 'Hey, Cass, what you got for me?'

'I'm working on those phone records, but I thought you'd like to know that I've found a Judith Farlow, who's about the same age as the lady you're looking for.'

'Quick work,' Jack replied, sending a nod of approval to the others in the room. 'Where does she live?'

'Portsmouth. Word to the wise though, Jack. I found her through the electoral register. There's a load of people with that name or close variations of it and it might well not be the same person. The reason I think it is, and here's the clincher, is that I found a landline for her and guess who's called it several times of late?'

The tension in the room felt palpable. Everyone in it appeared to hold their breath, realising that they'd finally caught a break. Even Silgo stopped panting and Cosmo sat up, skewering Jack's phone with a penetrating look.

'Emily Pearson,' Alexi said, punching the air. 'I knew it!'

'Right.'

'Thanks, Cass. Keep on those phone records for me, please, and let me have Judith's address.'

Cassie reeled it off and Alexi jotted it down.

'I guess we're taking a trip to Portsmouth,' she said, when Jack cut the call.

16

Alexi felt rejuvenated as she almost skipped down the hall and out into the car park. Silgo thought it was a game and jumped around her. Cosmo maintained his feline dignity and trailed well behind. Jack smiled at her enthusiasm. Alexi could sense that he too was on a high. They were both well aware that they'd got their first positive lead in the case.

Jack opened the back door of his car for the animals as Alexi slid into the passenger seat.

'I have to say, Cassie's good at what she does. Credit where credit's due.' Alexi programmed Judith's address into the car's sat nav. 'I may not like her much, but I was right to tell you to keep her on.'

'You were, but things will never be the same way between us again. Not after the way she tried to break us up.'

'For reasons that escape me, she seems to think you're worth fighting for,' Alexi said, biting her lip to prevent herself from smiling.

'Yeah, that one's got me stumped too.'

Alexi released the smile that seemed determined to make

its presence felt, relaxing in what felt like the first time in days as Jack drove them swiftly towards a village about five miles outside of Portsmouth. They hoped to find Judith Farlow at home and willing to speak with them. Alexi knew that Jack would prefer to take that chance, rather than phoning ahead and giving her advance warning. Or worse, having her refuse to see them.

'It's pretty here,' Alexi said, as Jack slowed to drive the narrow country lanes. 'Hard to imagine that it's so close to a big city.'

'I dare say the property prices reflect that fact,' Jack replied, obeying the instructions from his sat-nav and turning left, then almost immediately right. They had reached the centre of a village that sported a few upmarket shops, a small supermarket and a chemist. There was a village green that was occupied only by a couple of dog walkers on a chilly autumnal afternoon and a very old church that must have some sort of function going on, given the cluster of cars parked around it. The sound of singing drifted through the car's partially opened window, confirming Alexi's suspicion.

'Very middle-England,' she remarked.

Jack nodded. 'Judith must be doing okay for herself.'

'This can't be it,' Alexi said, when the sat nav told Jack he'd reached his destination. He pulled up outside a bungalow with a small van parked in the driveway, a disabled sticker clearly displayed in the back window. There was a ramp for a wheelchair leading to the front door. 'If it is the right place then she must be disabled,' she added, stating the obvious.

'Looks that way.'

Jack got out of the car and let the cat and dog out too. Alexi knew they wouldn't roam far and if not invited in, would sit patiently outside the front door. But quite often, taking them along broke down barriers. Most people were curious about Cosmo. A lot more had heard of him following the various Lambourn murders and the part the intuitive cat had played in solving them. He had his own Instagram page with more followers than Alexi herself had, which said all there was to say about his popularity.

Silgo lifted his leg against the gatepost and then trotted along beside Alexi, tail wagging, as always. He paused to sniff at a clump of bushes but rejoined them when Jack whistled to him.

'Here goes nothing,' Jack said, glancing at Alexi as he rang the bell.

The door was opened almost immediately by an older lady in a wheelchair. A lady with thick, brown hair that fell past her shoulders and a pretty face that was immaculately made-up. Her clothing looked new and expensive and there were no outward signs of her disability, if one discounted the expensive electric wheelchair she occupied.

'Ah, you must be Maddox and Ellis.'

Jack raised a brow, the only expression of surprise that he would likely allow himself. Alexi wasn't too shocked that their arrival had been anticipated, aware that Emily had been in recent contact with her.

'I thought you'd track me down. Come along in. Bring the menagerie. All visitors welcome.'

So saying she expertly turned her wheelchair and propelled herself down a wide hallway that led to a full width lounge at the back of the bungalow. Alexi shared a *what-the-hell* glance with Jack and followed along behind Judith, holding Silgo by his collar to prevent him from introducing himself to Judith at that precise moment. Jack closed the front door and brought up the rear.

Judith watched Alexi and Jack taking in their surroundings: everything fitted out for a person living with a crippling disability that allowed her to, presumably, live alone. There were no signs that anyone shared her space but then again, perhaps Judith was the neat and tidy type.

'Not quite what you expected,' she remarked, her mouth lifting up on one side into a cynical smile.

'We didn't know what to expect, truth to tell,' Alexi replied, seating herself when Judith indicated a couch.

'When people say, "truth to tell", in my experience, they're usually lying through their teeth.' Judith's light-hearted tone took the sting out of the words.

'I tend to agree, but for the fact that on this occasion, I was being truthful. We only learned of your existence today and certainly weren't aware that you're disabled.'

Alexi's mention of her disability clearly surprised Judith. Alexi assumed that most people avoided any direct comment in that regard. 'I know. That you've only just heard about me, that is.'

'Someone obviously called to warn you that we'd track you down,' Jack said. 'Can't help wondering why you needed warning.'

'You're here to ask about Frank, I gather,' Judith replied, avoiding a direct answer to Jack's question.

'When did you last see him?' Alexi asked.

'Twenty years ago.'

Jack simply looked at her. Alexi did the same and allowed the silence to work in their favour. Judith had been warned to expect them so would have had time to decide what, if anything, she intended to say to them. The fact that she'd let them into her house implied a willingness to talk. Whether she'd be candid or attempt to mislead them, Alexi had yet to decide.

Judith watched Cosmo as he found a patch of wooden floor that reflected weak sunshine and settled down, his gaze never wavering far from her. He hadn't reacted adversely to her, which meant that Alexi would give Judith the benefit of the doubt. For now at least. Cosmo was an expert judge of character, and she and Jack had come to rely on his instincts, which was undoubtedly why Jack had let him tag along. Silgo, on the other hand, had settled down at Alexi's feet, panting and still wagging his tail. Judith watched him from her wheel-chair, her expression softening. She clearly liked animals, which was a point in her favour from Alexi's perspective.

'There was an accident.' Judith's voice broke through Alexi's introspective thoughts. 'I fell and damaged my lower spine and... well, here I am.'

'An accident?' Jack quirked a brow, not wasting time with sympathy which Alexi sensed wasn't required and wouldn't be appreciated. 'What happened?'

'Why do you want to know?'

'Because we're trying to find out why both Frank and Stella have been murdered,' Jack replied, his voice firm and unrelenting. Alexi knew that he wouldn't treat her any differently to anyone else, simply because she was physically disabled. Her accident was connected in some way to Frank and Daventree and very pertinent to their investigation. If that wasn't the case then Daventree or Emily wouldn't have bothered to warn Judith to expect them.

'Murdered?' Judith narrowed her eyes. 'But Frank died in a climbing accident. I heard about it.'

'Possibly, but we had our suspicions even before Stella was

murdered,' Alexi said. 'We're now absolutely convinced that it was no accident.'

'Well, don't look at me.'

'What we need to understand is why Frank took himself off to Australia and how he just happened to meet the woman he married out there. A woman who hailed from the same part of England as him. What are the chances?'

'Coincidences happen.'

'Not when murder's involved,' Jack shot back at her. 'In that situation, there's no such thing as a coincidence.'

'I'll have to take your word for that.'

Alexi could see that the possibility of Frank being murdered hadn't previously occurred to Judith and for the first time, she lost a little of her poise.

'Emily didn't mention our suspicions?' Alexi asked.

'People think that because I'm disabled physically, I must also be mentally deficient, which is emphatically not the case. They're very protective of my finer feelings.'

'That must be irritating, people tiptoeing around you, I mean,' Alexi said.

'You have *no* idea.' Judith rolled her eyes. 'You appear to know that Emily and I keep in contact. We're good friends and have been for years. She told me you'd been delving into Frank's murky past, trying to make sense of his wife's murder. But she neglected to mention that you thought Frank had been bumped off too, probably because she thought it would upset me. I have absolutely no doubt that it upset her.'

Alexi nodded, when Judith glanced at her, clearly expecting an answer. 'You could say that.'

'Not that it would surprise me if he was done for.' A smile lit up her features and Alexi caught a glimpse of the beautiful woman she'd once been. A woman who'd been special enough to have two virile men fighting over her. 'Frank always did like to sail close to the wind. It was only a matter of time before he seriously pissed someone important off.'

'Any suggestions?' Alexi asked.

Judith flapped a hand, dismissing the question. 'Not the foggiest. As I say, I haven't laid eyes on him for twenty years. And obviously, I won't now. Not ever.'

'Frank clearly meant a lot to you, and still does today,' Jack said. 'Why did you break off contact? I don't believe he was directly responsible for your accident, otherwise you wouldn't still think of him so fondly.'

'Am I that easily read?' She chuckled. 'In that case, you might as well know,' she added, sighing. 'We were on a night out, the four of us. Daventree and me, Frank and Emily. We were all high on a combination of weed, booze and adrenalin. Frank was being especially outrageous and flirting with me like there was no tomorrow. And I'll confess that I played up to him. I liked Frank.' She fell momentarily silent. 'More than liked, but I knew he wasn't the settling-down type and if I responded to his very obvious come-on then he'd have me and lose interest. Besides, I knew he was only doing it to wind Daventree up.'

'Why would he do that?' Alexi asked, even though she suspected that she already knew.

'Daventree was really into me. He started talking about a future together and that scared me. I wasn't ready to put down roots with him, or anyone else, so I backed off a bit.' She sighed. 'I suppose I used Frank to send Daventree a message.'

'He wasn't the one who did it for you,' Alexi said softly. 'We all like a bad boy, but I gather that title applied to Daventree too. He said as much to us earlier today.'

'Not really. Frank was the leader of their gang of two.

Daventree wasn't as wild, as unattainable, and that's what the attraction was about Frank. We all want what we can't have, don't we?'

'So, the night of your accident. You were all out of it,' Jack said. 'What precisely happened?'

'We were in Brighton, under the pier. It was winter, and dark. A cold night with the wind whipping in across the sea but, of course, we weren't feeling it. There were some other people there too. It's quite a popular hangout, year-round. Anyway, Daventree suggested a climbing contest. Frank wasn't keen. I think he was more together than the rest of us and realised the dangers, but Daventree egged him on. He dared him, calling him a coward when he didn't bite.'

Judith sighed and closed her eyes for an expressive moment, lost in her own version of hell. 'Daventree was manic that night. He's not as good a climber as Frank but had some experience and was determined to beat Frank at everything they did, perhaps to make a point to me. I don't really know. It was partly because he was high but also because Frank was coming on to me so blatantly, I've always thought.'

'They were climbing the stanchions beneath the pier?' Alexi asked, when Judith paused, lost in reflection.

'Yes. They did it too. Frank easily beat Daventree, going up and down in the dark like a monkey. We knew that he would. Daventree must have known it too and so I've always wondered why he insisted upon doing it.'

'Perhaps he was planning for someone to have an accident, but it wasn't supposed to be you,' Jack said.

Judith blinked at him. 'I've often wondered about that too,' she said softly. 'Anyway, after that Daventree dared Emily and me to have a go. Frank said absolutely not but Daventree called him all sorts of insulting names. It got quite nasty and so I, ever the peacemaker, agreed to do it, if only to stop the guys from fighting. It was in danger of getting out of hand. Feelings were running high, at least insofar as Daventree was concerned. The other people there hadn't been taking much notice of us, up until that point. But some of them decided to join in with the climbing, so it became us and them, if you like. A contest.'

'Oh lord!' Alexi muttered.

'Daventree pushed me up a stanchion, climbing behind me, ready to catch me if I fell, or so he put it.' Judith shook her head. 'It sounds ridiculous now and I really shouldn't have got involved. Anyway, far from helping me, Daventree lost his footing, slipped and fell to the ground. I froze and couldn't move a muscle. I screamed, I remember that much. One of the strangers climbed up, grabbed my arm to steady me because I was feeling sick, swaying about, totally disorientated. But he was heavy-handed and only managed to dislodge my grip. I fell and... well, the rest as they say is history.'

'Frank wasn't responsible in any way for your accident?' Alexi asked.

'No. He yelled to me to hang on. He'd come and get me. But he was halfway up another stanchion at the time and the other guy got there first. Anyway, if anyone's to blame, it's Daventree and he knows it. It's what came between him and Frank.'

'Why didn't Emily tell us this when we called on her?' Jack asked. 'It sounds like a stupid prank that went disastrously wrong. Nothing more.'

'Not her story to tell. We all agreed that we'd never speak about it.'

Alexi knew they weren't getting the full story. There had to be a reason why they'd agreed upon a vow of silence. Judith must have been asked hundreds of times how she'd finished up in a wheelchair. If it was so innocent, why not speak about it? At first, Alexi supposed, that would have seriously upset Judith, but she seemed resigned to her situation now and had no obvious reason to still keep quiet.

'You might as well tell us the rest,' she said softly.

'I thought I was going to be okay after that fall. I didn't lose consciousness and just felt sore and bruised all over. It was only a couple of days later that I started to realise something wasn't quite right when my back played up and I lost feeling in my toes. If I'd gone to A&E immediately it wouldn't have made any difference. The damage had already been done but was slow to manifest itself.'

'I'm sorry,' Alexi said.

'Don't be. It wasn't your fault. I've made the best of things and lead as full a life as I can, given the circumstances. I'm independent and have plenty of friends. Do I wish I had use of my legs? You bet your life I do, but there's no point in dwelling upon the past. We were old enough to know better but still did ridiculous things, so I have no one to blame but myself. I'm not the type to bear grudges or ask, "why me?".'

'Come on, Judith,' Jack said. 'Something else happened. Tell us about it.'

She shook her head decisively. 'I think I've said enough.'

'Well, of course, you don't have to say anything more, and we can't force you to. But you might as well know that in light of Stella's murder, the police are officially taking another look into Frank's death. Frank's brother's name is in the frame for Stella's murder, you see, and we will do absolutely everything we can to make sure he isn't charged with a crime he didn't commit.' Jack's expression was set in granite. 'And if that means reporting this conversation to them, then we will not hesitate, unless you give me a reason not to.'

Judith shook her head again, but less firmly. 'All this happened twenty years ago. It can't possibly be relevant.'

'Then there's no harm in telling us,' Alexi said. 'We can be discreet and if it has no bearing on Frank's death, or on Stella's, then no one will hear what you have to say. You have my word.'

Judith sighed. 'You really don't give up, do you? Do you get off on delving into other people's dirty laundry?' she asked testily.

'Murder's a dirty business,' Jack replied.

Alexi and Jack once again remained silent, waiting for Judith to come to a decision. Alexi knew that Jack wouldn't hesitate to put Vickery onto Judith if she remained tight-lipped. He might very well do so anyway, depending upon what she had to tell them. Alexi sensed, and she was sure that Jack did too, that they were finally getting somewhere. An aggrieved person from all those years ago was finally getting revenge.

It all fit, but for the fact that Stella's death didn't tie in with those long ago hijinks that ended in disaster. The more they found out, the harder it was to arrive at any definitive conclusions.

'Oh, okay, I don't suppose it matters now that Frank's dead.' She let out a long breath. 'We'd established that I wasn't injured. Huh, or so we thought, and Frank went ballistic at the guy who'd knocked me from the stanchion, accusing him of deliberately letting me fall. I'll never believe that he did, nor have I ever understood why Frank was getting so het up.'

'He cared about you,' Alexi said softly.

'I don't know about that, but I do know that both men were riled, high and running on an overload of testosterone. Inevitably, their dispute got physical. The whole scene turned ugly and I thought it was going to descend into a free-for-all. Before that could happen, Frank hit the other bloke; I never did get his name. He hit him hard. The guy fell, struck his head on a rock and... well, he was dead.'

'Christ!' Alexi gasped. That revelation opened up a whole new can of worms, together with a potential motive for Frank's murder. *For Frank's*, she reminded herself, *but not Stella's*. What the hell was going on? The more they found out, the less clear it became.

'Yeah, that about covers it.'

'What happened?'

'I'm afraid we all scarpered. Not just us but the guy's friends too. Not sure why they didn't hang around, but I suspect they'd been thieving or were wanted by the police about something. I know they wanted badly to get up onto the pier and kept going on about avoiding the security guy who patrolled it. We didn't care. We were just larking about, but I think, and I've had a lot of time to contemplate, that those guys were hardcore criminals. So they left their dead mate where he was and we never saw them again.'

'No wonder you haven't spoken about it,' Jack said into the ensuing silence. 'Technically, Frank killed the guy, even though it was an accident, and the rest of you, by keeping schtum, were accessories.'

'You imagine we're not aware of that!' Judith snapped. 'I think about that guy whenever I'm in danger of feeling sorry for myself. At least I'm still alive, albeit not whole.'

'Did the case hit the papers?'

'I think there was an appeal for witnesses, but I'm told not much effort was made. By then, I realised something wasn't right with me so my priorities changed. I was hospitalised for ages and didn't have time to think about the man I'd been partially responsible for killing.'

'Did any of those guys get your names?'

Alexi knew why Jack had asked the question. Like her, he was wondering if one of them had claimed revenge twenty years after the event. It seemed implausible but stranger things had been known to happen.

'Not as far as I can recall. But bear in mind, we were all pretty wasted.'

'The dead man's name?'

'Gary Dexter. It was online. I looked months after my accident, when I came out of rehab.' She paused. 'I'm really sorry that Frank's dead. I liked him. I liked him a lot.'

'But you haven't seen him since your accident?'

'Like I say, I was hospitalised for a long time. He knew I'd never walk again, and I think that he partly blamed himself for joining in a game he didn't want to play in the first place. Frank did call me. He wanted to see me, but I wouldn't let him. There was no point. It would have been too painful for me at a time when I was still learning how to cope with a different sort of pain.'

'I hear you,' Alexi said, impulsively reaching across to touch her hand.

'My mother died not long after I had my accident and left me well provided for, so I was able to set myself up here and carry on working online for a publicity firm.'

'Emily and Daventree still keep in touch?' Alexi asked.

'Emily is the only one I see. I won't have Daventree anywhere near me. If anyone's to blame for my situation then it's him and he is well aware of that. He calls occasionally and we speak on the phone, but if he knocked on my door then I wouldn't let him in.'

'I think I get how you feel,' Alexi said.

'There is one thing though.'

Alexi and Jack both looked at her expectantly.

'Frank rang me when he got back from Australia. Said he was coming to see me and that he'd break the door down if I didn't let him in. He said there was something he'd wanted to get off his chest for a long time.'

'When was this?' Jack asked, sitting forward in his chair.

'The day before he died.'

17

'Now we really are getting somewhere,' Jack said, as they climbed back into his car and drove away.

'Are we though? I thought that at first when she mentioned the accident and the guy who died. But think about it, Jack. Someone connected to Gary Dexter came for their revenge twenty years after the event.' Alexi frowned. 'Is that very likely? And why now? How did they know to go after Frank? If this person was there, or spoke to someone who was, they will know that Daventree suggested the climbing malarky and was the one who failed to keep Judith from falling.'

'True, but it was Frank who hit the guy.'

'Okay, so even supposing that person found out who Frank was, went climbing with him twenty years later and pushed him to his death...'

'Yeah, put like that, I have to agree that it seems a bit far-fetched. But I still think that tragedy has something to do with the murders we're investigating now.'

'Even if you're right, it still doesn't explain why Stella was murdered. Surely the two crimes have to be connected. You've said yourself that it's too much of a stretch to be any other way.'

'I know. But we have another thread to follow. Let's see what it throws up.'

'Don't forget that we have yet to look into that failed climbing school in Wales that Frank wanted to set up.' Alexi rubbed her hands together. 'I'm going to get onto that the moment we get back. I have a friend at the paper who can trawl company records and find out far more than is available online.' She threw back her head, closed her eyes and sighed. 'Everything about these cases seems to revolve around climbing.'

'And unrequited love. Or lust. Or whatever.'

'That too.' Alexi nodded. 'I didn't like Andy Dawson. He's definitely hiding something. If I find out that he went into partnership with Frank in that failed venture, then I shall consider myself vindicated.'

Jack chuckled. 'Just because you didn't like him, that doesn't mean that he's done anything untoward.'

'We need to see Frank's bank records and find out if he borrowed heavily at any point.' Alexi grabbed her phone and made notes. 'Although, like you say, if he was in debt then it would have been a limb or two that was broken in an effort to remind him of his responsibilities, not his neck.'

'Calm down, darling. We'll check all this stuff out methodically.'

'I really, really want to know who backed Stella's company and got it off the ground before Frank threw his wedge into the pot,' Alexi said, ignoring Jack's attempts to stifle her enthusiasm. 'My money's on Emily. She was really stuck on Frank, but he was coming on to Judith in front of her, which would have rankled. Emily wouldn't appreciate coming out second best. She isn't the type to undertake a supporting role. Frank only fell back on her after Judith was injured and wouldn't see him. But I'm betting Judith was still the one for Frank. Emily couldn't compete with their injured friend, or bad mouth her in any way, but women always know when their guy's carrying a torch for someone else.'

'I'll bear that in mind.'

Alexi slapped Jack's thigh. 'Seriously though, Jack, I still think we had it right early on when we suspected that Stella killed Frank because she'd bled him dry, and he was of no further use to her. He'd become a liability, and his possessiveness was holding her back. She came back to England to get one over on Nick, the guy who'd dumped her, and a husband loitering in the wings would have not been a part of the game plan.'

'It would make more sense if Emily was Stella's backer. Bumping off Frank definitely wouldn't have been done on Emily's orders. She used her money to manipulate Stella, who she would have known somehow from around here, and pushed Stella in Frank's direction. Or rather, pushed Frank in hers, well aware that he couldn't resist a pretty face. Stella was probably told to milk him dry. All the time he had money, he could be a free spirit and Emily had no control over him. I'm not sure she intended for them to marry though.'

'Perhaps Emily implied to Frank that the police had new leads on Dexter's death and would be knocking at his door,' Alexi said, her eyes coming alight with speculation. 'We wondered why he went so far and so fast. Presumably, Emily told him that she had connections in that part of the world.'

'You could well be right.' Jack nodded emphatically. 'It

certainly makes more sense than assuming Frank and Stella simply met one another by chance in Australia.'

'Of course I'm right! You're not the only one with instincts.'

They both laughed.

'Emily wanted him back, broke and beholden to her,' Jack said, indicating to overtake a lorry. 'His dying would have broken her heart, but Emily had managed to convince herself that it really had been an accident. History repeating itself, if you like. But when we started asking questions, implying that Stella had actually killed him, there was always the possibility that the business under Brighton pier would come to light, endangering them all. They'd stayed quiet all these years but there's no time limit on murder and they all now have a lot to lose. Besides, Stella had to pay for killing the love of Emily's life.'

Alexi nodded. 'She knew we'd get to Daventree and there was every likelihood that he'd mention Judith. The fact that he did implies innocence on his part, which is annoying. I don't like him either and want him to be guilty of... well, of something.'

'I actually think that his conscience troubles him, if that helps at all.'

'Not much.'

'I'd give a great deal to know what Frank wanted to speak to Judith about,' Jack said, tapping his fingers against the steering wheel. 'Perhaps he was planning to ditch Stella. We've heard that the blinkers had come off. It was one thing, being seen with a young, good-looking woman in Australia, where everything's laid back and anything goes. But once he got back on home soil, I dare say the realities struck home. He'd run through a large amount of cash, more than he'd ever had at any one time before. He'd been conned out of it and returned home with nothing to show for his travels, other than Stella, who no one seemed to like. Perhaps Frank had decided to ditch her and wanted to see if Judith would have him back. He didn't seem like the type to go it alone.'

'Judith did say that he wanted to talk to her about something important,' Alexi agreed. 'But I guess we'll never know what. Not for sure. I don't suppose it matters though.'

'Perhaps Emily did use the threat of Dexter's death to persuade him into Stella's arms, in a roundabout sort of way. His conscience might well have been bothering him too and he was planning to 'fess up to the police. If that was the case then he would have wanted to warn Judith first. Her reaction would have been all that mattered and if she told him not to do it, then he probably wouldn't have.'

'That does seem plausible,' Alexi said, nodding. 'But of course, we will never know for sure now.'

'Okay, leave Frank and his motives to one side for a moment and let's come at this from another angle. Who benefits the most, financially, from Stella's death?'

'Nick,' Alexi replied without hesitation. 'But his whereabouts at the time of her death have been established, so he couldn't have killed her. Well, not himself.'

'No, but he runs a tight team. Most of them have been with him for a while. Nick put everything he had into that pitch, and they would have gone under if he hadn't won it.' Jack removed one hand from the steering wheel and rubbed his chin. 'It might be worth having Vickery run a check on cars parked around that block of flats close to the time of death. Someone who wasn't local wouldn't have worried too much about their car being seen but would have wanted to park as close as possible in order to make a fast getaway.'

'You think like a policeman.'

Jack chuckled. 'Is that supposed to be a compliment?'

'Anyway,' Alexi said, yawning behind her hand. 'What now?'

'It's late. We go home. You do some digging into Frank's climbing company that didn't get off the ground, pun intended,' Jack added when Alexi groaned, 'and I'll ask Vickery to take a look at suspicious cars. I'll also ring Drew and give him an update, just so he doesn't feel neglected.'

'Good plan.' Alexi yawned for a second time. 'Let's order a takeaway. I don't think either of us feels much like cooking.'

'That'll work for me.'

* * *

Once back at their cottage, and with a Chinese delivered and consumed, Jack and Alexi both got down to work.

'Drew was glad of the update,' Jack said, closing the call. 'But he still sounds as stressed as hell.'

'Then we have to get to the bottom of this mess, and I think I might have something.' Alexi spoke with a pencil clenched between her teeth, even though she was working online. Old habits, Jack assumed. 'I called my old pal from the paper, and he's already got back to me with the details of Frank's company.'

'That was quick.'

'What can I say? He owes me more than one favour and has resources that would make Cassie weep with envy.'

'Are you going to share what he told you, or make me guess?'

Alexi grinned. 'I was right. The company papers were lodged under the name Dawson Enterprises.'

'Clever girl!' Jack leaned across and kissed the top of her head.

'Yeah, that's me! The directors are named as Andy Dawson and Frank Hopgood. My friend did a bit of online sleuthing for me, and it seems the application for licences was opposed by a group of environmentalists who were worried about soil erosion, and the destruction of wildlife habitat that would have been caused by all those boots trampling over the site.'

'Frank couldn't have known that would happen.'

'Perhaps not, but if he'd done his research properly he'd have foreseen the problem.' Alexi scrolled down the screen she'd been reading. 'It seems there had been other applications to use the site for various outdoor pursuits, and those applications had all been successfully opposed. A snoopy journalist discovered that the failed applications had all come from non-Welsh.'

'Ah, now I see where you're going with this.'

'Right. A year ago, an application almost identical to Frank and Andy's was granted and guess what nationality the applicants are.'

'Welsh, I assume.'

'Right.'

'Do we know how much money Dawson lost?'

'Nope, but I'm guessing he put up the majority of the capital simply because Frank didn't have the dosh. Frank's job would have been to draw in the punters, which is what he would have done best, being so charismatic.'

'This is old hat, darling. Why would Dawson wait all this time to get his revenge?' Jack mused.

'He probably accepted defeat and put it behind him, I agree with you there, but it must have rankled. But then, if that new application was only granted a year ago and if the enterprise is doing well then Dawson's resentments might well have resurfaced.'

'Possibly,' Jack agreed, 'but it's thin.'

'Dawson could have been the person who went climbing with Frank that fateful day.' Alexi nodded, as though to reinforce the suggestion. 'Frank was telling the truth and did intend to climb with an old buddy.'

'Yeah, but I still can't see Dawson killing over the loss of his investment. He's supposedly a successful builder in his own right. We need to find out if he *is* successful, or if he just talks a good game.'

'I'm on it,' Alexi said, making a note.

'And of course, Frank did come on to Dawson's wife. I'd see that as more of a motive, especially if the wife in question still had a thing for Frank that she didn't hide from her husband as well as she thought she did.'

'All well and good, but if Dawson did kill Frank, then we don't have a hope in hell of proving it. We have no evidence to confront him with, other than that failed climbing school, which is hardly a smoking gun.'

Jack grinned at her. 'Who said anything about confronting *him*?'

'Ah, now I'm with you.' Alexi's eyes gleamed. 'You intend to corner his wife.'

'I rather thought we'd do it together tomorrow.'

'She may not be home, may not talk to us if she is, and Dawson might be there.'

'Good job one of us thinks like a policeman.'

* * *

Jack proved his point the following morning by calling Dawson and asking if they could have a few more minutes of his time.

'Sorry, I'm on a building site all day. I'm on my way there now.' Jack could hear that he was on speaker and in his car. The sound of traffic and wheels on tarmac was unmistakable. 'Anyway, what else do you need to know?'

'Not to worry. Just wanted to pick your brains about a few things, but it can wait. Sorry to have bothered you.'

'No worries.'

'Damn, you're good!' Alexi reached up to give him a peck on the cheek. 'But then, so am I. Dawson's company is in deep do-do. He's overstretched himself and is close to the brink.'

'Yeah, I thought that might be the case.'

'Well come on then, let's go and see Mrs Dawson. We just have to hope that she's at home and willing to talk to us.'

'I think it unlikely that she'll work. Dawson wouldn't give her that much freedom. And the best time to catch a person at home is early in the morning. Anyway, there's one way to find out.'

'I assume you have their address, so let's go and check it out.'

'After I've walked this guy.'

Silgo barked in agreement, making Alexi laugh.

'Perhaps I have underestimated his intuitiveness.'

An hour later, with Silgo's requirement for exercise satisfied, Alexi and Jack once again hit the road with the animals installed on the back seat. This time their destination was the small village called Kingsclere, forty-five minutes away. Picturesque, it looked rich and prosperous, the old houses – more like mansions in some cases – separated by swathes of land inevitably populated by leggy racehorses. A more modern development was the only blot on the tranquil landscape and that proved to be their destination. They pulled up outside a large, modern, detached house without an ounce of character that Jack could detect. It was expensive, that much was obvious, but there was little difference between it and the rest of the properties on the development.

'Ostentatious,' Alexi said, twitching her nose.

'If it's supposed to impress then it falls woefully short of the mark,' Jack agreed. 'You guys stay here,' he added, addressing the comment to Cosmo. 'I doubt if animal hair will be appreciated in this establishment.'

Alexi blew them both a kiss as she cranked open a window. She and Jack then walked up the path and rang the doorbell.

It was so long before anyone responded that at first, Jack thought his element of surprise had failed. He was about to ring for a second time when the door was opened but left on the chain.

'Yes,' the woman who'd opened it said on a note of suspicion. 'Can I help you?'

'Hi.' Jack turned on the smile that tended to settle nerves and get him what he wanted, especially when he directed it towards a woman. She was dressed in jeans and a white shirt. Her feet were bare and brunette hair hung in a tangle, falling below her shoulders. She wore no makeup but didn't really need to. A lot younger than Dawson, she was ageing well. Jack could understand Frank being attracted to her. 'Jack Maddox and Alexi Ellis. You're Mrs Sarah Dawson?'

'The last time I checked. What do you want?'

'A moment of your time,' Alexi said. 'We're making enquiries about Frank Hopgood's death.'

Sarah's face paled. 'Come in,' she said, taking the chain off and opening the door wide.

She led them through to a soulless kitchen – all stainless steel and granite surfaces – not an item out of place. It looked unused. She indicated stools around the central island but didn't offer them refreshment. Instead, she took up occupation of a stool across from them and fixed them with a wary look.

'Why do you think I can help you?' she asked. 'Besides, Frank's death was an accident and we've all moved on.'

'Is that what you really believe?' Alexi asked. 'That it was an accident, I mean.'

She looked away from them. 'Even if I doubted it, it's too late now.'

Alexi flashed a sympathetic smile. 'But you do have your doubts, don't you?'

'Look, why are you really here?' She leaned her forearms on the surface and pushed her face closer to Jack and Alexi, her expression a combination of curiosity and nervous anxiety.

'Cards on the table?' Jack asked.

'Always the best way.'

'Okay, we're told that you and Frank were tight.'

She sat bolt upright. 'Who told you that? Who have you been talking to? Did my husband send you? Is this some sort of sick joke on his part? It's just the sort of thing he would enjoy doing, winding me up, I mean.'

Jack could see that his words had scared her, which implied that she was afraid of her own husband.

'Does it matter who told us? As to your husband, hell no, he has no idea we're here.' Alexi spread her hands. 'You have nothing to fear from us. If you don't want to talk then we'll leave. But if you cared about Frank, which I think you did, then you'll help us get to the truth.'

Her affronted attitude didn't stand the test of time. 'What does it matter now?' she asked, clearing not expecting a response. 'Yes, Frank and I had a dalliance. I was feeling lonely and neglected and Frank was a breath of fresh air. He didn't take life too seriously and made me feel cherished in a way that I've never experienced before.' Her expression turned defiant. 'Is that so wrong?'

'You're not the first woman to have an affair,' Jack said, 'but you seem to have it all here. Weren't you taking a massive risk?'

'Ha! It's a gilded cage. I'd settle for a lot less.' She abruptly stopped talking, as though belatedly realising that she'd given too much away about her personal circumstances. 'Anyway, why rake up Frank's death now?'

Alexi explained about their connection to Drew, and his concerns about the cause of Frank's death.

'He thinks he was too good a climber to be so careless,' she finished by saying, 'and wants answers.'

'He came back from Australia with a young wife so had a lot to live for,' Jack said.

Sarah's expression closed down. 'Oh, I'm well aware of that,' she said bitterly. 'And if I hadn't been, you can be sure that my dear husband would have pointed the fact out to me and enjoyed rubbing my nose in it.'

'He knew about your affair?' Jack asked.

'It was hardly an affair. More of a fling and yes, he found out. Don't ask me how. I wouldn't put it past him to put spyware, or a tracker or something on my phone. Andy is *very* possessive.'

'I gather Andy and Frank tried to open a climbing school in Wales back in the day,' Alexi said.

'That was before we were married. It seems like a lifetime ago. But yes, they did and Andy blamed Frank for not doing his research properly. He never stopped banging on about it, which is perhaps why he was so furious when he found out about Frank and me. He said Frank had no real interest in me and that he'd only gone after me to wind him up.'

'I'm sure that isn't true,' Alexi said.

Sarah shrugged. 'Well, it doesn't matter much now, does it.'

'You know, I suppose, that Frank's wife was murdered,' Jack said.

Sarah's eyes widened. 'No, I wasn't aware of that.' She shook her head. 'That's awful. Do you have any idea who...' She blinked at Jack. 'You think Andy was involved? That's why you're really here.'

'Did you see Frank, with or without Stella, after he returned from Australia?' Alexi asked.

'Yes, just the once, for drinks, and it was torture. Stella was all over Frank and played up to the other men as well. She ignored me and Jan Green. But Frank... well, he sent me a lot of looks, as though apologising for Stella's bad behaviour.' She tilted her head to one side, as though reliving the moment. 'For what it's worth, I don't think he was that enamoured with Stella, not any more. But then again, perhaps that's what I wanted to believe. I mean, why keep sending me flirtatious looks if he'd found the perfect partner to keep him happy?'

'We're told that flirting was built into Frank's DNA,' Alexi said, and she exchanged a look with Jack.

'Even so.'

'When was this?' Jack asked.

'A couple of weeks before Frank died. The six of us met for a drink at Goodwood House. Frank was splashing the cash and showing Stella off but... I don't know, he was flamboyant and yet subdued, if that makes any sense. Almost like he was putting on an act. Anyone who didn't know him as well as I did would have said he was the same old Frank, but the spark had gone out of him, and I got the impression that he was simply going through the motions. I wanted to ask him if something was wrong but Stella and Andy between them ensured that I didn't get to speak with him alone.'

'You still cared about him?' Alexi smiled across the divide that separated them. 'I gather he was an easy person to like.'

'I fantasised about him rescuing me from all this, if you must know.' She gave a cynical little laugh as she waved an arm in a wide arc. 'Talk about living in cloud cuckoo land. Frank didn't have any money and if I try to divorce Andy, I won't get much. Not enough to live on at any rate and he makes sure that I know it. He wants to possess me rather than have an equal partner. His business is on the uppers, this place is mortgaged up to the hilt and any funds he does have are tied up in the company.'

'Ouch!' Alexi reached across and touched Sarah's hand.

'It's his way of controlling me. He knows I don't love him any more, perhaps I never did; I just fell for all the gloss and glamour of an older man who treated me like a princess, taking me to places where he could show me off to his friends. I should have picked up on the warning signs then, but still.' She let out a prolonged sigh. 'It was fun, until he got me where he wanted me, and then my life was no longer my own. Which is why I would have lived in a tent with Frank given half a chance.' She let out another long breath. 'But it was never to be, so that's that.'

'What did you make of Stella?' Jack asked.

'I wasn't impressed by what I saw, but then I wouldn't be, would I? I was biased against her before we'd even met. But in retrospect, I think I was right to be. There was no real affection on her part for Frank. I reckon she'd just latched onto him in Australia for some reason. But Andy was all over her in the way that he used to be with me before we married, and Stella lapped up the attention. I thought at the time that Andy was doing it to arouse my jealousy. I wanted to tell him he was wasting his time.' She flapped a hand, making the gesture somehow seem derisive. 'Stella was welcome to him.'

'Did you get the impression that they knew one another?' Alexi asked.

Sarah looked confused. 'What do you mean?'

'Stella was brought up in Lambourn.'

'Oh, I didn't know that. I assumed she was Australian. I didn't ask her because she barely spoke to me, and I had no interest in getting up close and personal with her. But yes, now you come to mention it, they didn't behave like people who'd just met for the first time.'

'In what way?' Jack asked.

'Well, the occasional knowing look.' Sarah paused, clearly lost in thought. 'And yes, he ordered drinks for us all and didn't ask her what she wanted. But Frank and Stella got there before us and had drinks in front of them when we arrived, so there was no way that Andy could have known what type of wine she was drinking. But I remember quite clearly him asking for Chardonnay. I almost corrected him because it used to be my tipple, but I went off it.' She tapped her fingers on her thigh, looking perplexed. 'What does it all mean?'

'What indeed,' Alexi replied, her mind whirling with probabilities.

'Did Andy climb with Frank once he returned?' Jack asked.

'Oh yes,' Sarah replied. 'I thought you knew and that was why you were here.' She lifted her head and looked directly at Jack. 'They climbed together on the day that he died.'

18

'Are you absolutely sure about that?' Alexi asked, recovering from the shock of the revelation first.

'Oh yes, he made a point of telling me that they'd be climbing together that morning, early, at first light when they'd have the place to themselves. He didn't need to because I heard them making the arrangements when we had those drinks. They were planning to free climb, which isn't illegal but is highly dangerous and against club policy, which would explain the need to be there before they got distracted by the arrival of others. Andy describes Reg Parsons as a right little jobsworth, a stickler for the rules, and he wouldn't have wanted him interfering, especially if...' She paused to swipe at a tear. 'Well, if he went there with the express intention of killing poor Frank, which I am absolutely convinced that he did.'

'But since no one else was there, there's no way to disprove the accident theory,' Jack pointed out.

'If Frank did fall, why didn't Andy hang about, call the emergency services and explain what had happened?' Sarah's tone had turned hard and aggressive. Appearances could be deceptive, Alexi decided. Beneath the fragile exterior, this woman was tough and resourceful.

'You really think your husband pushed Frank off that rock?' Alexi asked. 'Murdered him over an old business failure and his interest in you?' She drilled her with a look, challenging her to commit. 'Are you absolutely sure?'

'I am,' Sarah replied defiantly. 'In fact, I know that he did. I asked him about it when I heard of Frank's death. He just shrugged and said that he'd had it coming. No one took what was his, and no one ripped him off. He was proud. Boasting about what he'd done, if only in front of me.'

'You didn't say anything to the police though?' Jack asked.

'What could I say?' Sarah lifted her shoulders and gestured with her hands. 'I had no proof. Andy would have covered his tracks. No one knew precisely what time Frank died, but you can be sure that when his body was discovered, Andy would have made sure he was somewhere else, surrounded by people who could vouch for him. Anyway, Andy knew I wouldn't dare to speak out. That's why he boasted about what he'd done. It was his way of punishing me for daring to defy him.'

'He gets physically violent with you?' Jack asked, and Alexi knew he would be struggling to contain his anger as he waited for her response. Although violence against women was something he'd come across as a matter of course during his career as a policeman, he considered it to be the epitome of cowardice and it still wound him up.

'He makes sure the bruises don't show,' she said, a little too casually. Alexi hadn't taken a liking to Andy and was convinced that he did control Sarah, but whether he also hit her she was unable to decide.

'If you had spoken up in confidence,' Jack said, 'the police would have picked Andy's car up somewhere near the climb. Or tracked his whereabouts through his phone.'

'Ah.' She blinked as though confused, but Alexi didn't think she was that stupid. Was she making all this up, just to get back at her husband? Or was she telling the truth, glad to be able to finally get it off her chest. 'I didn't think of that.'

'Okay, but how could you carry on living with a man capable of murder?' Alexi asked. 'Of murdering a man who mattered to you.'

'You don't understand.' Her eyes flooded with tears. 'He owns me or thinks he does. If I left him then he'd find me, no matter if I took out restraining orders or whatever, and he'd make my life a living hell for walking out on him. He's told me so more than once and, take it from me, Andy doesn't make idle threats.'

'You're afraid of him?' Alexi asked.

'You bet your life I am! He's got a ruthless streak that he covers well. He's usually the quiet one in a gathering and lets the others do most of the talking. But he misses little and if someone upsets him, or goes against him, then his anger is terrifying. I think he's a bit unstable. Well, I know that he is, and I'm stuck here, almost afraid to breathe for fear of saying the wrong thing and tipping him over the edge.'

'We're on good terms with the police,' Jack said. 'I used to be a policeman, in fact. How do you feel about my telling the detective investigating Stella's death what you just told me? He's taking another look at Frank's death so now would be a good time. He'll be discreet and only speak with Andy if he can find sufficient evidence. And if he intends to do that, we'll give you the heads up first.'

'I'm... I'm not sure.' Genuine fear flashed through her eyes.

'He will know I spoke to you, and you don't know what he can be like if he thinks he's been betrayed.'

'Well look, don't make up your mind now.' Alexi reached into her bag and produced one of her cards. 'Think about it and call me when you've come to a decision. We won't do anything about what you've told us before that, and if there's insufficient evidence to give the police a viable chance of prosecuting then we might not do anything anyway.'

'Well all right, thank you.' She put Alexi's card in a holder on the kitchen surface and stood up to show them from the house. 'It's been a relief to talk about it, if nothing else,' she said, as she led them back through the ostentatious hallway with its marble floor and sweeping staircase that was clearly supposed to lead to a galleried landing. Unfortunately, the landing in question was so narrow that it nullified the intended effect.

'Well,' Alexi said as they got back in the car and greeted the animals. 'Now things are starting to make sense.'

'I agree,' Jack said, starting the engine and pulling away. Alexi raised a hand to wave at Sarah, who was watching them from a window.

'Do you think she told us the truth?'

'Oh yes! There's no question in my mind that Andy killed Frank. The question is, did he also kill Stella, and if so, why?'

'Where are we going now?'

'To talk to Stella's dad. I want to know if Stella ever mentioned Andy. It's a long shot, but if we can make the connection then there's a good chance that he pushed her in Frank's direction.'

'But why?'

'I have absolutely no idea. You'd have thought that he'd be glad to see the back of Frank when he went off to Australia but perhaps he deliberately manipulated him once he got there. He knew money was Frank's god and tasked Stella with relieving him of it.' He chuckled. 'If I'm right, then she did a first-rate job.'

'I don't get any of this,' Alexi admitted, after a short, reflective pause. 'If Stella didn't kill Frank, why did she need to be silenced?'

'A better question to ask is who backed Stella's business start-up?'

'Andy?'

'I doubt it. We know he's short of funds. My money's still on Emily.'

Alexi frowned. 'She assumed Stella was responsible for Frank's death and took her revenge.'

'But Stella knew Andy was climbing with Frank that morning. Sarah just told us they made the arrangements over drinks, so she could have set Emily straight. It certainly explains why no phone calls regarding meeting up to climb were discovered. Stella obviously couldn't tell the truth without dropping Andy in it and if he's half as lethal as Sarah implied when crossed, and if she knew him well enough to realise it, then she wouldn't have taken that chance. Besides, it probably suited her purpose to have Frank out of the way.'

'Andy had done her a favour, either with or without her collusion?'

'Yep. But what's bugging me is why attempt to frame Drew? Someone either forced Stella to ring him and plead for his help, or else someone imitated her voice. Drew didn't know her that well and wouldn't necessarily have recognised her dulcet tones.'

Alexi nodded. 'When someone tells you their name over

the phone, you tend to assume you're talking to that person. Anyway, voices can be deliberately distorted.'

'Exactly.' Jack paused at a junction and indicated left, pulling out after a van passed him. 'No, whoever stole that baseball bat did so knowing that Drew's prints were likely to be on it. Although it was kept behind the bar, it wouldn't be that easy for a customer to slip back there when the bar was open without being noticed by the barman.'

'This really is personal. Someone bears a grudge against Frank and Drew.'

'If we can figure out why then we'll understand what this is all about. I *will* tell Vickery what Sarah just told us. He can do a little digging, see if he can somehow place Andy anywhere near the climb, and take it from there.'

'Be careful. Sarah is petrified.'

'Is she?'

'You think she was putting on an act?' Alexi tilted her head. 'I did wonder about that myself. Her story was a little too glib.'

'No, I believe she told us the truth and she's scared of him. But she does desperately want a way out of her marriage and if Andy's banged up then she'll get her wish. So she told us what she knew and probably embellished the facts in the telling.'

'Our calling did her a favour, in other words.'

'Happy to oblige,' Jack replied cheerfully. 'I hate wifebeaters.'

'Yeah, I hear you.'

The rest of the journey was spent mostly in silence as Jack drove them rapidly to Ben North's abode. They found their quarry at home, feet up in front of a fire, watching a documentary on TV.

'You two again,' he said, not looking distraught at the violent nature of his daughter's demise, which they knew he would have been told about by now. 'What is it this time?'

'Sorry to bother you,' Jack said, not offering condolences that clearly wouldn't be welcomed. 'Just a quick question. Do you know if Stella had anything to do with this guy?' He pulled up Andy's website on his phone and enlarged the picture of a smiling Andy on the home page.

'Yeah. He gave Stella her first big break. She did all the PR for a housing development he needed promoting. The market crashed when the building was only half complete. I think the guy made a loss, or only broke even in the end. Stella did what she could to promote his cause. She mentioned him a lot at the time, I seem to recall. Why? What does it matter? Did he kill Stella?' he asked, as casually as if they were discussing the weather.

'Not as far as we're aware. It's Frank's death we're still looking into and we know Frank and this guy were buddies. We're squaring the circle, if you like.'

'Oh, okay.'

Ben seemed distinctly disinterested in the pursuit of his daughter's killer and kept glancing at the TV screen, as though sorry to be missing his documentary.

Jack thanked him for his time, and they took their leave.

'The plot thickens,' Alexi said as they drove away again. 'We can link Andy and Stella but we're no closer to knowing who actually killed Stella and tried to frame Drew, which is all we really want to know.'

'I still don't think that Andy payrolled Stella's company.' Jack shook his head to emphasise his point. 'But I do think they stayed in touch. We need to ask Mark if he can find any email or text messages between the two of them. She went to

Australia perhaps because she was chasing an opportunity there. We know she had to get away from England in case her father or brother told the police about their suspicions regarding their mother's death. Why Australia, though? What made her decide to go so far away?'

'Or who did? Perhaps she had contacts there. I don't think that really matters. What is important is who pointed Frank in her direction.'

'Agreed. Anyway, let's get back to Lambourn. At least we can tell Drew with a fair degree of certainty who killed his brother and why. That might give him some comfort.'

'Right.'

Drew and Cheryl were in the restaurant when they got back, chatting to some of their lunchtime clientele. Alexi was proud of the way in which trade had picked up since the hotel had become better known. Lunchtime catering in the past hadn't gone much beyond sandwiches for the locals, frustrating the hell out of Marcel, their chef, whose talents were thwarted. Nowadays, people from all over were required to make reservations sometimes weeks in advance to be sure of sampling Marcel's amazing cuisine. If people would only stop getting themselves murdered in and around the place, their future would be assured.

'Hey.' Drew saw them and raised a hand. Alexi, Jack and the animals made their way to Cheryl's private kitchen, secure in the knowledge that Drew and Cheryl would be close on their heels.

'You come with news, I hope,' Drew said, plonking himself down at the table and running a hand through his hair. He looked haggard, and Alexi knew that he probably hadn't achieved much sleep.

'We do,' Jack replied.

He proceeded to relate the main points of their conversation with Sarah Dawson.

'Blimey!' Drew looked totally flummoxed. 'And you say that he and Stella had a connection. What the hell!'

'We need you to have another think about who might have had a grudge against you and Frank, Drew,' Alexi said. 'And who could have swiped that baseball bat too. That's the key to all this.'

'Yeah, I know, and believe me I have been thinking about little else, but I just can't come up with the name of anyone who dislikes me enough to frame me for murder.'

Jack's phone ringing caused a hiatus in the conversation.

'It's Vickery,' he said, putting the call on speaker. 'Hey, Mark. Are you calling to tell me that you've caught the murderer?'

'I'm good, but not that good.'

'Well, maybe we're better than you are.'

'Because you don't have to abide by the rules.' A loud sigh echoed down the line. 'Okay then, give. What have you got for me?'

Jack once again related the substance of their conversation with Sarah.

'Bloody hell!' Vickery allowed a short pause. 'Hold tight. I'm not far away. I'll be there in ten. We need to talk this through in person.'

'That's the ultimate compliment to you, Drew,' Jack said as he cut the call.

'How so?'

'The lead detective in a murder you're suspected of

committing is about to come and discuss the investigation in front of you. That's a pretty clear endorsement of your innocence in my book.'

'Yeah, but—'

'He'd get hauled over the coals by the hierarchy if anyone finds out.'

'I guess he would.' Drew got up and went through the process of making fresh coffee. Alexi assumed he just needed to be doing something, anything, to distract himself from his problems.

'It's that baseball bat,' Jack said when Drew placed a steaming mug of coffee in front of him. 'If we can figure out who took it, I reckon we'll crack the case.'

'I can see that,' Drew replied testily. 'Like I say, I've been thinking of little else but nothing's sprung to mind.'

'Okay, let's go at this methodically,' Alexi said. 'The flap to the bar is usually down during opening hours so the chances of the bat being taken then and no one noticing a person behind the bar who shouldn't be there are slim. So, it seems logical that it must have been taken out of hours.'

'The cellarman is here then, the wait staff in the restaurant have access if they need anything for the kitchen, the cleaners and that's about it,' Cheryl said, glancing at Drew for approbation. He nodded.

'Well then, after Vickery's been, we'll run through that list of people and see if we can narrow the field down,' Jack said.

'But they've all been with us for a while!' Cheryl protested. 'And none of them have grievances against us. None of them even knew Frank, as far as I'm aware. And anyway, even if we'd unwittingly upset one of them, surely they wouldn't go to such lengths...'

Her words stalled when Vickery walked through the door.

He was alone, which didn't surprise Alexi. He was indeed breaking all the rules and wouldn't want to put DC Hogan in the position of having to lie for him if he was called to account for showing his friends too much leeway.

'Greetings,' he said. 'Is that coffee I can smell?'

'Easy to see why you're such a senior detective,' Jack replied, getting up to do the honours.

'Sometimes I surprise myself.' Vickery took an appreciative sip of his brew, helped himself to a biscuit and sighed contentedly. 'Okay,' he then said. 'Run the business with Andy Dawson past me once again. You're telling me that he agreed to free climb with Frank on the day he died and made that arrangement in front of Stella and Dawson's wife. And yet Stella insisted he received a phone call from a mate, which is how the arrangement was made. We've had a look at Frank's phone records and there was no phone call, so Stella obviously lied, which lends credence to Mrs Dawson's claims. However...' He held up a hand to prevent Alexi from interrupting him. 'From what you tell me, Mrs Dawson is a discontented wife, stuck in a brutal and loveless marriage. It will have occurred to you, no doubt, that this could be her way out.'

'Obviously. But it could also be that she's still in love with her husband and resented his interest in Stella. An interest that he didn't try to hide, according to her.' Jack rubbed his chin. 'But I believed her. She had no idea we'd be calling on her so no time to prepare what she intended to say to us.'

'Fair enough. I'll find out what vehicle he drives and see if it was in or around the climbing site at the time.'

'Is that still possible after all this time?' Cheryl asked.

'Not sure, to be honest, but I'll give it my best. Same with his mobile signal. But don't hold out too much hope, guys. I really need more than the word of a disgruntled spouse if I'm to get this past my guv'nor. And I can't speak to said spouse for fear of making the situation worse.'

'We understand that,' Jack said, speaking for them all. 'I'm more interested in the fact that Stella and Dawson were known to each other. That can be proven with a simple search into the building project she promoted for him. What I don't buy is that Dawson killed Frank and then Stella.'

'She knew that he climbed with Frank that morning and so she wouldn't need to be a genius to figure out that he also killed him,' Vickery said. 'She would have known that there was resentment there. He couldn't trust her to keep her mouth shut.'

'It's more likely that she put the squeeze on him,' Jack said. '"I won't tell if you pay up." She tried to do the same thing to Drew, remember, claiming that Drew had shortchanged Frank when it came to the division of spoils after their mother died. The woman seemed to be perpetually short of funds, so it wouldn't surprise me.'

Vickery inclined his head. 'Fair point. All that's missing is the evidence to back your theory up.'

'We were going to ask if you could check Stella's online communications,' Alexi said. 'See if there's anything between her and Andy.'

'I never would have thought of that,' Vickery replied, smiling to take the sting out of his sarcasm.

'Sorry,' Alexi said meekly.

'We think that someone else financed Stella's ambitions and pushed her in Frank's direction,' Jack explained. 'And it all hinges on that baseball bat. We're trying to figure out who could have had access to the bar at a quiet time and filched it. And more to the point, why. We'll get back to you on that one.'

Jack sat back in his chair and crossed one foot over his opposite thigh. 'Anyway, you had something you wanted to tell us.'

'Yeah. I've had someone trawling through Frank's bank records and you were right, Drew, he was almost skint. A lot of funds went out to Stella's company and little or nothing came in.'

Drew nodded in a resigned fashion. 'I guessed as much.'

'Interestingly, I took a peek at Stella's finances too and she had a regular income of a couple of thousand a month. We're trying to find out where it came from.'

'Her business was making money?' Cheryl asked.

'Not as far as we can see. She'd poured all her available funds into the pitch for that contract which went to Nick Fairburn. I had someone chat with the CEO of the company who hired him, and they reckon that Nick would have got it even if Stella had been able to make her pitch. He said that Nick's track record was solid, but Stella was still a start-up and wouldn't be a safe pair of hands for such a big contract.'

'Perhaps suggesting that she was a blackmailer wasn't so far off the mark,' Alexi said.

'I've got people trying to trace the origin of those payments, but it's hidden.' Vickery yawned as he stood up. 'Keep me updated people, and I'll do likewise. Adios.'

19

'Don't look so downhearted, Drew.' Jack's voice broke the heavy silence that pervaded following Vickery's departure. 'We're making good progress now.'

'Actually, that's my thinking face.' Drew dredged up a half-smile. 'I can see that the plot is most definitely thickening, and I know you'll get to the bottom of things. In the meantime, Cheryl and I will try to figure out who could have taken the bat. That's something we can do to help. I'll get Marcel involved. He can grill his kitchen staff, pun intended.'

Drew looked more upbeat and positive now that he had a purpose. He and Cheryl bustled from the room, both talking at the same time.

'Okay,' Alexi said, 'I'm going to do a little online sleuthing. Or rather, Ed at the paper is going to undertake it for me. I'm becoming increasingly convinced that Stella was a black-mailer, which would account for those regular payments that someone went to a lot of trouble to hide the origins of.'

'How will he know where to start?'

'Well, it seems Mark carelessly left this printout of Stella's account behind,' she said, grinning as she picked it up from the table and brandished it above her head.

Jack chuckled. 'Gotta hand it to Mark. He's not above asking for a favour or two. Without actually asking, that is.'

'Same goes for me and my friend Ed still owes me a few.'

'He must have paid up by now, giving all the times you've called on him,' Jack replied, grinning. 'You sure you don't want me to put Cassie on it?'

'Let Ed have a go first. Cassie has enough on her plate.'

'Fair enough.'

Alexi placed a call to Ed's mobile, had a short chat with him, told him what she needed and left him to work his magic.

'He's on it,' she said, cutting the call.

'I don't think we should lose sight of Daventree,' Jack remarked pensively. 'He put Judith's name out there, aware that the business beneath Brighton pier would probably come out if we tracked her down.' He tapped his fingers restlessly on the tabletop, frowning as he articulated his thoughts. 'I'd love to know why he did that. There's just something about that guy that doesn't sit right with me. All that sanctimonious, born-again malarky makes me feel ill.'

'It was Frank who hit the guy and caused his death, so even if it all comes out, there's very little that Daventree can be prosecuted for. Failure to report a death, I guess, but I don't suppose they'd bother to take him to court for that, especially given what happened to Judith that night. The press would have a field day.'

'Thinking like a journalist, darling?'

Alexi blew him a kiss. 'Always.'

'You think he wants to clear his conscience?' Jack asked, after a brief pause in their deliberations.

'Perhaps, given that he's gone all, as you put it, born-again and sanctimonious.'

Jack snorted. 'Well anyway, we now know that Stella has a connection to Andy Dawson. I'd really like to tie her in with Emily as well but I've no idea how.'

'I think—'

A yell from the restaurant area caused Jack and Alexi to share a concerned glance and simultaneously leave their chairs. Before they could reach the door, it flew open and Drew and Marcel barged through it.

'It's Amber,' Cheryl said breathlessly, bringing up the rear. 'She's run off.'

'The cleaner?' Alexi looked confused. 'Why? What happened?'

'She was hoovering the dining room while the waiters were setting the tables for tonight's sitting,' Marcel explained. 'I went out and asked them if anyone had seen that baseball bat being taken. Amber overheard. She went as white as a sheet, knocked a table sideways and ran off.'

'She's been here for a couple of years,' Cheryl said, shaking her head. 'She's a single mum, but reliable and, I thought, honest.' She frowned. 'But it must have been her. Why else would she have reacted that way?'

'You have an address for her?' Jack asked.

'She lives in a flat in the village, over the bookies.'

'Alexi and I will go and see her.'

'Best if I come with you,' Cheryl said. 'Despite everything, I still find it hard to believe that she'd do something like that. If she did then she must have been coerced. She'll be afraid, but she knows me well and is more likely to tell me the truth.'

'I'll stay here then,' Alexi said. 'We don't want to go in mob-handed and spook her. I have plenty to keep me occupied.'

'I'll keep an eye on Verity,' Drew said, even though Susie was back on duty. It was a constant source of friction between her and Drew; Cheryl insisting upon working as hard as ever through her second pregnancy and dealing with the demands of a lively toddler outside of Susie's hours. Drew wanted to employ a full-time, live-in nanny but Cheryl was adamant that her children wouldn't be raised by a stranger. It was as though she had a point to prove to herself, Alexi often thought, but being a bit of a workaholic herself, she was in no position to criticise her friend.

'Wish us luck,' Jack said, picking up his car keys and opening the door for Cheryl.

'You're quiet,' Alexi said to Drew, once they were left alone with just two dogs and a cat for company. 'What is it?'

'Cheryl's right about Amber.' Drew rubbed his jaw. 'Someone must be pulling her strings. She came to us about two years ago now, just after her baby was born, desperate for work. She'd had a spot of trouble with the law when she was a teenager and, credit where credit's due, she told us about it up front. She got in with the wrong crowd. There was some shoplifting and anti-social behaviour, I think. Nothing too serious, but then she got pregnant.'

'Ah,' Alexi said, sighing. 'I see.'

'She was still in her teens then and had no one to help her. No idea where her parents are but she was alone, living in one tiny room with a newborn baby. Cheryl felt sorry for her so gave her a chance to clean for us and she's never let us down.' He shook his head. 'She's grateful to us for giving her a chance. And because we've employed her and are willing to give her references, she's managed to get work elsewhere.' Drew shook his head. 'I just don't see her repaying us in this way, unless she's being threatened, or something.'

'Where's the baby's father?'

'Long gone. I don't think she's even sure who he is.'

'Right.'

'Don't judge her. I gather she grew up in and out of care, with no real guidance from anyone in authority. It's hardly surprising if she went off the rails.'

'Believe me, I'm not being judgemental.'

'Anyway, what are you up to?' Drew asked, peering over Alexi's shoulder at her laptop screen.

'Trying to get a handle on the source of the regular income that Stella was getting, or rather my friend at the paper is, but he's just sent me a message to say he's going round in circles and getting nowhere.'

'Someone didn't want to be identified.'

'Right.'

'Well, I wouldn't know where to start looking so I'll stop distracting you and get on. I have plenty on my to-do list.'

Alexi waved over her shoulder and went back to reading everything she could find online about Emily Pearson. The woman was a manipulator and Alexi was absolutely convinced that she was somehow involved with Stella. When nothing sprang out at her, she transferred her search to Emily's late husband, Nigel, about whom she knew absolutely nothing, other than the fact that he'd made a lot of money.

Another ten minutes of reading and she struck paydirt. Nigel was an entrepreneur and non-executive director of, amongst other interests, a successful PR company in Sydney.

'Gotcha!' she cried, waving a fist triumphantly in the air. It couldn't possibly be a coincidence.

She continued to read. Nigel, it seemed, had his fingers in many pies and also appeared to have the Midas touch. Every company he became involved with had been a success. And yet he'd died young from a degenerative heart condition. All the money in the world couldn't keep him healthy. *A timely reminder to make the most of every minute*, Alexi told herself, as she sat back and stretched.

Her phone rang, distracting her thoughts away from Emily and the connection she'd now made between her, Stella and Australia. She glanced at the screen. It wasn't a number she recognised but with a shrug, she took the call anyway.

'Alexi Ellis.'

'Alexi, I need to talk to you.'

'Who is this?' Alexi asked, unable to identify the anxious, female voice, even though she was pretty sure she'd heard it somewhere recently.

'Oh, sorry. Sarah Dawson.'

'Is everything all right, Sarah?'

'Yes, fine. But I've been thinking a lot about what you said.'

'Okay.'

'You did say it was all right to call you any time.'

'I did and it is. How can I help you?'

'Well, I've found something that I think you should see. I want to... er, talk to you about it, woman to woman.' Her voice caught and she stumbled over her words. 'Can you like pop over sometime soon, before Andy gets back tonight?'

'I can come now,' Alexi replied without hesitation. If Sarah was having a change of heart and would be willing to speak to Vickery, and if whatever she'd found backed up her account, then Alexi wouldn't give her time to change her mind. 'I'll be there in about forty-five minutes.'

'Thank you.'

Alexi realised she didn't have a means of transport. She went in search of Drew, told him what had occurred and asked if she could borrow the Land Rover that was the hotel's general runaround. It was a bit of a bone-shaker but still sound mechanically.

'Shouldn't you wait for Jack and go together?' he asked, looking dubious.

'No, best I go alone. She said she specifically wanted to speak to me, and she might open up more on a one-to-one basis. Dawson's away so I want to catch her before he returns and intimidates her.'

'I could come with you.'

'Thanks, but no. But I'll take my security detail.'

Since Cosmo was already standing at the door with Silgo faithfully behind him, she had no choice anyway.

'Well okay, if you're absolutely sure.'

'Let Jack know where I've gone when he gets back. Oh, and tell him I've found a link between Emily and Stella. Well, a potential link.'

'Care to elaborate?'

'Her late husband was only a non-executive director of a PR company in Sydney.'

'Bloody hell!'

'My thoughts precisely. It should have occurred to me to look into him before now.' She grabbed the keys to the Land Rover from the hook in the kitchen where they were kept. 'I hope not to be too long.'

'Be careful. I'm not happy about this.'

Alexi stood on her toes and kissed Drew's cheek. 'You worry too much. What can possibly happen to me when I have my Mace, to say nothing of my personal protection squad to have my back?' She nodded towards cat and dog.

'Don't forget that I've kept my martial arts classes up, too. Jack bullied me into it.'

She waved over her shoulder and made her way to the car park with Cosmo and Silgo to keep her company.

She drove swiftly towards Kingsclere, wondering what Sarah could possibly have found in the short time since she'd seen her that had resulted in Alexi's summons. She didn't believe that Dawson would be daft enough to retain anything incriminating. Perhaps there was some communication between him and Stella. Vickery hadn't had a chance to look yet but presumably Dawson had a computer at home and Sarah had been able to get into his email. That seemed like the most likely explanation.

There were no traffic delays and Alexi arrived at the Dawson's home for the second time in the same day. This time, she allowed the cat and dog to leave the car and follow her up the path.

'Stay here,' she said to them, just before she reached the front door. Silgo obediently lay down. Cosmo got the message too and climbed the nearest tree in hot pursuit of a squirrel. Silgo wouldn't move a muscle unless summoned and Cosmo instinctively knew when his services were required. That knowledge helped to quell the fluttering in Alexi's belly. Not that there were any obvious reasons for her to be nervous. There were no new vehicles parked on the drive: only the Volvo that had been there that morning. 'Stop seeing shadows on a cloudy day,' she told herself as she rang the bell.

Alexi gasped when the door was opened by Sarah, who looked terrified. Mascara ran down her face in black streaks and clothing that had looked pristine earlier was now crumpled and disarrayed.

'What is it?' she asked, instinctively taking Sarah in her arms. 'Has something happened?'

'I'm sorry, Alexi,' she said, fresh tears tumbling down her face. 'He made me call you. I had no choice.'

'Who did?'

Fear streaked through Alexi because she knew very well who Sarah must be referring to. She had the presence of mind to kick the door backwards, making it appear as though it was completely closed but the latch hadn't clicked. Silgo barging into it would open it without a problem, but she'd give it a minute before calling on her canine protector. Dawson must be desperate and the journalist in her badly needed to know why. She'd stupidly left the Mace in her bag in the car, but she had the keys in her hand and they could be equally dangerous when used as a weapon.

Hold that thought.

'When will you learn to mind your own damned business?'

Dawson loomed in the open kitchen doorway, his expression set in granite as he grabbed Alexi's forearm in a harsh grasp and dragged her into that room.

The stairs leading to Amber's little flat were narrow and rickety. The handrail was coming away from the wall, creating another hazard. Jack could see that they were a challenge for Cheryl and her baby bump to negotiate but there was insufficient space for them to climb side by side so that he could help her.

'Okay?' Jack asked, taking her elbow as she puffed her way up onto the tiny landing outside the door to Amber's abode.

The door itself looked flimsy and the paint was peeling. The landing smelled faintly of urine and fried food.

'How can she live here in such squalor?' Cheryl shook her head. 'I had absolutely no idea. She told me she'd found a nice place and that the rent was affordable.'

'The second part is obviously true.' The sound of a child crying echoed from behind the fragile door. 'Ready?'

'As I ever will be.' Cheryl straightened her shoulders. 'Let's do this.'

Jack rapped his knuckles against the flimsy wood and the crying abruptly stopped. The door was wrenched open by a young woman Jack recognised from the hotel. She had a toddler balanced on her hip. 'I've got your rent... oh!' Her face crumbled and her shoulders sagged when she realised that her caller wasn't her landlord. 'You know? I... that is to say.' She shook her head. 'There isn't anything I can say, not really, but you'd better come in and I'll try to explain. I *want* to explain.'

The room, and it was only one room with a miniscule kitchenette in one corner and what was obviously a makeshift bathroom in the other, was spotlessly clean. A sofa doubled as a bed for mother and child and was piled with colourful cushions. There was a small TV, a table and two mismatched chairs and a box of toys. The original floorboards had been varnished and were partially covered by a faded rug.

'Sit down.' She pointed to the chairs, put the child on the floor, handed her some building bricks and herself perched on the edge of the sofa.

'I'm so very sorry, Cheryl,' she said, tears tumbling down her cheeks. 'I had no idea what she wanted it for. If I had known, then I never would have...' She paused to sniff and wipe her eyes. 'When I heard the gossip about a baseball bat putting Drew's name in the frame for murder, I was beside myself.'

'It's okay, Amber,' Cheryl replied in a placating tone. 'Well, actually it's very much not okay. I don't understand any of this. Why didn't you say something when you realised Drew was in so much bother?'

'Because I need my job. If you sack me, all my other clients will let me go as well and then where will I be? This place isn't much but it's all I have and it's mine. But I struggle to make ends meet and got myself into serious debt. If I work then Ellie has to be in day care and it's expensive. I got into arears with the rent as well. Then one of my clients asked me if I could get a souvenir from the hotel for her. She was most specific about what she wanted. She'd seen Drew brandishing the bat once, larking about for the punters, and knew where it was kept.'

'You didn't think that was odd?' Cheryl asked.

'I've given up trying to figure out the way the rich and privileged work.' A slight edge underscored her tone. 'I didn't want to steal but she didn't give me much choice. Do it and I'd get a five hundred quid bonus. That's more money than I've ever seen in one go before and the answer to my prayers.'

Cheryl just looked at her. 'You should have come to me if you were having problems. We could have worked something out.'

'You've already done enough for me.'

Cheryl glanced at Jack, clearly thinking that she had an odd way of showing her appreciation. Neither of them felt the need to voice that opinion and left the floor open for Amber to continue.

'That amount would mean I could get myself straight. Besides, I wasn't given much choice. It was made clear to me that if I didn't do it, she'd sack me for stealing and make sure all my other clients knew it.' Amber spread hands that had nails chewed down to the quick. 'She left me with no option.'

'Who is this "she" you keep referring to?' Jack asked, already convinced that he knew the answer to his own question.

'Emily Pearson.'

20

Alexi's mind went into overdrive. She glanced at Sarah, who stood helplessly behind her husband, frozen with indecision. There was no possibility of her doing anything to help Alexi as Andy's fingers dug relentlessly into her forearm and he dragged her into the kitchen. Help, she reminded herself, was just outside the front door and would spring to her aid without hesitation.

But she wouldn't call on her protectors just yet. Andy wouldn't be stupid enough to seriously hurt her, here in his own home. He must realise that she'd have told Jack where she was going, and why. That being the case, she'd hear him out first, try to get him to admit that he'd killed Frank, then get herself out of this pickle.

'Is this how you usually greet your wife's guests?' Alexi asked, striving to find her dignity in a far from dignified situation. She knew that it would be a grave error to show any fear in front of a man who liked to dominate women and got off on intimidating them.

'It's how I greet interfering journalists who can't keep their noses out of other people's business,' Dawson snarled. 'Get in here!'

'How kind of you to invite me,' Alexi replied, her voice oozing sarcasm as she stumbled into the kitchen and almost tripped over her own feet. *Way to go, Alexi!*

'Get in here too!' Dawson yelled at Sarah.

In Sarah's situation, she would have told Dawson to take a hike, but he obviously realised that Sarah would do no such thing. Instead, she meekly followed Dawson into the kitchen, where he thrust Alexi against a work surface and held her there with the weight of his body. His harsh breath peppered the side of her face. She turned her head away, disgusted.

'Right. Care to tell me what you were doing here earlier today?' he demanded in a harsh tone.

He clearly expected her to show surprise and ask him how he knew about her visit, but Alexi hated being predictable and refused to rise to the bait. She had known the moment she walked through the door, even before then when she saw the state Sarah was in, that Dawson had somehow found out about her visit with Jack.

'You're not quite so clever as you thought you were,' Dawson growled. 'So I'll ask you again, and I'm not in the habit of repeating myself. Why were you here?'

'To find out why you killed your friend,' Alexi replied, turning to look directly at him as she sent him a scathing look and lifted her chin defiantly. Sarah would already have told him that much, Alexi figured. She glanced at the other woman, barely suppressing a gasp when Sarah turned her head. The gesture moved the hair away for the side of her face and revealed swelling where bruises were already forming. The sight served to fuel Alexi's anger.

And defiance.

'Well, are you going to hit me as well?' she asked. 'You get off on dominating women, don't you. I expect it makes you feel like the big man that you'll never be. Frank was better looking than you, more popular with the opposite sex and a better climber. That must have infuriated you and you eventually took your revenge.'

'Even if I did kill that miserable excuse for a human being, there's no way in this world that you'll ever be able to prove it. It went down as an accident and the case is done and dusted.'

'That was before Frank's wife was murdered. The police don't believe in coincidence and so his case has been reopened. Didn't Sarah tell you that?' Alexi asked sweetly. 'Anyway, your name's now firmly in the frame. There's a great deal of circumstantial evidence, which may be sufficient to see you convicted in a court of law.'

'Not a chance!' Dawson spoke with authority, but Alexi was encouraged to see the doubt creeping into his eyes.

'Perhaps not, but then the court of public opinion is so much more effective I find, and I just happen to be a respected journalist.'

Dawson's jaw dropped open and his expression darkened.

'Your reputation would never survive the fallout and what's left of your business would be yesterday's news. You're on the brink of bankruptcy as it is, and any adverse publicity would be the final straw.'

Dawson's scowled intensified as he pulled his weight away from her and appeared momentarily lost for words. It felt good to confront him. She suspected that few people, and no women, ever did. Would she have been so cavalier if she hadn't had Silgo and Cosmo waiting in the wings? Very probably not. She didn't have a death wish. But they were there, and their presence gave her the courage to goad a thoroughly despicable person into indiscretion.

'Leaving aside whatever my clearly delusional wife might have said to you, what makes you suppose I'd have any interest in killing my old friend?'

'Because you lost money on your Welsh climbing school venture and blamed him for not being diligent enough in the research department. Because he had an affair with your wife. And because your own lover, Frank's wife, had no further use for him.' Alexi counted the points off on her fingers. 'How am I doing so far? You must see what a compelling story it would make. The tabloids would lap it up. It has everything. Sex, greed, a trophy wife, and revenge.'

Dawson snarled and lunged for her, which is when Alexi realised that she'd driven him too far. She managed to evade his fist and responded with a swift knee to his groin, which he didn't see coming and which caused him to double over, howling with pain.

'Don't be so stupid!' she said derisively, watching him as he clutched his scrotum and turned the air blue with his language. 'You can't kill or even harm me and expect to get away with it. Everyone at Hopgood Hall knows where I am and why I came here.'

'That may or may not be the case,' he replied, puce in the face, presumably because she'd had the audacity to fight back. Alexi realised that might not have been the smartest move on her part. He would never let her win. It would be a matter of pride for him to have the last word. 'The thing is, I watched you arrive in that old heap of a car. All sorts of mechanical failures can happen in vehicles of that vintage.'

She laughed in his face, even though fear had now overcome her initial bravado. 'You really think I'd willingly drive off in it, aware that you'd tampered with the brakes? Or something.' She sent him an imperious look. 'Get real.'

'Who said anything about you being conscious at the time?'

Alexi shook her head. 'You really are something else. If I'd had any doubts about your having killed Frank when I got here, then you've just eradicated them. I know you did it and I know you want to tell me why. You might as well, seeing as how you're convinced I'll never live to tell the tale.'

'No one takes what's mine: money or wife,' he snarled. 'Frank was a real piece of work but for reasons that escape me, the ladies were all over him. What happened to him was his own fault. He had it coming. I just made sure it happened and did the world a favour.'

'Frank hit on the ladies a bit like you were all over Stella when she worked on your PR campaign.'

He sent her a derogatory look, but a lot of the confidence had left his expression. 'You have been a busy little bunny.'

'I do my research.'

'Sure, Stella and I were an item for a while, until her mother had her accident, and she felt the need to get away from a family who blamed her.'

'You pointed her towards Australia?'

Dawson looked surprised by the suggestion. 'Not me,' he said.

Alexi felt that he'd told the truth on that one. But at least he'd admitted to killing Frank.

'You disapproved of his behaviour, but it was no different to yours, it seems.'

'Stella wasn't married.'

'But you were. You obviously have double standards.'

'I've had enough of this!'

Alexi saw his fist coming but wasn't quick enough to completely evade it this time. Stars exploded behind her eyes as she crumpled to the floor, struggling to hang onto consciousness. She was aware of Sarah crying out but also knew she'd do nothing to help her. Time to call for her secret weapon.

Alexi inhaled sharply, fighting dizziness as she let out a piercing whistle.

The sound of the front door crashing against the wall caused Dawson to pause with his fist drawn back.

'What the...'

No further words passed his lips before a whirling dervish flew into the kitchen, growling, teeth bared, and leapt at Dawson's forearm, sinking his teeth into it and not letting go.

'Get this wild beast off me!'

'Now you know how it feels,' Alexi said, sending Sarah a collusive look.

Dawson's wife still appeared shellshocked and watched proceedings without moving a muscle. She wondered if Sarah was enjoying the show as she observed her husband finally get a taste of his own medicine.

Blood dripped from Dawson's forearm as Silgo continued to hold on. Alexi would have called him off, but for the fact that he tried to kick her beloved dog, and that she simply wouldn't stand for. Silgo, having previously been owned by a crooked trainer who kicked him as a matter of course, had experience of evading such brutality and easily managed to keep clear of Dawson's foot.

'Get this damned creature off me! I'll sue.'

Finally, Sarah cracked a smile. She actually laughed when Cosmo leapt from the floor, landed on Dawson's shoulder and swiped at his eyes with vicious claws.

'Okay, boys,' Alexi said. 'I think that will do for now.'

Silgo and Cosmo obediently left Dawson to fall to the floor clutching his forearm, blood now also spilling from scratches on his face that had narrowly avoided his eye.

'Did you really think I was stupid enough to come here alone?' Alexi asked, watching Dawson dispassionately as he writhed about on the floor.

Slowly, the fog left her brain and she felt in command of herself again. She'd have a bruise where Dawson had struck her, Alexi accepted, but it could have been a lot worse. She realised now that she should have called her protection detail in a lot sooner. One of these days, the journalist in her that made her determined to get the full story, no matter what the risk, would be her undoing. She inwardly sighed, resigning herself to a lecture from Jack.

'Get me something to tie his hands with,' she said, glancing at Sarah. 'Not that Silgo or Cosmo will let him move a muscle, but still...'

Sarah snapped out of her catatonic state and did as Alexi asked. With Dawson bound hand and foot, Alexi withdrew her phone from her pocket and called the cavalry.

* * *

'It was generous of you to agree to let Amber continue working at the hotel, Cheryl, given the circumstances,' Jack said as he drove them back to Hopgood Hall.

'You saw her living conditions. She's not a bad kid and was clearly put in an awkward situation. I believed her, as well, when she said she would have spoken up if any charges were brought against Drew.'

'Yes, me too. Shame she didn't speak up a little sooner.'

'It has all happened very quickly.'

'Well, it seems Emily either killed Stella herself or, more likely, had someone do it for her. The question is why.'

'I assume you'll have Vickery ask her.'

Jack grinned. 'Count on it.'

They arrived back at the hotel to find Drew in the kitchen with Verity on his lap. He was singing to his daughter, some ridiculous song of his own composition that made Cheryl and Jack smile.

'Where's Alexi?' Jack asked.

Before Drew could respond, Jack's phone rang. 'Never mind. This is her. Hey,' he said, taking the call. 'What's happening?'

His mouth fell open when she told him. 'You've called 999, I take it.'

'They're on their way.'

'So am I. I'll call Mark too.'

'What?' Drew and Cheryl asked together.

Jack grabbed his discarded keys and gave them a brief account.

'Blimey! Good old Silgo,' Drew said, chuckling. 'Is Alexi okay? I told her not to go on her own, but she insisted she could take care of herself. Seems she was right about that.'

'She says she isn't harmed but you know Alexi.' Jack's anxiety went off the scale. 'I have to go. See you later.'

'Alexi discovered after you left that Emily's late husband had a PR company in Australia. It's all coming together, Jack.'

'Later. We'll talk later.'

Jack absorbed that information as he left room at a run, needing to be with Alexi. She'd just taken on a dangerous and unpredictable man and there was bound to be a reaction.

When he arrived at Kingsclere, a whole raft of emergency

service vehicles were already there, lights flashing. Dawson was being attended to by a paramedic, shouting about dangerous animals attacking him in his own home and threatening to sue.

'He's playing the part of victim,' Vickery said, walking up to Jack the moment he left his vehicle, 'but don't worry, the wife's backing Alexi's account.'

'Where is Alexi?'

Vickery pointed to the house and Jack approached it at a run. He found Alexi and Sarah in the kitchen drinking tea. Silgo was sitting at Alexi's feet, rubbing his head against her shin, as harmless as a puppy. Cosmo was on the island that served as a table, consuming what appeared to be a bowl of tuna.

'Hey,' Jack said, crouching beside Alexi and ruffling Silgo's ears. 'I hear you've had quite an adventure.'

Alexi smiled at him. 'I had the presence of mind to bring these two so there was no real danger *and* Dawson admitted to killing Frank in front of us both.'

'Even so, you should have waited for me, and we'd have come down together.' He gently stroked the curve of her face, tutting at the swelling that had formed. 'Your injuries need to be photographed, both of you,' he said. 'Just in case Dawson tries to duck out of an abuse charge.'

'I hear you,' Sarah replied. 'He had some mad scheme to tamper with Alexi's brakes and have her die in a car crash, having beaten her up first.' She shook her head. 'He seemed to think he'd get away with it, too. He never dreamed anyway that I'd find the courage to testify against him, so he was able to boast about what he'd done, supposedly secure in the knowledge that he'd beat the system.' Sarah straightened her shoulders. 'Unfortunately for him, I've decided to follow

Alexi's example and stand up for myself. I've been too afraid of Andy to exert myself for far too long.'

'He says that he didn't kill Stella though,' Alexi said. 'And I believed him. His reaction when I threw that accusation into the mix was about the only genuine one I saw from him the entire time.'

'Well, I have news in that respect.' Jack related what Amber had told them.

'Emily. I knew it!' She bounced on her seat. 'We have to confront her.'

Jack held up a hand in an effort to stem her enthusiasm. 'No more confronting dangerous criminals. We have to do this one by the book and get Vickery to take the lead. Hopefully, he'll let us be there before he interviews her formally, given that we've done all his leg work for him. He's made that concession before.'

'Drew told you about Stella's late husband having a PR company in Australia?'

Jack nodded.

'It's all starting to make some sort of convoluted sense.'

'It is, darling. Anyway, let's get you home. Are you okay to stay here alone, Sarah?'

'Actually, I've invited her to stay at Hopgood Hall for now. I don't think she should be here without company.'

'That's a good idea. Go and pack a bag, Sarah. We'll wait for you,' Jack said.

'Are you really okay?' Jack asked, taking both of Alexi's hands in his once they were left alone. 'I could throttle that bastard with my bare hands for hitting you.'

'Let the law take its course. That will be far more satisfying.'

'Yeah, okay, I guess.' Jack wagged a finger at her. 'But don't do anything that rash ever again.'

'I probably shouldn't have come here alone; I will admit that much. It seemed too convenient, that call coming through when it did, I mean, and I was suspicious. But no one could have known that you weren't there at the time and aware of my location. Besides, the journalist in me took over. I just figured that Dawson was too shrewd to do anything rash. He's not stupid and would have realised he'd never get away with killing me.' She grinned. 'Anyway, like I say, I had help at hand.'

Jack dropped a hand to ruffle Silgo's ears. Cosmo had finished consuming his snack and sat on the island fastidiously washing his face, looking oblivious to all the fuss and flashing lights. He very likely was. Before Alexi had adopted him, Cosmo had been a feral street cat, a real bruiser, who could take care of himself. It appeared that he could also take care of any human who met with his approval.

Sarah reappeared, carrying a holdall which Jack took from her. 'All set?' he asked, smiling at her. There was a spring to her step now and she suddenly looked a great deal more confident.

'Yep, relieved too. I should have found the courage to walk out on him years ago. Better late than never.'

'That's the spirit!'

'We'll all go in my car,' Jack said. 'I'm not having you drive the Land Rover, Alexi, just in case Dawson got at it.'

'He can't have done. He didn't leave this house once I arrived but yes, let's all travel together.'

'I'll get one of Vickery's men to drive the Land Rover back,' Jack replied.

21

Vickery and DC Hogan arrived at Hopgood Hall early the following morning.

'Dawson's locked up and due to appear before the magistrates on Monday morning. He'll be our guest over the weekend.'

'I'm sure you'll make him comfortable,' Jack replied. 'What does he have to say for himself?'

'He's lawyered up, naturally. He admits to climbing with Frank on the fatal morning but insists his fall was an accident. He didn't report it because there was nothing he could do for Frank, and he didn't have the time to get involved. He says he was boasting to Alexi because she'd interfered in his marriage but now denies pushing Frank to his death.'

'Well, he would say that, wouldn't he,' Drew replied morosely.

He was delighted to have found out what had happened to his brother and even happier to have his name completely cleared, Alexi knew. It would take him a while to process things though, and that couldn't really happen until they'd untangled Stella's part in the sordid affair.

'Dawson found out you'd been there, Alexi,' Vickery explained, 'because Sarah left your card in her kitchen and forgot to hide it away. Dawson made a habit of checking up on her activities, apparently.'

'That I can believe,' Jack said. 'He could do as he pleased but his wife had to account for her every move.'

'Will he get away with simply not reporting an accident?' Alexi asked.

'Unlikely, just so long as Sarah is willing to testify against him.'

'I think she will,' Alexi said. 'We had a long chat last night and she realises now that she's allowed herself to become controlled. She can taste freedom and is thirsting for revenge for all the humiliations she suffered at Dawson's hands.'

'He's complaining bitterly about being attacked by wild animals that ought to be destroyed.'

'Ha! Sarah can confirm that he attacked me, intended to kill me and the animals only came to my rescue when I was in fear for my life.'

'Don't worry,' Vickery said in a placating tone, 'he will definitely face charges for attacking you, but early indications are that the CPS will prosecute him for murdering Frank, too. There's enough circumstantial evidence, now that he's admitted to being there. And with you two ladies repeating the events of yesterday. Well...' Vickery paused to sip at his coffee. 'Problem is, he's denying having anything to do with Stella's murder.'

'Ah, we can help you there,' Jack said.

He proceeded to explain the presence of the baseball bat at the scene of Stella's murder and who had procured it.

'That lets you off the hook, Drew.'

'Yeah, thank God,' Drew replied. 'What we don't understand is why Emily felt the need to either leave it at the scene herself or have someone do it for her.'

'Our money is on someone else committing the deed, with Emily pulling their strings,' Jack said.

'Well, there's only one way to find out.' Vickery drained his coffee and stood up. 'Fancy tagging along while we call on the lady? Unofficially, of course.'

Alexi grabbed her bag. 'Try and keep us away.'

* * *

They travelled to Emily's house in separate cars.

'Amber won't have warned Emily to expect us, will she?' Alexi asked Jack.

'No. I hope not. Cheryl's been very generous keeping her on and Amber knows it. We told her specifically not to get in touch with Emily. If she has then she'll have well and truly burned her bridges. She must realise that Emily will be called to account for wanting the bat at the very least. Probably much worse than that. Anyway, there will be no further work for Amber at Emily's and none at all anywhere else if she lets Cheryl down for a second time. Cheryl will make sure of that.'

'As will I,' Alexi said, firming her jaw.

Vickery stood back while DC Hogan rang the doorbell. Emily answered it promptly, presumably because she'd observed their arrival.

'Mrs Pearson,' Vickery said. 'Detective Inspector Vickery and DC Hogan. I think you are acquainted with Mr Maddox and Ms Ellis.'

'I am, but I'm at a loss to know why you've arrived at my door mob-handed, so to speak.'

'We have news for you regarding the death of Frank Hopgood. We now believe it was no accident,' Vickery said. Alexi watched Emily's response, which seemed to be one of genuine shock. But then, if she'd already known it was murder, she would have had time to prepare her reaction. 'May we come in?'

'Please do.'

She opened the door wide and ushered them into a pristine lounge that looked more like a room from a showhouse than a place to relax. There was nothing personal that Alexi could see, and if Emily used the room on a regular basis, then she hadn't bothered to stamp her personality on it. Or, then again, perhaps it told Alexi everything she needed to know about the personality in question.

'Who do you think killed Frank?' she asked, seating herself with elegance and crossing her legs at the ankle. 'That ambitious wife of his, one supposes.'

'Actually, no.' Vickery paused, watching the woman as closely as Alexi. 'It was Andy Dawson.'

'Dawson? I know that name.' Emily plucked at her lower lip with a well-manicured finger. 'Didn't they used to climb together?'

'I think you know very well that they did.'

'Possibly, but I don't recall ever meeting him.' She remained calm and outwardly in control. 'I can't think why he would have done such a thing but there you have it. There's no accounting for the depths some people will stoop to when they have grievances, real or imagined.'

'Something you would know all about, madam.'

Emily blinked and stared directly at Vickery. She was

good, Alexi thought. Her expression of mild affrontery was almost convincing.

Almost.

'Now is your opportunity to tell us why you had Amber steal a baseball bat from Hopgood Hall.'

Emily's face drained of all colour and her hands trembled. This time, she stared blankly at them all and had nothing to say.

'This is an informal interview, but charges will be brought,' Vickery continued. 'If you would prefer for me to arrest you now and take you to the police station to make a formal statement under caution then that is your right.'

Emily dropped her head and examined what was probably a very expensive rug beneath her feet.

'Did you kill Stella Hopgood?' Vickery asked quietly.

'Don't call her that! She didn't deserve to share Frank's name, or his bed, or any part of him!' she cried frantically. 'She was a glorified gold-digger,' she added with a derisive sniff.

'Whom you deliberately put on Frank's tail,' Alexi said. 'We are aware that your husband had a PR company in Australia. We're just a little unsure how you came to know Stella.'

'She did some work for my husband in this country,' Emily replied. 'I met her a few times at social occasions and saw how the men were drawn to her like flies to you-know-what. That was several years ago, obviously. Anyway, she tracked me down, told me she had decided to leave the country and wondered if Nigel would have any work for her in Sydney. I did a little digging, discovered that her mother had died of an accident and... well, it didn't take a genius to join the dots.'

'Go on,' Vickery said, when her words stalled.

'Nigel was dead by then. She didn't realise it. If he hadn't been, I wouldn't have let her within a mile of him. He was the faithful sort, but every man gets tempted from time to time. Anyway, the company was still running so I gave her a recommendation.'

'Why?' Jack asked.

'You know, I've often asked myself the same question. I suppose I saw a little of myself in her when I was her age. The ambition, the determination to have her own way. I liked her.' She paused. 'And I figured that everyone deserves a second chance.'

'Even though you obviously suspected her of killing her own mother?' Alexi asked, scowling.

Emily shrugged. 'I asked her about it. She said they'd argued, and it was an accident but that her family didn't believe her account and had disowned her.'

'Did you bank roll her start-up company?' Jack asked.

'No, not me.' She shook her head emphatically and Alexi sensed she was telling the truth. 'But I'd kept tabs on her, knew she'd set up on her own and guessed she'd be short of funds. When Frank got his hands on his inheritance, he had no further need for me and cast me aside like a worn-out shoe.' Her face coloured and she looked furious. 'I wasn't about to put up with that and so I got in touch with Stella. I told her that Frank would be coming her way. I'd pointed him in that direction, you see, telling him of fictional opportunities for investments, and knew he'd take the bait because... well, because I'd always looked after him and he trusted me. He had absolutely no idea that he'd broken my heart.' She let out a slow breath. 'Again.'

'You offered Stella a great deal of money to cultivate Frank's friendship,' Alexi suggested.

'And instructed her to bleed him dry,' Jack added.

'It was less than he deserved after he'd leeched off me for years. I needed him back where he belonged. Here with me with his tail between his legs, willing to toe the line. What I didn't expect was for him to come back married to that hussy.'

'You realise you've just given yourself a motive for her murder,' Vickery said. 'Be careful what you say without legal representation.'

'What does it matter now? Besides, I didn't kill her.'

'Perhaps not,' Vickery replied. 'But you know who did and put Drew Hopgood's name in the frame.'

'Well, if he'd done as I suggested and withheld Frank's inheritance then none of this would be necessary.'

Jack and Alexi shared a glance. Drew hadn't mentioned anything about deliberately withholding Frank's share. Alexi wondered if she'd made that part up in an effort to justify her actions.

Emily sat with her hands primly folded in her lap, appearing to think that her explanation was both plausible and reasonable. Alexi wondered if she was mentally unbalanced, or simply a rich woman used to getting her own way.

One who reacted violently when she did not.

Frank had clearly been the love of her life, she had already admitted as much, but he'd used her and then married someone else. To Emily, that would represent the ultimate betrayal and could not be permitted to go unpunished. But her idea of punishment was to fleece him so that he was obliged to come back to her.

She had not been involved in his murder.

'You assumed Stella had arranged for Frank to die, now

that she had his funds and no further need for him,' Vickery said. 'Is that why you arranged for her to die?'

Emily flashed an evil little smile, one that probably reflected her true character, Jack thought. A character that was as warped as it was unpredictable.

'She was a nasty piece of work. Frank, the fool, told her about what happened in Brighton all those years ago and she was attempting to blackmail me over it. Me!' Emily pointed at her own chest for emphasis. 'After all I'd done for her.'

'You paid up?'

'I didn't.'

'Daventree,' Alexi said into the ensuing silence. 'He started to pay her; we saw the payments coming in on her bank statement but couldn't trace them to source. But the more he paid, the more she would have wanted. Besides, she was going to blow your secret. You couldn't let that happen.'

'And so Daventree did the deed and you insisted upon the baseball bat to get back at Drew and to divert attention.'

'Oh, what's the point.' Emily flapped her hands. 'Daventree is weak. He'll tell you the truth if I don't. Yes, you're right. We couldn't let that tart get the better of us. Besides, I did think she'd had a hand in Frank's death. She certainly didn't mourn his demise. Daventree said he'd make sure that her spirit passed on to the next plane, or some such nonsense. His conscience was bothering him, you know. That's why he told you about Judith. I realised you'd ferret around and get to the truth, and I think Daventree would have been glad to have it out in the open now that he projects himself as purer than the driven.'

'His conscience was bothering him, yet he was willing to kill Stella?' Jack asked, frowning.

'He couldn't afford to be blackmailed indefinitely. His

business isn't doing as well as he'd like the world to think. As for me, I have a reputation to maintain, so Stella had to go to avoid her speaking out. And to prevent her from blackmailing us both, of course.' Emily tossed her head. 'And because she deserved to. She was a thoroughly unpleasant woman.'

'And you wanted to implicate Drew, too,' Alexi said, through gritted teeth.

'If you hadn't interfered then Drew Hopgood would have been charged with murdering Stella.' Emily glowered at Alexi. 'He had more reason than anyone for wanting her out of the way. I heard she was putting the squeeze on him as well, insisting that Frank hadn't received his fair share of their joint inheritance.' She sighed. 'My retaliation was perfect and should have worked.'

Vickery stood up, read Emily her rights and arrested her. The woman sent Alexi a condemning look but seemed resigned to her fate. 'I'll call my lawyer,' she said.

22

'You guys are amazing,' Drew said the following day. 'I'll never be able to thank you enough.'

'No thanks are necessary,' Alexi replied, grinning at him. 'I have a stake in this hotel too, don't forget. I can't afford for profits to decline.'

Everyone laughed.

'I still can't believe that Emily wanted to frame me simply because I gave Frank what was rightfully his. She did mention to me one night in the bar that it wouldn't be safe to let him loose with so much dosh and that I ought to find a way to drip feed it to him. But I'd forgotten all about that. Like I say, it was spoken in jest, or so I thought. I had no idea she was serious.' Drew scratched his head. 'It just goes to show.'

'You were a convenient scapegoat,' Jack said. 'You hated Stella, she was trying to put the squeeze on you and you thought she'd killed your brother. Reason enough for the police to think that you'd killed her and probably enough to get a conviction, what with the baseball bat and all.'

'But unluckily for Emily,' Alexi added, 'the police in question are on our side. Anyone other than Vickery might have taken the easy option.'

Drew shuddered. 'Don't remind me.'

'Daventree's been arrested and is singing like the proverbial canary,' Jack said. 'He says it was all Emily's idea. Anyway, the early signs are that they will both be charged with Stella's murder.'

'Good!' Cheryl and Drew said in unison.

'Dawson will be charged with Frank's murder too. He denies murder but Vickery tells me he might be willing to plead guilty to the lesser charge of manslaughter. It will still get him a good stint behind bars. He'll be charged with assaulting Alexi, too. Sarah doesn't want to press charges for spousal abuse.'

'However long he gets won't be long enough,' Cheryl complained. 'Where does that leave Sarah?'

'I think she's going to take a restraining order out, so even if or when Dawson's released, he won't be able to go anywhere near her. He'll be on probation, so if he does, he'll go straight back inside. That will give her time to sort her life out.' Alexi smiled. 'I had a long chat with her this morning. Her house is mortgaged up to the hilt but there's a little bit of equity. Enough for her to buy somewhere modest and start again. Dawson will have to agree to sell. His company is almost bankrupt, and he can't afford the mortgage, so if he doesn't agree, it will be repossessed.'

'What about Amber?' Jack asked.

Cheryl shook her head. 'I hate the thought of her living in that awful room. I won't dignify it by calling it a flat. So Drew and I have been talking. There's that small cottage in the grounds that used to be a tennis pavilion. It's much nicer than where she's living now. We thought that we'd take her on full time as a cleaner and part-time barmaid. Her daughter can be with Verity while she's working. Our helper can look after them both and yes, before you ask, I am considering Drew's suggestion of taking on a full-time nanny. It's not as though I'll be working in an office somewhere miles away so will still be able to interact with my children on a daily basis.'

Drew gave his wife a smacking kiss.

'Anyway,' Cheryl added. 'Amber won't have to fork out for childcare and can get her life on track.'

'You're very generous, all things considered,' Alexi said, squeezing her friend's hand.

'Well, her life hasn't been easy. Someone needs to give her a chance.'

'I have a feeling that she won't let you down,' Jack said.

'That flat in Newbury. Who did it belong to?' Jack asked.

'Emily's company. It seems Frank and Stella had been house sitting for an old friend of Emily's. She suggested it when they came back and wanted somewhere to stay,' Alexi replied.

'She was still keeping tabs on Frank,' Drew said, shaking his head. 'That level of devotion has to be admired.'

'Well anyway, the house sit came to an end. Stella went to Emily, wanting a base in this part of the world. Apparently, she wanted to try and mend fences with her family, if you can believe it.'

'And Emily had her own reasons for wanting to keep Stella in this part of the world,' Jack added. 'I think she was already considering bumping her off. I'm betting her phone records will show that Emily called Stella the day before that pitch, asking her to be in Newbury.'

'And Stella wouldn't be able to say no,' Cheryl said,

nodding. 'But she didn't know that by agreeing, she was signing her own death warrant.'

Everyone fell momentarily silent, contemplating the greed, jealousy and obsession that had ended two lives.

'Anyway.' Drew broke the silence. 'Let's express our admiration for the real stars of the show. Without those two, I dread to think what might have happened to you, Alexi.'

Silgo sat up and woofed in agreement. Cosmo merely sent them all an "it was nothing" look, turned in a circle and settled down for a well-earned snooze.

ACKNOWLEDGEMENTS

My thanks as always to the amazing Boldwood team, and in particular to my fabulous editor, Emily Ruston, who manages to create order out of my chaotic scribbles.

ABOUT THE AUTHOR

E.V. Hunter has written a great many successful regency romances as Wendy Soliman and revenge thrillers as Evie Hunter. She is now redirecting her talents to produce cosy murder mysteries. For the past twenty years she has lived the life of a nomad, roaming the world on interesting forms of transport, but has now settled back in the UK.

Sign up to E.V. Hunter's mailing list here for news, competitions and updates on future books.

Follow E.V. Hunter on social media:

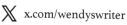 x.com/wendyswriter

facebook.com/wendy.soliman.author

bookbub.com/authors/wendy-soliman

ALSO BY E.V. HUNTER

The Hopgood Hall Murder Mysteries

A Date To Die For

A Contest To Kill For

A Marriage To Murder For

A Story to Strangle For

A Deadly Affair

A Deadly Legacy

Revenge Thrillers

The Sting

The Trap

The Chase

The Scam

The Kill

The Alibi

Poison
& Pens

POISON & PENS IS THE HOME OF
COZY MYSTERIES SO POUR YOURSELF
A CUP OF TEA & GET SLEUTHING!

DISCOVER PAGE–TURNING NOVELS FROM
YOUR FAVOURITE AUTHORS &
MEET NEW FRIENDS

JOIN OUR
FACEBOOK GROUP

BIT.LYPOISONANDPENSFB

SIGN UP TO OUR
NEWSLETTER

BIT.LY/POISONANDPENSNEWS

Boldwood

Boldwood Books is an award-winning fiction publishing company seeking out the best stories from around the world.

Find out more at www.boldwoodbooks.com

Join our reader community for brilliant books, competitions and offers!

Follow us
@BoldwoodBooks
@TheBoldBookClub

Sign up to our weekly deals newsletter

https://bit.ly/BoldwoodBNewsletter

Printed in Great Britain
by Amazon